Profited

Bound Together Book 2

Lacey Black

Everyone loves the asshole!

♡ *Lacey Black*

Lacey Black

Index

Also by Lacey Black 5
Dedication.. 6
Prologue... 7
Chapter One... 29
Chapter Two 48
Chapter Three 62
Chapter Four.. 78
Chapter Five 84
Chapter Six 94
Chapter Seven.. 101
Chapter Eight... 108
Chapter Nine.. 114
Chapter Ten 122
Chapter Eleven 131
Chapter Twelve 140
Chapter Thirteen.. 146
Chapter Fourteen 156
Chapter Fifteen 170
Chapter Sixteen 175
Chapter Seventeen 183
Chapter Eighteen 195
Chapter Nineteen 213
Chapter Twenty 220
Chapter Twenty-One 230
Chapter Twenty-Two... 244
Chapter Twenty-Three.. 251

Chapter Twenty-Four...261
Chapter Twenty-Five 267
Chapter Twenty-Six..276
Epilogue...283
Acknowledgements...295
About the Author 296

Also by Lacey Black

Rivers Edge series

Trust Me, Rivers Edge book 1 (Maddox and Avery) – FREE at all retailers

> *~ #1 Bestseller in Contemporary Romance & #3 in overall free e-books on Amazon*
> *~ #2 Bestseller in overall free e-books on iBooks*

Fight Me, Rivers Edge book 2 (Jake and Erin)

Expect Me, Rivers Edge book 3 (Travis and Josselyn)

Promise Me: A Novella, Rivers Edge book 3.5 (Jase and Holly)

Protect Me, Rivers Edge book 4 (Nate and Lia)

Boss Me, Rivers Edge book 5 (Will and Carmen)

Trust Us: A Rivers Edge Christmas Novella (Maddox and Avery)

> *~ This novella was originally part of the Christmas Miracles Anthology*

Bound Together series

Submerged, Bound Together book 1 (Blake and Carly)

Profited, Bound Together book 2 (Reid and Dani)

Music Notes, a sexy contemporary romance standalone

*Coming Soon from Lacey Black

Entwined, Bound Together Book 3 (Luke and Sidney)

Book 1 in the Summer Sisters series, a new contemporary romance series

Dedication

To my dear friends Amanda and Jo.

From random texts and emails to the daily PM's, we've laughed, cried, and shared incriminating evidence. I never imagined that this journey would bring me two amazing friends that I will cherish for the rest of my life. When I look back, I will always know that I profited from your friendship.

Love,
Sweet Cheeks

Prologue – I Don't Want This Night

To End

Reid

More Than 8 Years Ago

"I'm running back to grab another beer," I holler over the loud, thumping country music piping through the massive collection of speakers next to the stage. The guys just give me a head nod before turning back to enjoy the view of a luscious Sara Evans performing in short shorts and cowboy boots on the main stage.

I start to push my way through the masses, taking in the country music lovers around me. Girls in bikini tops and barely-there shorts. Guys in Wranglers and boots and big Stetsons to protect them from the intensity of the desert sun. Their cowboy appearance definitely makes me feel slightly out of place in my khaki shorts and blue and tan polo shirt.

We're only a few hours into the music festival located on the northern part of the outskirts of Phoenix, Arizona in the Sonoran Desert. My buddies Jon, Cory, Scott and I drove the almost five hours south to attend this massive two-day country music festival. For me, it's not about the music though. I've never been a huge fan of country music. For me, it's about freedom. With graduation from UNLV in my rearview mirror this past May, I'm soaking up every ounce of freedom I can before officially giving my soul to the devil incarnate. The devil being my father.

Joseph Hunter has owned me since I was born. With a degree in business management, I've been groomed since the moment I entered the world to join him at the helm of the family casino, The Chameleon. My grandfather, Harmon, at a very young age started the casino with his father back in the day where gangsters walked the streets wielding tommy guns and flapper dresses were all the rave. When his only child, Scarlett, married a nobody from the wrong side of the tracks, Harmon didn't bat an eye. He took the young boy under his wing and showed him life from within the casino. Joseph took to it like a fish to water, and together Harmon and Joseph developed and grew The Chameleon into one of the largest casinos on the Las Vegas strip.

This past summer, since my college graduation, Grandfather has allowed me to travel and enjoy a little free time. A two-month backpacking trip overseas was his gift to me, and that was the only way I was able to enjoy my summer. My father wouldn't permit me to take time off unless it came as an order from Grandfather. He was ready to have me join him at the company, but he would never challenge a decision made by my grandfather. However, come Monday morning, my freedom ends. From that point on, you'll find me Monday through Friday, eight to six, sitting at a desk in the office next to Joseph's.

I make my way to the massive area of land designated for tents. Tents of all shapes and sizes are littered everywhere. Fire pits, lawn chairs, and coolers adorn each campsite. Most of the open area is deserted right now as the concert dwellers are enjoying the third act to take the stage since we've been here. Some of these entertainers I haven't heard of before, yet that didn't stop me from jumping in the passenger seat of my buddy Jon's three-year-old Chrysler 300 and riding for hours to enjoy this final little taste of liberty.

Nearing the sliver of land we claimed as our own, movement out of the corner of my eye draws my attention. I can't exactly ignore the person just off to my right, as I'd prefer to do; nor can I backtrack and find another path. I've already committed to this one and I'm not that far from our campsite now. Besides, I could really use that beer.

Even though the sun is starting to set, I can tell instantly that the individual is a girl. A woman. She's petite with long, blond hair pulled tightly into a ponytail at the nape of her neck. Her thin blue tank top dips dangerously low in front, giving off a lustful view of creamy, smooth cleavage. The woman is wearing shorts, but hers appear to be a little more modest than the ones other girls are sporting. A pair of worn cowboy boots and socks lies in the dirt next to where she's sitting, clearly tossed aside in search of a more comfortable option. She doesn't notice me as I approach, which works out perfectly for me as I intend to slip by her unnoticed.

Just when I'm a few feet away, she startles and glances up. Crystal blue eyes the color of the ocean slam into me with so much force, it stops me in my tracks. The stifling summer desert air lodges painfully in my throat as we stare at each other, neither of us moving or speaking. Her sparkling eyes are wide with innocence and shock, but that's not what holds my attention. No, her eyes shine brightly with sadness and unshed tears. Something foreign grabs ahold of me, deep in my cold-hearted chest, and I suddenly want to make her smile.

And shit if that doesn't piss me off instantly.

"I'm sorry, I didn't mean to startle you," I say, still unable to move a single muscle. I should keep walking; walk to our campsite and grab that beer. Instead, I find myself stepping closer to this stranger to get a better look at her.

She's breathtaking in a simple, effortless way. She's not caked in makeup or with her hair teased into some fancy hairdo. She's sitting on the ground, in the lumpy dirt, covered in sweat, and drinking a Dr. Pepper while holding a cell phone. And the sight of her practically knocks me on my ass.

"It's okay. I thought you were someone else," she mumbles softly.

Without giving it any thought, I take another step into her campsite. I don't know why, but there's some crazy cosmic pull happening right now, and I'm unable to walk away from her. The sadness in her eyes guts me to the core. That alone completely catches me by surprise since I haven't felt emotion in years. Well, except towards my little sister, Tara.

"Are you okay?" I ask her, squatting down in the dirt next to her.

She seems leery by my sudden interest in her wellbeing. After all, she doesn't know me. The woman gives me a questioning look before running her eyes down my body. My entire being suddenly burns with want as her blue eyes peruse me. They linger on my chest and trim waist for several moments as if she's picturing what I look like beneath my clothes. My cock thickens instantly as those blue eyes continue to my open legs and down to my sandal clad feet. If I were a damn woman, I'd feel a little violated, but since I'm a man–a red-blooded, horny man–I fucking love it.

"Are you done?" I ask, unable to mask the smile on my lips.

Her stunning eyes move swiftly back up and slam into my own. The most beautiful pink blush settles in as she stumbles on whatever it is she's trying to say. "I'm sorry," she mumbles before turning away.

"Don't be. I'm not," I reply with another coy smile.

Without standing up, I reach forward, extending my hand. "Reid," I tell her.

She hesitates, but only for a moment before reaching forward and placing her petite hand inside of mine. "Dani." The instant we touch, my blood starts to boil. My gut rages with fire and it has nothing to do with the sweltering heat under the desert sun. No, it has everything to do with this beautiful woman in front of me. Her touch causes me to flare to life for the first time in a long, long time. Suddenly, I don't want to let her go.

"Nice to meet you, Dani. Is there a reason you're sitting in the dirt by yourself instead of enjoying the concert with everyone else?" I ask her, shifting so that I drop down on my ass in the dirt next to her.

Dani laughs, but it lacks humor. "You wouldn't believe me if I told you," she says with a little punch of venom. Apparently whatever has her on the verge of tears also has her pissed off.

"Try me," I find myself saying.

Dani takes a deep breath as if weighing her options. No, she doesn't have to tell me, and I'm not going to push her, but part of me–a very foreign part–hopes that she humors me and tells me what's wrong. "I came here for the weekend with my boyfriend," she starts. Another emotion I'm completely unaccustomed to tingles in my chest and punches at my gut. Jealousy.

"Anyway, we really hadn't been seeing each other very long when he invited me to come here." Dani laughs again. "I take that back. He really didn't invite me, he more like hinted around about how bad he wanted to go and how much fun it would be, but he didn't have the money for the tickets."

"So, let me guess. You bought them?"

"Ding, ding, ding. We have a winner," she says as she points to me. Her face lights up as if I'd just won the big prize on one of those daytime game shows, and for some reason, I feel like I have. "Stupid, right? You can say it. You're probably not going to say anything that I haven't already thought."

"I'm not going to put you down right now. It looks like you're already doing a good job of it," I say with the slight raise of the corner of my mouth.

"I am. Anyway, we weren't here an hour when a group of college girls set up their camp right next to us. Next thing I know, Bryson has his tongue down one of the girl's throat."

"Are you kidding me?" I ask, incredulous.

"Wish I were," she mumbles, dropping her eyes back down to the cell phone clutched in her hand. "And to make matters worse, I can't get ahold of my sister to come get me."

"Wow. I don't even know what to say to that," I tell her, shaking my head. "So, he went off to enjoy the concert with some girl he met five seconds ago, and you're here at the campsite because you can't get a ride home?"

"Basically. My older sister is the only one I can think of who has a car besides my dad, and there is no way in hell I'm calling him tonight to drive out to the desert to pick me up. He wasn't a fan of Bryson anyway, and frankly, I don't want to listen to it the entire ride home. A cab would cost too much money."

"Where's home?" I ask.

"Here in Phoenix. I'm a senior at Arizona State."

"So, you're stuck here while your *ex-boyfriend* is off having fun with someone who's probably half as good looking as you? And I'm assuming he's your ex-boyfriend now, right? Unless you're into that sort of thing," I joke. Not that sharing a woman would be a bad

12

thing, but the thought of sharing this particular woman makes me want to lose my mind.

"Yeah, he's definitely my ex-boyfriend now. Not that he was a very good one to begin with, but at least he finally showed me the full range of his douchery."

Her comment makes me laugh again, which is another surprise. I've laughed more in the last 10 minutes than I have in the last four years of college combined. Serious by nature, I've always been more of the quietly observing type. Never quick with a smile or laugh, my humorous side has always taken a distant backseat to my desire to get to the bottom line. Down to business. No pleasantries. That's what makes me damn good at what I do. There's always an angle and never any need for the other shit.

I've had a few girlfriends, mostly in high school, though. In college, I focused on getting my degree in the manner that my father deemed appropriate. Late nights in college were spent with random girls to scratch a particular itch, never allowing any of them to get too close. I never stayed the night and never allowed her to either. In fact, I was usually gone before the sheets started to cool down. Sure I developed a reputation, but I didn't give a shit. There was always a girl willing to indulge in a night of no-strings sex. Half of them were just as interested in keeping it as casual as I was. The other half were hoping to be the one to change me. None of them were.

"I've got an idea," I start as I stand up. "Come on." Extending my hand down towards her, I wait for her to grab ahold. The thing she doesn't realize is that she's not the only one taking a chance here. I am so far outside my comfort zone right now that I can barely see the line anymore.

"Where are we going?" she asks with a curious look. She hesitates, but only for a few seconds.

"We're going to have fun," I tell her as she places her warm hand inside of my own. Again, at our contact, an electric current shocks my system.

With ease, I pull up until she's standing. Dani doesn't hesitate as she slips her socks and cowboy boots back on her feet. I've never been into the cowboy and cowgirl movement, but seeing those worn, dark boots on her feet makes my dick thicken in my pants once more. I'm suddenly picturing her with those long, tan legs wrapped firmly around my waist while she's wearing those boots and nothing else.

She's a vision. Like staring at the sun; I know I should look away before I get burned, but I can't.

"That jackass doesn't deserve any more of your thoughts. We're going to go out there and listen to a few bands, drink a few beers, and have fun. You can hang out with me and my buddies tonight," I tell her.

Still, she hesitates a little. I'm assuming it's a safety factor, you know? Mom and Dad all but beat it into her head from the moment she can walk that you never talk to strangers. You never get into a vehicle with someone you don't know. And you never go off with a strange man at a concert even when you're surrounded by thousands of others. Ever.

Yet, here I am, asking her to throw caution to the wind and come with me. I can practically see her wheels spinning as she weighs the odds, mentally listing the pros and cons. I can tell that what she needs right now is reassurance; to know that not every guy out there is a douche like the man she came here with.

"Dani, I promise to watch out for you tonight. My friends are good guys. I'll be a complete gentleman the entire time, unless you don't want me to be," I add with an ornery smile. Her sweet laughter fills the campsite moments before she places her hand inside of mine once more.

"Let's go," she says, awarding me with a warm smile. I suddenly feel like I just won the damn lottery as her eyes twinkle with the same excitement that her smile carries. My breath hitches inside my chest, and unexpectedly, I'm feeling lightheaded.

I lead Dani towards our makeshift campsite. We've got two tents that Jon bought specifically for this trip, a cooler filled with enough beer to keep us hydrated for a few days, another with food and bottled water, and a small fire pit; not that you need it in this heat, but the desert does start to cool down once the sun disappears. And besides, we need it for cooking. Four bag chairs that Scott borrowed from his parents complete our set up. It's nothing fancy but it'll get the job done tonight and keep us from sleeping in the dirt or being eaten by mosquitoes.

"Want one?" I ask as I fish a Coors Light out of the cooler.

"Um, sure," she replies in a smaller voice laced with uncertainty.

"You don't have to if you don't want to. I have water," I tell her.

Taking the proffered can from my hand, she says, "I just don't drink that much."

"Ahh, a lightweight," I reply with a grin.

"Exactly," she laughs.

"Well, then here's to letting down your hair and having fun," I toast with my full can of suds.

"To having fun," she says just before tapping her can against mine. Instantly I want to push the limits and see what kind of fun she's willing to have with me. But I promised to be a gentleman tonight, and I'm not about to go back on my word. If I'm anything, I'm honest. Sometimes, brutally so.

Lacey Black

"Come on. Let's go find the guys and I'll introduce you," I say as we make our way towards the crowd. Dani threads her small fingers between mine as we make our way through the mob. I'm sure it's because she doesn't want to lose track of me, but a part of me is still hoping it's because she just likes to touch me. God knows I like touching her.

When we make our way to the spot I last saw my friends, I see they wasted no time filling my absence with some girls. A short brunette with large tits has them pressed firmly against Cory's chest while she whispers in his ear. The smile he offers me tells me it has nothing to do with whatever story she's sharing and everything to do with the fact that her tits are smashed pleasantly against him.

"Hey, guys, this is Dani. This is Jon, Scott, and that one there is Cory," I tell the girl at my side, pointing to each of my friends.

"Hi," she says, offering them each a pleasant smile.

While night falls around us, the temperature only continues to climb. With each band or performer that takes the stage, more bodies seem to flock to the large grassy area we're all standing in.

An hour ago, we ran back to the campsite and cooked a bunch of hotdogs. Dani didn't want to impose, but I wasn't about to let her starve tonight because her asshole ex didn't care enough to make sure she was eating or had a place to sleep. She sat in my chair while I straddled the cooler beside her, munching on hotdogs and potato chips.

Now, Dani is plastered against my side, gently swaying to the beat of the music. She wasn't kidding about being a lightweight. Three beers in and she's already showing signs of a healthy buzz. The crowd around us is getting more belligerent and a little closer to out of control. We've seen several fist fights, a bunch of shouting matches, and are doing everything we can to stay out of the line of

16

fire. The more alcohol that flows freely in the crowd, the closer to chaos we get.

"Good evening, Phoenix," the announcer says into the microphone, ringing out loud enough that I'm sure everyone within a five mile radius can hear. "I'm excited to present our next performer. Are you ready? Give it up for Tim McGraw," he says as the shorter cowboy takes the stage. The crowd erupts into hoots and hollers, and from somewhere over to the left of the stage, a bikini top flies on stage and lands at his feet.

"Oh my God, I love him," Dani announces excitedly. She starts to bounce up and down, and I can feel the moment she completely lets go.

Tim walks up to the mic and offers a greeting to the crowd. Then he starts to play "I Like It, I Love It." The similarities between my situation and the words in the song don't go unnoticed. The woman next to me has completely wormed her way into my frigid heart. No, I'm not making any declaration to anything, but for the first time, I realize I might be capable of feeling something for another person who isn't family.

And that thought terrifies me.

Dani sings along, a little off key, but neither of us cares. She's finally having fun and letting loose, and that's all I've wanted since I invited her to spend the evening with me. Well, that's not *all* I wanted, but it was all I was prepared to have. And I got it.

A few songs later, I find myself dancing along with Dani. I don't dance. Ever. I only went to my prom because I was planning on getting laid that night. The guys and I spent the night on the balcony with a flask of some cheap dime store tequila while our dates danced to the DJ. But now, I find myself swaying in rhythm to the music, singing along to songs I don't even really know. It's exhilarating.

17

When Tim starts a slow song, Dani wastes no time grabbing me and pulling me against her smaller frame. My six-foot body is much taller than hers, but we fit together perfectly like puzzle pieces. My chin falls at the top of her head and we gently start to move to the music. A song about finding love and the effects of said love blares through the darkened sky. I can feel Dani's breath against my arm, and I can't control the direction that my mind wanders. Holding her in my arms, feeling her body against me, causes every ounce of blood I possess to run south of my belt. I don't mean for it to happen, it just does. It's out of my control, just like my future.

Apparently, Dani notices at that moment, too. She pulls back ever so slightly and gazes up into my eyes. Her blue eyes shine with excitement and curiosity. I wish I knew what to say to her. I mean, "Hey, that's my hard-on pressed against your stomach," just don't seem like the right words. Yet, for the first time in my adult life, the right words don't come.

Realizing that we've stopped dancing, I pull her body firmly against mine. There's no mistaking the hard ridge between us now as it's practically thumping against us, begging to be released from my shorts. And fuck if I don't want to release it from its confines with this woman.

Dani's eyes darken into a deep navy blue as her pupils dilate. Her breathing comes out in short pants that pepper the five o'clock shadow on my chin. I feel her hands flex against my back, gripping at my shirt. It takes every ounce of control I possess to not take her mouth in the fierce kiss I'm suddenly fantasizing about. Her lips are parted and glisten with moisture as I imagine what it would be like to claim them for the first time.

"Do it," she whispers just loud enough for me to hear.

"Do what?" I ask hoarsely. Suddenly, my brain isn't quite working properly; like there's some sort of short circuit. The only thing it can focus on is the woman I'm holding in my arms.

"Kiss me," she says as if daring me. *Well, honey, it's a challenge I'm more than willing to take.*

When my lips meet hers for the first time, something crazy happens. Fireworks. Seriously, fucking fireworks burst in the night sky, drawing the attention upward of everyone at the concert. Everyone but us. I zone in solely on her lush lips and claim them for my own. There's no hesitation in her kiss. Only matching hunger and need. Dani's tongue slides against my own, and I damn near explode in my pants. I've never experienced anything like this kiss in my entire life. It's raw and hungry and teasing me in the best damn way possible, as if to say "more is yet to come."

I nip at her full bottom lip before sucking it into my mouth and soothing the sting with my tongue. Her moan is loud, but thankfully, everyone around us is focused on the night sky. I feel my shirt being pulled out of my shorts moments before Dani rakes her nails down the bare skin of my back. *Fucking all things holy, does that feel amazing.*

"I made you a promise tonight," I mumble, trying to clear the sexual fog from my lusting brain. The problem is that my big brain isn't doing any of the thinking at this point; it's all about the smaller one. Pulling back, away from her fantastic body, is the hardest thing I've never done, but it's necessary. The only way I'm going to keep the promise I made is to distance our bodies right this instant. A lot of distance.

"What if I don't want you to be a gentleman, Reid?" she whispers. I search her eyes, looking for any sign of doubt or hesitation. But the only thing I see is desire. Want. That same hunger I'm sure is evident in my own eyes.

"Are you sure?" I ask her, giving her one more chance to back out. I'm not about to force myself on anyone, especially Dani. I want her to trust me and know that I would never do anything to harm her.

"I've never been more sure of anything," she answers with a smile. I lean forward and place a gentle kiss on her lips, cementing my intent to take care of her tonight. Sexually, yes, but also emotionally. Considering I've never thought about taking care of another woman emotionally, that's saying a lot for the woman I'm holding in my arms.

Taking Dani's hand in mine, I turn to my friends. "You're rooming with them tonight," I say to Jon.

"No. Bullshit, Reid. We're not sleeping three guys in one of those little tents," Jon says with a little heat. Too bad I don't give a shit.

"Yes, you are," I tell him with a pointed look before turning back to Dani and leading her away from my friends. I don't even hear what they say behind my back, but I'm pretty sure it's not about how great of a friend I am right now. I couldn't care less. Being with Dani is the *only* thing that matters at this moment.

I barrel through the crowd of people all focused upward on the bright lights bursting in the night sky. My primary focus is getting this beautiful woman naked and underneath me. It suddenly feels like it's the only reason I was put in this very place at the exact same time she was.

When we reach our campsite, I finally slow down. Having dragged her along behind me, Dani is breathless and sweating. That's nothing compared to what she's going to be like shortly. Stepping towards the small tent that Jon and I were supposed to share, I turn towards her, giving her one final chance to walk away.

If she does, I'll deal with it, but I'm praying to God and anyone else who'll listen right now that she doesn't.

She doesn't hesitate as she steps forward and wraps her arms around my back. Her lips are still swollen from our earlier kiss, and I can't fight my need to kiss her once again. Her mouth opens immediately, allowing me to explore and taste her. My hands slide into her long, blond hair, pulling and tugging on the elastic band holding her hair back. I toss it somewhere into the night as my hands dive into her lush locks. Instantly, I'm assaulted with the scent of something fruity. It takes everything I have to pull my lips away, but I crave her scent. I place tender kisses up her face and towards her hair. I inhale a deep breath of her sweetness, and the action isn't lost on me. I've become that guy who smells a woman's hair. Again, I don't give a shit.

Breaking the contact of our bodies, I turn towards the zipper of the tent and give it a pull. The slide against the teeth echoes in the night and for some reason, sounds magnified against our surroundings; like a beacon drawing all attention towards our tent, as if announcing what's about to happen.

Inside the tent is sweltering, the air stagnant. We should have probably left the small windows open to allow any air movement to travel through the small space, but that's hindsight now. I sit down in the middle of the floor, an unrolled sleeping bag on either side of me. Dani straddles me, wrapping those long, tan legs around my waist. I can practically feel the heat from her pussy through our clothes. She grinds her sweetness against my aching cock, sending every ounce of blood I possess to that one concentrated area. All thought evades my mind as she grinds and moves against my dick, mimicking the act I'm so anxious to engage in. Suddenly, it's sizzling in here and it isn't from the humid air.

"I want you just like this when you come," I tell her hoarsely, not really able to recognize the sound of my own voice. Lust has completely taken over, leaving behind a trail of molten fire.

Her moan is the only reply I receive before I steal another life-altering kiss. There's something about the way she kisses; like I'm the very air she breathes. It's intoxicating. Exhilarating. Fucking Heaven.

Quickly, I flip us around until she's beneath me; another position I can't wait to enjoy. Her legs remain wrapped around my waist as I grind my dick against the V of her legs. Shit, I'm going to explode in my pants if I'm not careful, and there's no way in hell I'm going to let that happen.

Grabbing the hem of her tank top, I lift it up, exposing mounds of firm, fleshy tits. Her bra is black lace and teases just enough creamy cleavage to make my mouth water. The little plastic clasp in the front holds my attention now as I kiss my way down her neck and towards the closure. Her hot skin is an intoxicating combination of salty and sweet with a hint of bug spray, and I'll damned if the mixture doesn't turn me on that much more. With precision, I flick that clasp open and jimmy the pieces until it springs apart, freeing her beautiful tits.

I'm hypnotized instantly, her pull like nothing I've ever experienced before. There's something so very different about Dani, and I do everything I can to push it to the back of my mind. Now isn't the time to try to rationalize and compartmentalize whatever is brewing between us. Monday is the start of a new chapter for me. Tonight, I don't see any reason that I can't close out my old life with Dani. Getting lost in her sweet body is the perfect way to end this chapter.

Taking one of her pert rosebud nipples in my mouth, I suck and lap at her sensitive skin. Her moans of pleasure are the only encouragement I need right now, but the feel of her hands holding onto my head, as if ensuring that I don't move, only fuels my burning fire. After a few minutes of showing one nipple attention, I turn to the other. Dani's legs tighten around my waist as she pulls me tighter against her, creating as much delicious friction as possible.

Her shorts are next. My mind practically short-circuits at the thought of seeing her bare for the first time. I reach down and flick open the single button, followed quickly by lowering the zipper. A hint of black lace peers out at me through the opening of the denim. My throat is suddenly dry and my hands have a slight tremble to them as I grip her shorts and tug. When they're removed completely from her body, she sits up and removes the wrinkled tank top and her bra. She now lies before me in nothing but a tiny black lace thong that is soaked through. The scent of her arousal fills the tent, replacing the stale air with only her.

I waste no time discovering what's hidden underneath that lace. Smooth, bare skin glistens back at me when I move the material to the side. A strangled growl erupts from deep within my chest. She feels like silk against my fingers. Hands that are manicured and well groomed for the business world slide effortlessly through her wetness. Dani wriggles against the assault of my gentle caress.

"I need to taste you," I confess. Her blue eyes are dark with desire as she gives me a little head nod. *Silly vixen, I wasn't asking for permission.*

The first swipe of my tongue is electrifying; like being caught in a lightning storm and I'm holding a metal pole. Her essence is everywhere: my tongue, the air, my mind. She has penetrated my being so deeply, I worry I'll never eradicate her.

Pushing that thought aside, I dive into her wet center. I use my tongue to lick, tease, and pleasure her, pulling out every trick I've learned in the past few years when it comes to seducing women. Her small hands find their way into my hair as she rides my face. Dani's moans fill the tent and can probably be heard from outside, but it doesn't matter because giving her the most pleasure I can manage is my single focus. She's all I want.

Sliding a finger inside of her, her internal muscles instantly grip me, pulling me in deeper. "Oh, God," she moans, crushing her pussy against my hand.

"I want to hear you let go. I want everyone outside to know what I'm doing to you right now," I demand as I continue my assault. Her pussy grips my finger as I flick my tongue over her swollen clit. And that's all she wrote.

Her cries of ecstasy fill the small tent, and do weird things to my once-hollow chest. It makes me want to pound on my chest like a caveman or fluff my feathers like a peacock. It must be some crazy male pride thing.

"Don't get too comfy," I tell her as I kiss my way back up her stomach and towards her mouth. I don't even wipe off my mouth before I plunge my tongue inside. She's panting from her orgasm, but latches on to my mouth instantly, sucking off her own juices.

Dani's fingers grip and pull at my shirt. With one swift yank, I've removed my polo shirt. Her hands burn my chest as she slides them along the contours of my abs. I work damn hard to keep my body in great shape, almost as hard as I worked the books in school. I've also learned that a physically trimmed body can be like catnip to women.

I make quick work at stripping my khaki shorts from my body as if I couldn't get rid of them fast enough. My cock throbs to the point of pain in my boxers. Gripping them in my hands, I slide them down my legs, maneuvering myself around in the confined space. Dani's audible gasp pulls my attention back to her where I find her eyes firmly locked on my dick. I'll be honest; I'm not a little man. I'm not conceited or exaggerating; I'm hung like a damn race horse, and the thought of sliding inside this tight woman before me has my mind all sorts of fucked up. The Lord gave me more than my fair share, and I'm damn sure gonna use it to my advantage as much as humanly possible tonight.

The lust and excitement in her eyes pulls my attention. I crawl back up her body and revel in the feel of her flesh against mine. My cock is practically hammering against her stomach as if begging for me to give it what it wants; and fuck, if I don't want that too.

Taking her sweet lips against mine once more, I hold on to Dani with everything I've got. Cradling her in my arms, I shift my weight to my elbow and slide my dick through her wetness. Yeah, she's ready to go again.

Positioned at her entrance, I suddenly stop. Her blue eyes are fire and her breathing is labored in anticipation. "I can only give you tonight, Dani," I mumble moments before I take her lips once more. "I wish I could promise you more, but I can't. I'm not from here."

"I know," she whispers. "Give me tonight. That's all I want," she adds. Her eyes are softer, her sweetness tugging at what little heart I have.

Without saying another word, I slide forward, enveloping my dick in her tight wetness. Fucking heaven. The feel of her body wrapped around me steals my breath. Her own breath hitches, causing her to grip down on my shaft. Thankfully, I don't lose the precious self-control I'm barely holding on to as I give her a few moments to adjust to my size.

When I feel her relaxing underneath me, I slowly pull out and push forward again. Dani locks those long legs around my waist giving me the perfect angle to slide in deeper. My body is sweating and my mind is blank as I savor the feel of her body against mine.

She's a little slice of heaven on earth, and it pains me that I can't keep her. Because for the first time in my life, I wish I could. I want to spend more time with her, getting to know her and exploring her body.

Dani's gasp against my ear pulls me out of my internal turmoil. Now isn't the time for sappy shit; shit that I can't control. Now is the time to fuck this beautiful woman. To leave my mark on her, hopefully with a memory she'll carry for the rest of her life.

Sliding myself completely out, I slam back inside of her. I swear I hit her stomach as she moans her pleasure in my ear. My pace suddenly becomes swifter and more precise. I'm on the verge of losing control as I grasp at her perfect tits. Wishing I could suck them again, I latch my mouth onto the only thing it can find right now: her mouth.

The kiss is potent, passionate. It's so intense and fierce, I'm afraid the flame-retardant vinyl of the tent might actually burst into flames. The sounds of skin slapping against skin and labored grunts fill the smoldering confines of the space we occupy. She grips my shaft hard with each thrust bringing me one step closer to losing my fucking mind.

I realize a change of pace is needed if I'm going to last longer than a few more seconds. Gripping Dani around the waist, I roll us over until she's straddling me, without breaking our connection. When her legs are positioned next to my outer thighs, I thrust up into her body hard. I grasp Dani by her hips and hold on while she takes me for a ride. She lifts up slowly and slams her body back down on mine, gyrating and grinding against me. Un-fucking-believable. My eyes roll back in my head.

Not only does this position send me deeper than ever, but it also gives me the perfect angle to stroke that sweet spot deep inside her.

And if the way she's riding me like a bucking bronco at the rodeo is any indication, I'd say I'm hitting it perfectly.

Dani's legs grip my outer thighs as I bring us both closer to climax. My moans mix with hers as I feel her muscles grab ahold of my dick and squeeze the life out of it. Dani all but screams as another powerful orgasm rips through her body. I latch my lips onto hers to swallow the sounds of her pleasure, though I'm sure it's fruitless. As I thrust up into her body once more, Dani bites down on my lower lip. Not enough to draw blood but enough to cause an sharp sting. The moment is more intense than anything I've ever experienced as I follow her over the edge, head first into blackened oblivion.

I hold on tightly as we both try to slow our racing heartbeats. She sags against my chest, spent and sated. I slowly roll us over until we're lying side by side atop my sleeping bag. Dani stretches like a cat while I wriggle the lightweight sleeping bag open. Holding it, I wait while she slips inside and gets comfy. Opening the tops of the windows in the tent, cooler night air finally penetrates the confines of the muggy tent.

Before I climb inside my bag next to this beautiful, naked woman, I hear the guys outside the tent. Jon's clearly still unhappy about being booted from his own tent, but I couldn't care less. Balling up his sleeping bag, I unzip the entrance to the tent and toss his bag out, careful not to expose myself.

"Thanks for something," Jon slurs as he retrieves his sleeping bag from the dirt. I don't answer, just zip back up the entrance, closing off my friends from the naked woman in the tent with me. He may be pissed, but he'll get over it. Jon never stays mad for too long.

I slip inside the sleeping bag and snuggle up as close as possible to the beautiful woman beside me. Her body is warm and wet, but I think it only makes this moment that much more perfect. So this is what snuggling is like, huh? I've never done it. Never even wanted to try it. A girlfriend in high school used to want to cuddle on the couch while watching movies, but I always considered it useless. I was usually there for one thing, and cuddling together under a blanket–clothed–wasn't it.

Dani sighs loudly as I pull her into my arms and tuck her back against my side. She fits perfectly. My eyelids are suddenly heavy as exhaustion from the drive, the drinking in the sun, and the best fuck I've ever had takes a toll on me. My body is spent.

Dani mumbles softly as she drifts off to sleep, bringing a smile to my lips. Lips that still feel her body against them. I'll never forget this night. This moment. This woman. As I succumb to sleep, thoughts of how I wish my life were different plague my mind. I wish I didn't have to go to work for my father on Monday. I wish I could take Dani out on a proper date. I wish I could stay right here, right now, forever.

She's the last thing I think about as I fall into a deep sleep.

In the morning when I wake, she's gone.

Chapter One – Blind Date From Hell

Dani

Present Day

"So, you're a teacher?" my date asks while chewing a mouthful of sloppy Chicken Parmesan.

"Yes," I confirm for the second time tonight, all the while moving my baked halibut around on my plate in an effort to hide the fact that I haven't eaten more than a few bites. Greg's open trap of tumbling food is enough to turn my stomach and dissolve any appetite I had when I walked into this restaurant.

"That's pretty cool. I bet you're a great teacher. I mean I would have loved to get you as my teacher back in the day. I never had a hot teacher," he mumbles while chewing. Chew. Chew. Chew. I swallow the bile that's threatening to make an appearance when his bushy eyebrows wiggle like some sort of caterpillar walking across his forehead.

I hate my sister. It's official. I have the worst sister in the world. I don't know what I ever did to Trysta to make her hate me enough to subject me to this kind of torture. "Go on a blind date," she said. "It'll be fun," she said. "Greg's so adorable; like a puppy," yada yada yada. Apparently my sister is mean *and* blind. And don't get me started on her lack of hearing, because if she really had to sit in the same room with this guy while he ate, there's no way in hell she ever would have set me up with this clown.

"So, what do you do at The Mirage?" *Please let him say pit boss. Please!*

"I'm a custodial engineer," he says while shoveling a heaping pile of steamed broccoli into his face.

"Custodial engineer?" I ask more to myself than to him. I have a pretty good idea where this is going.

"Yeah. I clean the restrooms, mop the floors, and pick up after the rich gamblers. But I'm not a maid," he informs me sternly. "No, I don't clean the rooms. I do more of the general grounds of the casinos. I've been there for six years now, and have worked my way up to the blackjack room. Someday, I hope to hit it big and get the High Roller Room. But, the guy that cleans that room now is really good and has been there for like twenty years. Your sister is one of everyone's favorite cocktail waitresses in the High Roller Room. Nice girl; big boobs like yours."

"Wow, that's…yeah."

"Have I told you that I have a teacher fantasy?" Greg asks, a few pieces of cheesy noodles flying from his pie hole.

"Excuse me?" I ask, praying to God that this conversation isn't about to turn in the direction I'm fearing.

Greg leans forward enough so that his blue and green polka dotted tie featuring two animated dinosaurs on the front dips into his plate of cheese sauce. "Oh, yeah. Hot teacher asks me to return after class. When I walk in, she's got her long ruler in her hand and uses it on my -"

"That's nice and all, but it's getting late," I say with a little more force than I intend.

"Oh. But we're still eating the main entrée. We haven't even gotten to dessert yet," he says with an insinuating smile while wagging those caterpillar-like eyebrows again.

"Yeah, well, it's getting late and I have class tomorrow," I reply while depositing my cloth napkin down on the tabletop. Greg doesn't realize that it's Friday and I don't actually have class tomorrow. If he asks, though, I'm pleading Saturday detention duty.

Greg stands up when I do and walks around to my side of the table. A drop of the sauce is sitting on his chin like a big neon sign. Like a zit, my eyes are glued to that little dripping of food. In fact, I'm staring so long that it takes me a second to realize that the drop of goo is moving towards me. I snap out of my trance just in time to divert my lips away from Greg's. He places a wet kiss that reminds me of a dog, on my cheek.

"Are you sure you have to go home now? I thought maybe we could go back to my place tonight. My mom is out at Bridge Club so she won't be home for at least another hour. Plenty of time to drive home and get disciplined by a hot teacher," he says, baring his coffee stained teeth. And that's the moment my stomach actually rolls and I fear I'm going to blow chow all over the front of his dull white shirt, elementary neck tie, and wrinkled khakis; all in front of Vegas' middle class at a mom and pop Italian restaurant.

"Oh," I start with a laugh. "I don't think so, Greg. It was really nice to meet you," I lie while digging out a handful of bills from my pocketbook. I drop just enough to cover my portion of the bill and a tip. Let Mr. Can't Chew With His Mouth Closed pay for his own meal.

"It was really nice to meet you, Dena," he says.

"It's Dani, actually," I mumble while grabbing my wrap from the back of the chair and whipping it over the shoulders of my navy blue dress.

"Dani? Are you sure? I could have sworn your sister said your name was Dena."

"Nope, I'm pretty sure it's Dani," I reply, voice dripping with sarcasm, before turning and walking away. I don't stop. I keep walking straight out of the restaurant, even though Greg is still talking behind me. I don't stop until I'm sliding into the driver's seat of my 6-year-old Toyota Camry. My hands are still shaking as I slip the key into the ignition and start the car. I'm definitely ready to go home and drown in a bottle of wine and a bubble bath.

But first thing's first…

"It's barely eight o'clock," my older sister, Trysta, says in way of greeting.

"You set me up with a troll. A troll, Tryst. He talked with his mouth full the entire time. He spit food particles while trying to show me some new video game app on his cell phone. He lives with his freaking mom for God's sake!"

"Hey, now, Greg isn't that bad. He's always so nice when he's vacuuming and cleaning up the trash around the room."

"He's repulsive. I was afraid one of his eyebrows were going to crawl off his forehead and land in his dinner," I yell at my sister, which instantly makes her laugh.

"Yeah, those things are a little on the creepy side," she adds through her laughter.

"I'm glad you think this is funny. Laugh it up, Tryst. Enjoy this moment. Because I assure you it won't ever happen again. I will never, ever, *ever* let you set me up on a blind date again. Got it?"

"Yeah, I got it," she says when her fit of laughter is under control.

In Trysta's defense, she never has to work for a date. She doesn't know what it's like to be looked over once, sometimes twice. She is the epitome of beautiful. Her long blond hair is more platinum than my honey-colored locks. Her figure is that perfect hourglass shape with not an ounce of fat on her. Well, except her boobs. They practically have their own zip code. And don't get me started on her legs, which extend for miles and miles, as she parades around on four-inch heels all night long.

Trysta is two years older than me, and we are as different as night and day. I'm quiet to her openly friendly. I prefer books to her manicures. I love to throw my hair up in a ponytail while she makes sure not a speck of makeup is out of place before she leaves her bedroom. But for all of our differences, she's still my best friend and has been since our mom left before we were teenagers.

I'm just a little plainer than my supermodel-worthy sister. I stand a few inches shorter than her at five foot, five inches, and while I don't lack in the chest department, my double D's still don't compare to hers. My hands haven't seen a manicure since she treated me to a spa day two years ago for my twenty-seventh birthday.

"I'm heading home now," I tell my sister. "I'm picking up a pint of Chunky Monkey at the corner market. Do we need anything else?" I ask.

"No, I don't think so. I don't go in until eleven, so I have plenty of time to hear all the details of your date," she says with a chuckle.

"Fine, but I'm not telling you about it until after I have my ice cream." The last thing I want is to lose my appetite *before* I've indulged in my favorite dairy treat.

"Deal. See you in a few," she says before signing off.

I drive home to the comforting sounds of Dierks Bentley and Lady Antebellum. Even though I've been in Vegas for almost five years now, I still can't turn my back on my country roots. Even in the middle of the Vegas strip with bright lights and dancing showgirls, I feel most comfortable in a pair of worn boots.

Thinking of my favorite pair of worn cowboy boots reminds me of Country Fest. It was the last concert I've been to, more than eight long years ago. Before my life changed forever. For the better.

As I pull into the driveway of our cute little yellow bungalow house, my mind can't help but return to that one moment in time. That one night when everything was perfect, even for just a little bit. Reid. The one man that I will never forget. His touch, his scent, his eyes. Even if I wanted to, I'll forever hold his alluring gray eyes in a special place in my mind. Though, that moment in history is something for me and me alone, I try to keep his memory locked away.

Something magical happened that night we shared a tent. A life was created.

One that Reid knows nothing about.

* * *

I just get settled into my chair at the kitchen table when the back door flies open with a loud bang as it bounces off the wall. "Hey Mom," my seven-year-old son, Ryan, says as he walks through the open doorway, trailed behind by my exhausted looking dad.

"Hi, Ryan. Were you good for Grandpa?" I ask, standing up and walking over to the love of my life.

"Yeah, we watched *Pawn Stars* all night. He even let me stay up til ten o'clock!" Ryan exclaims, obviously very happy that his grandpa allowed him to break bedtime by two hours.

"Ten o'clock? Really?" I ask, fretting mock dismay.

"Yeah, did you know that Chumlee once called in sick but was really home playing video games?" Ryan asks, his eyes lighting up with laughter.

"I did not know that," I tell him, fighting the smile that's playing on the corner of my lips.

"Grandpa said that you can get fired for that," Ryan adds with a decisive head nod as confirmation. Ryan has always looked up to the only man in his life–his grandpa. Whatever Grandpa says is practically law. I've used that logic in my favor a time or two in the past when it comes to dealing with my rambunctious son. Ryan definitely isn't a difficult child, but sometimes his strong will can be challenging to deal with.

"Grandpa is very smart. Usually," I reply before giving my son a big squeeze. "Why don't you go put your bag in your room." Ryan starts to take off down the hallway that leads to the bedrooms in our modest sized bungalow home. "But be quiet. Don't wake Auntie Trysta." Ryan throws me a quick nod over his shoulder before he takes off down the hardwood hallway at DEFCON Seven, each step echoing off the white walls like a fighter jet taking off from an aircraft carrier. The entire place practically vibrates.

"Ten o'clock, huh?" I ask, not able to mask my smile at the older version of myself, as I walk over to the coffee pot.

"What can I say?" he asks while nodding his head in confirmation when I hold up the almost-full coffee pot.

"It's fine. What time did he get up?" I ask, already knowing the answer to that question. I can tell by the way Ryan was practically bouncing off the walls that he didn't get much sleep. Some people get cranky, some full of energy. But I know his energy levels are short lived. Wait until about six o'clock tonight. Then, he'll drop like a lead balloon.

"Six," he winces. "And of course he wanted waffles."

"Of course." I smile knowing that his waffles were probably topped with plenty of sticky syrup and either strawberries or bananas just like mine were when I was his age.

"How'd last night go?" he asks, taking a cautious sip of his black coffee.

"Horrible. I hate Trysta. I can't believe she set me up with that guy," I tell my dad while stirring a heaping spoonful of sugar into my coffee cup.

"She meant well," Dad confirms.

"I know." And I do. Trysta hates the idea of me sitting at home every weekend while Ryan's father is off doing God knows what, living his life. It's not that I'm not living the life I want, it's just that I didn't have a choice on which road I was to follow. I was twenty-one years old and pregnant. There was no decision to be made. I was having a baby. She doesn't broach the subject too often, but will occasionally use my lack of knowledge pertaining to Reid against me. Case in point: last night's blind date. She caught me at a weak moment.

Dad doesn't know the real story. How can a daughter in her early twenties tell her dad that she slept with a guy she didn't know, didn't use protection, and wound up pregnant? She can't. Trysta is the only one who knows the truth about Ryan's dad. That morning when she picked me up at the main gate of the festival, she knew something was up. We've always been close, in tune with each emotion, facial expression, and basically every thought that went through the other's head. She's been my best friend since I was ten years old and our mother left for places unknown.

"Thank you for humoring her," Dad says as he slides down into an empty seat at the kitchen table. "It's difficult to be set up like that."

"You have no idea," I mumble. The look Dad gives me tells me that maybe he *does* have an idea. "How do you know?" I ask, noticing that he's fidgeting something fierce and unable to hold eye contact.

Finding our little bungalow was sheer luck. Our first week in Vegas, Dad took a wrong turn, winding us into a cul-de-sac with cheerful, family-friendly homes. While turning around, this cute, yellow house caught my eye. What drew my attention more than the white shutters on the windows was the For Sale sign in the front yard. I made Dad stop while I wrote down the number of the realtor on the sign. An hour later, I was scheduling an appointment with some woman named Sherry to tour the house the next day.

Dad had to work so Trysta went with me. She seemed just as excited as I was as we walked around the fifteen hundred square foot home. Two decent sized bedrooms downstairs and one upstairs in a large, loft-style space. From room to room, I took in every nook and architectural charm that this house possessed. I was in love. I had to have it.

I didn't need anyone to co-sign the mortgage loan. I have excellent credit and pride myself on making sure I pay off any debt I incur right away. I knew the payment would be tight under my teaching salary, but I was determined. I would eat Ramen noodles every night if I had to, as long as Ryan had everything he needed and I had this house.

Trysta presented me with an offer I couldn't refuse right after the ink was signed on the papers. Taking the loft room upstairs, suddenly I had a roommate. Plus, she was willing to help with Ryan, and that alone was way more than I could have ever asked for. When she landed her job at the Mirage casino, it was practically written in the stars. She worked nights, slept during the day while I was at work, and watched Ryan in the afternoon after school. We were a match made in heaven.

"Mom, are you ready to go swimming?" Ryan asks from the kitchen entryway. He's already wearing his Batman swim trunks, brown hair tussled from changing his clothes.

"I'm grading the last paper now. Give me five minutes and then I'll run and change into my suit," I tell my son.

Like many houses in the Nevada desert, this house came with a pool. I was terrified at first to have a pool with a toddler, but after speaking with a colleague, whose husband is a general contractor, I paid to have a fence installed around the in-ground pool. It helps me sleep at night knowing that Ryan can't slip out the back and fall into the water, unknown.

After my last paper is graded and the lot stuffed back inside my satchel bag that I use for work, I quietly sneak into my bedroom to change. The black and hot pink polka dot bikini is my favorite. It accentuates all of my curves without making me look like I'm trying too hard. My body definitely changed after birthing my son, but when I wear this suit, it gives me the confidence boost that I desperately need, even if I'm the only one to see and appreciate it.

"Mom, I'm ready," Ryan hollers from his position by the back door. Armed with a couple of dry beach towels and grabbing the bottle of SPF 50 sunscreen off the counter by the back door, I follow my son into the bright desert sun. Not a bad day for mid-May.

Reaching around the backside of the gate, I fumble until I release the latch. When I installed the fence, the first thing I had the contractor do was add the latching mechanism to the backside. It was one of the only ways I could safeguard my son against the water on the other side. You have to be able to reach around and release the latch. Little hands are unable accomplish the task.

Placing my towel on the chaise lounge already reclined from previous use, I lather up my son in sunscreen. As soon as I give him the signal, he takes off towards the water's edge. He's been swimming like a fish for years. The first thing I did after we moved to Vegas was sign us up for swimming lessons at the YMCA. Those lessons helped ease my mind where the pool was concerned.

"Oh, he was a shameless flirt and almost as handsome. Asked for my number no less than a dozen times. Said I was breaking his heart," she says with a laugh.

"And?"

"And I gave him my number," she says. Even though she's wearing sunglasses, I can tell she offers me a wink.

Hot guys flock to Trysta like ants to a picnic. I've never felt wild and reckless like she does so often in life. No, I take that back: I've felt that once.

Reid.

That night, I was alive. I was free. I was irresponsible and wild. The irony of that one night is that my irresponsibility led to the most responsible thing I've ever had to do.

My son. Ryan.

Chapter Two – Business As Usual

Reid

"Carly, can you come in here?"

The phone buzzes instantly with her reply. "Right away."

My personal assistant, Carly, hurries through the heavy wooden door that separates her workspace from mine. She has been at my side for three years now, and honestly, she's the best fucking assistant I've ever had. Hands down. She's not afraid to get her hands dirty, stay late, or slap me upside the head when I need it. She works hard and is loyal to a T. She's devoted to this company right alongside of me. The difference? She works eight hours. I work sixteen.

I was concerned about her having a young child, of course, but Carly does everything she can to ensure that she's at work as much as possible. Her mother is very active in her life and helps as much as possible with Carly's daughter, Natalia. And of course, I value her too much so whenever she needs time off here or there, I'm always willing to help her out. I'm not a complete bastard. At least not to her.

Of course, the dynamics of everything changed last fall when Carly reconnected with Nat's father. Blake is an FBI agent who was going undercover when he met Carly. They shared one night together, which resulted in Natalia. Two years later, they found their lives twisted together tighter than a bread tie when he found himself undercover in a world to take down her father. It was a tangled mess. Total *Days of Our Lives* shit. But they've seemed to come out on the other side semi-unscathed. They're getting married next month, and even though that shit isn't for me, I'm truly happy for her.

"Yes, Mr. Hunter?" she asks as she takes the leather seat across from my expansive desk. Her pen and paper poised on her lap, ready to write down anything that I ask of her. I've tried to buy her a tablet to take notes on numerous occasions, but she won't have it. She'd rather handwrite her notes and says she gets joy from flipping through the pages. I enjoy ruffling her feathers every now and then about it, though. I even went as far as to have a tablet delivered to her desk via courier after one stressful afternoon where she misplaced notes on the eve of an important meeting. I still smile inwardly when I think about her wrath practically busting through the wall that day like the Kool-Aid Man.

"How many times do I have to tell you to call me Reid?" I ask her. Another old argument.

"Don't start, *Reid.*" I can't help the corner of my lips turning upward ever so slightly at her snarly attitude.

"Cruz wants to meet tomorrow morning. I'm tired of him dragging his feet. Every time we get close, he starts renegotiating the terms. We've been working this deal for more than seven months now, and I'm done. Either we sign tomorrow or we walk."

"Can I speak bluntly, Mr. Hunter?" Carly asks from across the desk. The thing is I already know what she's going to say. She's been opposed to this deal since it was presented last fall.

"You're going to anyway, so get on with it." My tone is clipped, I know it. I can't help it. Even as my little sister's best friend, I still keep Carly and anything else personal separate from business. Carly has made her opinion of the Cruz deal very clear. She hates it. She hates the fact that I've considered this deal, and even more so that I'm probably going to sign.

"Don't do it. Don't sign those papers. Just walk away from this one. You don't need Bravado Resorts. I know this would fit into your plan for world domination, but it's not right, and you know it." Her face is hard, yet so full of concern. Concerned for me as her boss, sure, but also as her friend. Over the last three years, we've worked side by side. We've developed a friendship that goes beyond employee and employer. She cares about me the way I've come to care about her. I will always protect her the way a brother would protect his sister.

"Carly, I appreciate your concern, really. But I've had months to think about this deal. It's perfect for my life."

"It's all wrong for your life," she whispers. The look of sadness completely transforms her beautiful face. Carly is a very beautiful woman with dark, exotic features. With long black hair and dark chocolate eyes, Carly is a walking fantasy. You'd have to be blind not to see it. But that's not how I see her. Since the day my little sister, Tara, brought her home, I've wanted to help her, protect her. Besides my right hand man, Jon, and Steven, she's probably the closest person I have to a friend. I don't need friends. Friends always want something in return. Acquaintances: that's what I have.

Carly's incredibly gorgeous, yes, but she's also caring and sweet and wears her heart on her sleeve. She reminds me of one other woman. A woman from my past that I have to occasionally push to the far recesses of my mind.

"Duly noted. Call Cruz's office and set up the meeting. I want it here. I'm not going to his office or to another luncheon. I want it on my terms, in my terrain. If he bitches, cancel the whole thing. Make it clear that this is his last choice. *He* sought me out to purchase his company, not the other way around. I've already spent more man-hours on this deal that I've ever put into a contract, and I've reached my limit. This is his final chance. Tomorrow, we either sign or we walk."

Carly writes furiously on her pad of paper. When she looks up, she gnaws on the end of her ink pen. Brown eyes search my face, and the intensity in her gaze leaves me feeling uneasy and undone. Like she can see everything deep inside that torments me, churning in my gut and robbing me of sleep. I guess if anyone can see it, it's probably her. Though I do a damn good job at masking it from everyone else in my life, I've come to realize that I do a piss-poor job at hiding it from her.

Maybe I don't want to.

"I'll take care of it, Mr. Hunter," Carly says. "Anything else?"

"That'll be all for now. Have Jon bring in the final contract. He was supposed to get it from legal yesterday, and I have yet to see it."

"He mentioned yesterday afternoon that it was supposed to be on his desk by five o'clock. I'll check with him right away," she says before standing up and heading towards the exit. "Oh, I delivered your tuxedo upstairs an hour ago." With that, Carly leaves the office, shutting the heavy door behind her.

Silence fills my massive office space. Walking over to the glass wall facing the downtown business district of Las Vegas, I take in my impressive surroundings. Off in the distance, I spy the building that was supposed to become mine. The man who gave me my last name currently occupies the space, dictating and dominating everyone within his sights. Getting out from under his grip was one of my greatest accomplishments. Taking down one of his companies and watching him unravel under my hands was another.

Stepping back over to my desk, I get busy reviewing a new proposal from Jon. A small casino just off the strip is floundering, and Jon thinks it's perfect for Hunter Enterprises. According to his proposal, Jon thinks we can get the property for a steal. It sits adjacent to a larger casino pulling a substantial profit. His plan is to purchase the older one for pennies, remove it from the lot with explosives, and sell off the lot. Mark the property high enough and dangle competition in the face of the adjacent property's owner, and you have the recipe for a multi-million dollar deal with a lucrative bottom line.

A hard knock sounds at the door. I don't even look up as I wait for my right hand man to enter. There's only one person that Carly allows into my office without an announcement first. Jon walks into the room like he owns it before dropping a manila file folder on top of the papers I've been reading for the past ten minutes.

"Well, hello to you too, Jon," I say with a clipped tone.

"Contracts for Bravado. Legal amended the hell out of it and went over it with a fine-toothed comb. They have assured me that every I is dotted and every T crossed. The last round of stipulations are outlined, as per your request. If he so much as breathes funny, we'll slap him with a breach of contract so fast, he'll have whiplash before he can even fucking think about moving money to an offshore account," Jon says as he plops down on the leather seat across from me. This is why he's my right hand. He lives and breathes this company. He has questionable morals at times and a deep desire to better our bottom line. He's also almost as ruthless as I am in business, and our joined deals are somewhat legendary in the small business world. Plus, he's one of the only men I'll ever trust with everything I have.

"Did you review them?" I ask without raising my eyes.

"You know I did," he comments.

After a few minutes of silence while I skim the noted changes, I finally look up at my best friend since college. He sits casually with one leg propped up on his knee in an impeccable designer suit and imported Italian loafers. "Good work."

"Tonight's the fundraiser for the Children's Museum, right?"

"Yeah," I say before diving back into the contract. Every year I make a sizable donation to the Las Vegas Children's Museum. It's a cause that is near and dear to my heart. It's also something closed off so damn tight in my heart and mind that you'd need a pry bar and a big truck just to peek inside. Every year I go to this event. It's the one I never miss.

"Who's the hot date for tonight?" Jon asks with the hint of a cocky grin.

"No date," I tell him. I never take a date to this particular fundraiser. I don't want some plastic doll arm candy draped all over me like a cheap suit.

The package might be different with each woman, but they're all the same on the inside: money-hungry socialites who are looking for that perfect piece of man willing to share their riches. Every one of them easy, offering to drop to their knees before the limo even pulls out of the parking lot.

I've enjoyed the hell out of plenty of willing women. A single date. That's all they get. At the end of the night, after fucking away whatever weighs down my mind, I head home. Alone. That's the way I want it, and that's the way it will always be. I make it crystal clear at the beginning of the night what I'm offering. One night. Period.

The problem that I've discovered somewhat recently is that no amount of fucking really kills that ache in my chest. It only masks it for a little while, bringing me a temporary reprieve. It's usually about the time I hit the car for the ride home that the loneliness and emptiness set in. That's when the night starts to swallow me whole, leaving behind an empty pit of darkness. But I don't fight it. It's what I deserve.

Some women try to change me, sure. Plenty think that I'm controlled by my dick, not my head. While I might lose myself in their sweet bodies for a while, I always come back to my senses. The fact remains that I'm a cold-blooded asshole who only wants one thing from them. Then, I want them gone. End of story.

The thing I've discovered about women, especially the older I get, is that they don't give a shit if you're an asshole. As long as they think you have money to throw around and the dick to back-up your talk, they'll throw themselves at you and say just about anything they think you want to hear; just as long as the checks keep coming. Even the ones who aren't exactly single.

"What time is Cruz going to be here tomorrow?" Jon asks, snapping me out of my funk.

"Carly hasn't confirmed the time yet. I want to meet with him first thing in the morning, but knowing him, he'll put it off as long as he possibly can just to fuck with me some more."

"So…you're really going to go through with this deal? I mean, you're sure this is what you want?" Jon asks, raising a well-manicured eyebrow up towards his dark hairline. He has been surprisingly quiet about this deal since the very beginning, so it pisses me off that he's actually starting to grow a fucking conscience right before the deal is done.

"Yes." I'm curt. There's no other answer to give him. *Except maybe* no. *If he were to ask me that question in the dark of night when I'm being strangled by the silence and sleep fails to find me. That's when I'd actually consider telling him no.*

"Well, I just want to make sure you're one-hundred percent in this thing. There's no room for half-assed when it comes to this deal, Reid." Jon starts to stand up, bringing his full six-foot height towering before me. It's an intimidation tactic we've both used since we were old enough to use our height in our favor. But Jon's stature does anything but intimidate me. Especially when I'm a good three inches taller than he is.

Standing up to face him, I answer, "I'm in. One-hundred percent."

After staring at me for several heartbeats, he finally throws me that cocky smile. "Good." Turning and heading towards the door, Jon throws a final, "Have a great time tonight," over his shoulder before leaving my office.

My heartbeat has kicked up as I stare at the doorway my best friend just went through. Shit, my only friend. Even the guys I hung out with in college have moved on with their lives. Married, divorced, moved away for jobs, working seven days a week to support the lifestyle they've always wanted, it's all part of the reason we've become estranged over the years. And that's okay. It's not like I have time for friends, anyway.

After confirming tomorrow's meeting with Cruz, Carly headed out at about five-thirty. She was mumbling something about an appointment with the wedding venue for next month's big day. It warms my heart to see her so damn happy. Even if that happiness is something I don't want or need, I'm pleased that Carly has finally found her bliss.

At six-thirty, I head upstairs to the apartment I keep for late nights. Swiping the keycard in the private elevator in my office, I'm silent as the elevator sweeps me up to the floor above my office. Stepping inside, I can smell the stench of expensive perfume. My stomach instantly rolls with disgust. After firing off a quick text message to Carly to have the cleaning crew scrub down my apartment as soon as I leave tonight, I grab the glass decanter of scotch. Pouring two fingers into the tumbler, I relish in the feel of the burn as it slides down my throat. The welcomed pain reminds me that I'm alive.

Refilling my glass, I head into the only bedroom in the apartment. The stench of last night's date still fills the room. Rebecca is the soon-to-be ex-wife of a business associate. Not only did I take his company from him, but I bedded his wife the weekend after I took the company that he'd spent a decade building. I say wife only because they haven't finalized their divorce yet. Rebecca had been anxiously waiting for the moment we signed the papers so she could get her half of the 3.5 million dollars I just shelled out for the floundering casino.

Pushing the thought of Rebecca and the deal out of my mind, I strip down to jump in the shower. Taking another pull from the crystal glass, I walk naked into my bathroom. My phone dings with a text message, and I read Carly's confirmation that the cleaning crew would arrive at eight o'clock tonight. Excellent.

Thirty minutes later, I'm dressed in the new tuxedo I had delivered for the fundraiser, and I'm ringing Steven to bring the car around. It's a short drive to the Children's Museum, one that I fill with sending more emails from my phone.

The limo pulls up in front of the massive building, and I put away my phone. Steven is at my door moments later and opens it. These fundraisers always draw a large crowd of local media and paparazzi. Celebrities and the rich and famous always show their faces at big fundraisers, dropping big money on over-priced vacations or exotic cars. The only reason they come out to these events is to be seen, not to support the charity at hand.

Jesus, when did I become so cynical? Oh, the answer would be always. I've always been this way. Well, except for one night…

Pushing that night out of my head, I flash my full-watt smile at the flashing cameras as I step inside the museum. The room is packed with high society. Designer dresses and custom made tuxedos are everywhere; it's wall-to-wall money. A passing waiter offers me a glass of expensive champagne. The liquid courage is just what I need before diving deep into surrounding conversations of business and money.

After talking with several area business owners about their latest contracts to take over the world, I make my way over towards the silent auction tables. Spying a trip for two to the Caymans, I throw my name down on the sheet of paper with an obscene dollar amount next to it. It'll be a great wedding gift for Carly and Blake. I know she's talked about holding off on taking a honeymoon, saying that with Natalia being so young and the purchase of their new house, they both decided to wait on a big, expensive trip.

"Hello there, handsome," I hear behind me in a seductive, sugary sweet voice moments before claws dig into the arm of my tux.

"Good evening, Gabrielle," I say without a smile.

Gabrielle and I spent a night together a few months back. She was definitely one of the women who didn't want me to leave. After begging me profusely to stay the night with her and her offering up every sexual favor known to man, and me still refusing, I've found her at several of the events I've attended since our night together. She always seems to appear right when I least expect it. Each time, I get that uneasy feeling in the pit of my gut that tells me our meeting is definitely not a coincidence.

"You look well," I tell her automatically.

"Thank you," she whispers as she leans in, offering me a cheek.

I cringe inwardly as I lean forward to place a peck on her cheek. Her perfume assaults my senses as my lips reach her skin. At the last possible second, Gabrielle turns, leaving my lips against hers. I fight the desire to push her off me; I'm in the middle of a room full of money and cameras. Instead, I keep my mouth closed, even though she clearly has every intention of deepening the kiss.

"Darling?" I hear behind me. Thankful for the save, I look up and see the son of one of Vegas' largest casino owners. Broderick Flanders stands behind Gabrielle looking pissed as hell.

"Broderick, darling. I was just saying hello to a dear friend. You know Reid Hunter, right?" she says with a wicked smile. She's playing her date like a fiddle as she strokes my arm up and down. Broderick's eyes are instantly ablaze with heat as he watches her hand settle on my bicep.

Pulling myself out of her talon claws, I extend my hand towards the young man. He practically glares at my proffered hand as if it's a snake about to bite him. Reluctantly, he places his wet hand inside of mine. His handshake is firm; almost too firm, as if he's squeezing a bit to flex his muscles or mark his territory.

Take her, buddy. Been there, done that.

"Yes, of course I've heard of Reid Hunter. Good to meet you," he says with a touch of venom in his voice.

"Good to meet you, too," I lie. I couldn't care less.

"I was just saying hello to Reid for ol' times sake," Gabrielle says with a sweet smile, but it's the underlying meaning that has Broderick's ears practically smoking. "We're old friends, Brod," she adds. The innuendo is crystal clear, and I'm instantly wishing I hadn't taken her to dinner that night a few months ago. The sex was good, but definitely not worth all this bullshit that has followed.

"Yes, it was good to see you again. If you'll excuse me, I see someone I'd like to say hello to," I say with a head nod. I extract myself from the conversation quickly and stroll away with purpose before Gabrielle has another opportunity to sink her claws or lips into me.

Another two hours later and I'm at the end of my rope. I've listened to everybody talk about all of the money they've made and all of the women they've bedded, all while trying to convince

"Perfect. Much better than the pressed chicken patty sandwiches they're serving today in the lunchroom."

"Eww. I didn't even like those in school. There's no way I would willingly eat one now," she says as she dribbles Italian dressing over her salad.

"No kidding. A couple of weeks ago, I forgot my lunch and I had to suffer through meatloaf. I still don't even know what they put in it," I say as I grab the ranch dressing out of the bag.

"Gross. Did you decide on what you're doing for Ryan's birthday next month?" she asks before taking a bite.

"Yeah, I'm going with the superhero theme. I figured we'd just do a pool party at home this year instead of going somewhere."

"I like that idea. I've already taken that weekend off from work so I'll be able to help you set up and watch all the kids. I can probably ask Sadie to come over, too. She was a lifeguard for a few years at the Y."

"What if I pay her? Do you think I could just hire her to watch the pool for me? There's going to be so many little kids there that it would make me feel better if I had someone solely watching the pool."

"I'm sure she'd do it. I'll text her when I leave here and ask," Trysta says with a nod.

"Thanks. He wants a Batman cake this year. I don't even know where to begin to get a Batman cake," I tell my sister.

"Call that bakery that did it last year. I'm sure they can come up with something. These bakeries nowadays can do just about anything, Dani."

I nod my acknowledgement at her and finish up my salad. Whatever happened to the days where you just had a plain chocolate cake with candy letters on the top? Nowadays, cakes are bigger, each one more spectacular than the last. I went with Ryan to

Emma's birthday party a few weeks ago and her cake was bigger and more complex than half the wedding cakes I've seen. And don't get me started on the chocolate fountain…

"Oh, I almost forgot!" Trysta exclaims before diving into her huge shoulder bag while I bag up our empty plastic containers. "When I stopped for gas earlier, they had newspapers out on the shelf at the register. When I glanced down, I saw this!" Her excitement was contagious. I prepare myself for whatever image she's about to show me.

Except, I'm not prepared at all for *this* image…

"This is that guy I was telling you about Saturday morning. His friend kept calling him Hunter, but his name is actually Reid Hunter. He's gorgeous, isn't he?" she asks while white dots pepper my eyesight. Shit, I can't see a damn thing.

I suck in air greedily, trying to inflate my lungs with precious oxygen. This can't be happening.

"Dani, are you alright?" Trysta asks, worry marring her face.

"Let me see that," I whisper almost inaudibly as I reach for the newspaper. There on the cover is a picture of the man I remember from eight years ago. The man I left sleeping in his tent on that fateful September morning.

"He's hot, right?" Trysta asks again with a big smile.

I study the strong lines of his handsome face, the steel edge in his eyes, and expensive tux he's wearing. Even though his smile is wide, it looks fake and forced. It looks nothing like the smiles I was awarded with that night so long ago. My stomach rolls and I fear that I'm about to lose the salad I just ate. I drop down onto my chair, still not able to look away from the picture.

Reid Hunter.

"Dani, what the hell is wrong with you?" Trysta asks, voice full of concern.

He continues to stare at me as if waiting to hear where I'm going. Definitely not happening.

"Listen, Doug, I don't want to be rude, but I have to get going so I'm not late for my appointment," I tell him politely.

"Oh, sure thing, Dani. I just wanted to stop by and see how your weekend was. I heard they were having a big Star Wars convention in a few weeks. I thought maybe you'd want to go with me," he says very eagerly.

"Oh, well, I'm not really much of a Star Wars fan," I tell him. His face falls. The look of devastation on his face reminds me of how I felt when Trysta told me there was no Santa Claus.

"Really? Like…at all?" he asks, his mouth hanging wide open.

Doug is a nice guy, really. He's just a little on the geeky side. His Dockers are always finely pressed, while his button-up shirt is always rumpled with the back pulled out of the waistband of his pants. Then there's the fact that his dark-framed glasses are continually slipping down his long nose and have to be readjusted. And if that doesn't scream geek, the pocket protector with exactly three black pens and two red pens, in order with alternating colors, is like a flashing neon sign. Plus, he wears black socks with his brown loafers for Christ sake.

"Yeah, like at all. Listen, it was nice seeing you again, but I really have to go." I push my way past him, pulling my door closed as I go. After making sure it's locked, I throw Doug a wave and a polite smile over my shoulder as I head out to my car.

The drive to Hunter Enterprises is nerve-racking, to say the least. I almost turn the car around at practically every intersection I pass. But the thought of Ryan being able to have a father in his life is too great of an opportunity to pass up. God, I just pray I'm making the right decision here.

I find a parking garage down the street from the building I'm looking for. When I reach the front of the glass building, my heart is practically beating out of my chest. I'm afraid I could stroke out at any moment or that I'm going to have a panic attack right here in the middle of the business district. Somehow finding my inner courage, I open the massive heavy door.

Inside, the building is masculine. Beautiful tile floors and white marble for as far as the eye can see. A security counter with two well-built men stationed behind it sits just over to the right. Three elevators are situated on the back wall, but before I can make my way over to one of them, a voice draws my attention just over to the left of me. "May I help you?"

A young secretary sits at a reception desk in the middle of the lobby. Her dark hair and makeup is as perfect as can be, as if she just stepping off the pages from one of Trysta's fashion magazines.

"Uh, hi. I am…I was hoping to speak with Reid Hunter," I tell the fashionable brunette.

"Do you have an appointment?" she asks with a raised eyebrow. The look on her face is clearly one of utter annoyance. She must get strange women stopping in to see Reid often.

"Uh, no." I'm almost embarrassed by my lack of proper talk. It's as if just by being here, I've been robbed of any ability to properly form adult sentences.

"You can't go up without an appointment," she says briskly before turning her attention back to the computer in front of her.

"If I can just steal a few minutes of his time, I'll be out of here before you know it," I tell the woman.

"Listen, honey. Mr. Hunter doesn't see anyone without an appointment. Unless you can produce a name that's on my schedule for this afternoon, you're going to have to leave," she replies with a clipped tone.

Great, I make it all the way to his building and I can't even get past the first obstacle. How in the hell am I supposed to see a man who won't talk to anyone without an appointment? And how in the world am I supposed to get one of those? Call up his office and say, "Hi, I'm a girl he slept with eight years ago and we share a son. Can he squeeze me in at three p.m. today?"

I give it one last shot. "I'm an old friend of Reid's. I really won't take up much of his time if you'll just let me -" I start, but am cut off.

"Not happening, sweetheart. Do you know how many *old friends* of Reid's show up here every day to speak with him? No one, not even you, gets in without an appointment."

It takes every ounce of politeness I possess not to stick out my tongue. Instead, I give her a polite smile. As I turn to walk out the way I entered, an older man along the security counter catches my attention. He's staring at me, question clearly written all over his handsome face. I stop in my tracks as he starts to approach me. *Great, just what I need now. Security.*

"I was just leaving. You don't have to escort me out," I tell the gentleman.

His eyes are soft and the lightest shade of blue as he gives me a smile. It's then that I notice he's wearing a suit, not a security uniform like the other two guys at the counter. He doesn't scream security, but has that fatherly feel to him. My racing heart instantly starts to calm down a bit.

"I'm not going to escort you out, Miss. I'm Steven," he says as he offers his hand. His hand is warm, yet a bit rough as I place mine within his.

"Dani Whitley."

"Did you say you knew Reid?" he asks, as he leads me away from the nosey secretary. I can't help but notice that her interest is piqued as she watches Steven and I converse.

"Yeah. Well, I haven't seen him in years. I met him a few years ago, and I was hoping to have a quick meeting with him." Honestly, I don't know what the hell I'm doing. Do you think he can see it written all over my face?

He must be able to because he leads me over to the sofa along a sidewall back by the elevators. "You said your name was Dani?" he asks with a curious look.

"Yes."

Something changes in his demeanor. He suddenly stands up and looks down at me like he's seeing a ghost. "I see. How about I take you upstairs to see Reid?" he offers, his face softening again as he gives me another friendly smile.

"Really? Are we going to get in trouble?" I ask, looking over at Miss Snippy over at the front desk.

Steven chuckles as he notices where my eyes have settled. "No, we won't get into any trouble. If you need to go up and see Reid, then I'll take you up there." Steven extends his hand towards me, assisting me up from the couch.

"Miss Whitley needs a visitor's pass," Steven tells the brunette at the counter.

"Sir?" she asks, clearly not happy with the fact that Steven is going around her and taking me upstairs.

"This is Reid's friend, Dani. I'm taking her upstairs to see him."

"I need to call Carly first," she said in a clipped tone as she reaches for the phone on the desk.

"I'll take care of Carly. No need to call upstairs," he says as he helps secure a visitor's badge around my neck.

As we walk towards the elevators, Steven places a friendly hand on my back. It's a gesture that instantly calms my racing heart. He uses the keycard in his pocket and ushers me inside of the far left elevator. This one only has buttons for two floors. Steven pushes the first button and we suddenly start our smooth ascent towards Reid.

My breathing is suddenly labored again. I can't believe I'm about to do this. As if sensing my internal turmoil, Steven reaches over and squeezes my wrist. "Don't worry, Dani. He'll be happy to see you," Steven says, offering me another friendly, fatherly smile.

When the elevator opens, I can instantly hear the voice that has haunted my dreams for eight years. Reid is standing behind his desk, addressing someone on the phone in a not-so-friendly manner. Hearing the elevator open, he slowly turns towards me. As I take a few shaky steps into the room, our eyes lock for the first time. The electricity in the room crackles to life, and I can't stop the audible gasp that slips from my dry throat. Those steel gray eyes are locked on mine so intently that I'm afraid I'll never be able to speak again.

"I'll call you back," he says abruptly into the phone receiver in his hand before placing it down on the carriage without even looking.

Steven places a hand on my back and encourages me to take another step into the room. White spots dance before my eyes again and I realize I'm not breathing. I suck in a huge gulp of precious air before taking my eyes off Reid for the first time. I turn to look at Steven. Why? I have no clue. Maybe for a little direction? Maybe for an acknowledgement for his sudden support. Maybe just to give myself a few moments to collect myself before I look over at Reid again. I offer him a small smile in silent thanks.

"Dani?" Reid whispers in the hushed room, drawing my eyes back to his.

"Hi," I mumble as I study the man before me. He reeks of power and money. While the Reid I knew eight years ago permeated the same, this Reid is so very different. He looks almost…angry.

"I found this little lady down in the lobby. I thought maybe the two of you could use a moment to say hello," Steven says. When I turn back to him, he's smiling again. It's as if he knows more than he's letting on.

Then, he turns and walks back towards the elevator. I want to grab ahold of him and beg him to stay. Suddenly, the idea of not having this stranger's support is unnerving. The thought of being left alone with Reid is terrifying.

"You got this," he mumbles before slipping inside the elevator and disappearing from sight.

I turn back around and find those deep, soulful eyes focused on me once again. Neither of us speaks as I slowly take a few shaky steps towards his desk. I step around and lower myself into one of the chairs before his desk. I'm not sure how much longer my legs could support me anyway.

When I sit down, Reid slowly sits down in his massive leather chair. His mouth opens and closes a few times like a fish out of water. I know he's wondering what the hell I'm doing here–in his office. I wish I knew the right way to do this. I've wondered about having to tell him about his son for years, never really thinking that I'd have to do it. Now, I stare at the very reason I have a seven-year-old son.

"I'm sorry for just dropping by like this. I'm sure you're a busy man," I start.

"What are you doing here?" he asks as he runs a hand through his dark hair.

"I, uh…I just needed to stop by and thought that -" I suddenly stop talking. I have no freaking clue what to say to him. Do I make small talk for a few minutes, or do I just blurt it out? God, I wish Steven were here. I could use a reassuring look from his kind, blue eyes right about now.

Reid's eyes darken, but not in the way I remember from that night. They look intense, sure, but almost filled with fury. "I have a very busy afternoon. I need to call back the gentleman that I just cut off. Is there something you need today? Otherwise, I'm going to have to cut this reunion short."

I almost slink down into my chair from his rudeness and clear dismissal. Out of all of the ways I thought this could go down, him not wanting to give me the time of day wasn't really one of them. I thought he'd at least let me get out my news before he kicked me out of his office.

Suddenly, this feels all wrong. Do I want my son to have a father who's this brash and abrasive that he won't even give me five minutes of his time? His eyes hold nothing but annoyance and anger at this moment, and abruptly, telling him that he's a father seems like the worst thing in the word to say.

"I'm sorry, I didn't mean to disrupt your afternoon. I just wanted to say hello. I see you're a very busy man, and I won't take any more of your time." I get up out of the chair and make my way towards the elevator.

I push the button repeatedly to go down, all the while feeling Reid's gaze on my back. He doesn't say anything, and neither do I. It takes hours before the elevator arrives in his office. Okay, in reality it's probably about ten seconds. I slip inside without turning around, fearing that if I turn around and see that dismissal in his eyes again, I'll break down.

The elevator doesn't move. Clearly needing to push the button to descend, I turn around and find that magic button. When I hit it, I lift my eyes and see him. He's standing behind his desk again, watching me. I can't tell what his eyes are saying this time. It's part confusion, part anger, part longing. At least that's what it appears to me.

As the elevator door starts to close, I whisper, "I'm sorry," once more as a single tear slips unchecked down my cheek. This was not how it was supposed to go. I wasn't supposed to chicken out this way.

Just as the door gets ready to close, Reid takes a step forward. "Dani," he says, the look of pure angst filling his beautiful features. The look on his face in this moment will forever haunt me. I will never forget today for as long as I live.

And then the door closes…

I step out into the marble foyer and find Steven leaning against the security counter. When he sees me, his smile instantly falls. He rushes towards me as I move on autopilot towards the doors. All I want to do now is leave this building. I need to get away from Reid's unexpected anger at seeing me. I know I left him in the morning without a goodbye, but I didn't expect him to be so upset about my appearance. Hadn't we agreed it was just one night? I made the wrong choice in coming here.

"Dani?" Steven says as he grabs ahold of my upper arm, as if to help keep me upright.

"I'm sorry. I need to go," I tell him quickly as I pull my arm out of his gentle grip.

"Do you need a ride somewhere?" he offers. The softness in his eyes and the tenderness in his tone break me. Several tears start to slip from my eyes as I stumble backwards towards the exit.

"No, thank you. I'll be fine," I tell him as I stagger out into the May afternoon sun.

I don't turn around for fear that Steven will be following me. I make my way as quickly as possible towards the parking garage where I left my car. Once inside, I can have my breakdown. Right now, I need to just make it to my car.

Finally slipping inside of my car, I don't even put the keys in the ignition. My hands go up to my face as the dam breaks and the tears fall. I cry hard. I cry at the thought of Ryan not having his father. I cry at the recollection of Reid's clear resentment at my presence in his office. And I cry for the memory of our perfect night together that's now tainted.

After several minutes, the tears start to ebb. Placing my key in the ignition, I turn over my car and wipe my face. It's time to go home. Go home to my son. Go home to my life and push the memory of Reid Hunter as far from my mind as possible.

I only wish it were going to be easy.

Chapter Four – Dreams and Nightmares

Reid

I stand there for maybe ten minutes? Ten of the longest damn minutes of my life as I stare at the elevator door, praying that it opens again and that Dani is standing before me once more. I'm painfully aware of her lingering presence in the room, not only smelling the familiar scent of her perfume, but my dick is so damn hard, I could jackhammer concrete. It blows my mind that my body remembers her so vividly, so perfectly.

When the elevator opens, I pull in a deep breath. Unfortunately, the door reveals my driver, Steven, and I instantly want to punch a puppy. I watch as he strolls into the room like he owns the place and sits down in the seat across from my desk. His blue eyes, which remind me so much of the woman's who just ran from my office, are studying me intently.

"So, that was Dani?" he asks quietly, though it wasn't really a question.

Unable to form words for maybe the second time in my life, I give him a head nod in confirmation. The only other time I've been incapable of speaking was when I first saw her sitting in the dirt eight years ago.

"And I take it by the way she ran out of here crying that your reunion wasn't a happy one?" Instantly, my gut tightens and nausea sets in. She was crying?

Closing my eyes, I'm haunted by the look on her face when I was so rude to her. She completely caught me off guard this afternoon. One minute I'm signing the documents to take over Bravado, which put me in a fouler mood than I expected, then the next minute Dani is walking in. That changed everything. I was ready to throw that damn contract straight out the window, and that thought pisses me off. I've worked for months on this damn deal, and the fact that I actually contemplated walking away, even after the papers were signed, left me completely unsettled.

But, damn the look of hurt in her eyes...

"What brought her here after all these years?" Steven asks as he casually crosses his arms across his chest.

Steven's the only one besides Jon that knows about Dani. Jon was there that night eight years ago, but never brings it up. When I woke up alone in the tent, I felt like my heart was cut out of my chest. I looked for her around the campsites, including the one where her douche of an ex was sleeping, but never saw her again.

Steven caught me in a weak moment not long after he started driving for me six years ago. He had waited for me outside of some woman's apartment while I tried to fuck away her memory. Of course, it didn't work.

When I got back into the car, he gave me that pointed look that told me how disappointed he was in me. He didn't even have to say anything. It was written all over his face. But for the amount of disappointment he felt in me that night, it didn't hold a candle to how disappointed I was in myself. I ended up spilling my guts about the one girl who got away. The one that I was prepared to change everything for. The one girl that I could actually see falling in love with.

That's also the last night Steven drove me as I met up with women. Driving my own car may not have been able to hide the distress I felt in myself, but at least I didn't have to see it on his face anymore.

Now, I'm witnessing that same look from the man who is practically the only father I have left. He's staring at me from across my desk, waiting to hear what I have to say. The thought of disappointing him leaves me troubled, especially since disappointing my real father was the furthest thing from my mind.

"I don't know what you want me to say. She didn't have an appointment," I tell him, doing everything I can to keep my gaze neutral.

"Really? That's the card you want to play right now? She didn't have an appointment?"

"It's not a card, it's a fact. I was on the phone with a potential new client, and I cut him off rudely. Now I have to call him back and pray he doesn't take his business elsewhere."

"Screw that client, Reid. And screw you if you think her showing up here–*now*–isn't a sign. I saw the way you looked at her. So what the hell happened between the moment I left you here and the moment she came running downstairs crying?"

Taking a deep breath, I know there's no way the old man is going to let me get back to work without giving it up. For the sake of the remainder of my workday, I start talking. "She didn't say what she wanted. I might have been a little rude to her." The look Steven gives me has me squirming in my chair. "I panicked when I saw her, Steven. I just signed the Cruz deal, and suddenly, there she was. Why me? Why now?" I ask more to myself.

"Now I guess you'll never know, will ya," he states matter-of-factly.

I'm quiet, as I consider never seeing her again. The next phase of my life is all set–typed out in Times New Roman, size 12 font, with my signature and that of Douglas Cruz's on the bottom line. I've never backed out of a deal, and I'm not about to now.

"I guess I'll just head back downstairs. Call me when you're ready to leave," Steven says before getting up. He doesn't even look back as he heads towards my door, out into the front to see Carly.

I stay until eight o'clock. Carly left hours ago, and I sent Steven home not long after that. My plan is just to work until I can't see straight, and then crash in the apartment upstairs. The problem with my master plan is that I can't seem to concentrate on a single word of anything in front of me. Blue eyes and blond hair fill my mind on repeat. Dani is still the most beautiful woman I've ever seen in that simple way. She doesn't need to be done-up in tons of makeup or dress to impress. Even sitting in my office in her simple black dress slacks and purple ruffled tank top, she's the most stunning woman ever.

I decide to just head upstairs since work is fruitless at this point. Stepping onto the only elevator that goes up to the top floor, I remove my jacket and loosen my tie before it even makes it up to the next floor. Once inside the apartment, I instantly notice the scent of cleaning chemicals, which is a huge relief. I'm not so sure that smelling some other woman's perfume right now wouldn't completely send me straight over the edge of insanity and to the liquor cabinet for a very tall drink.

Instead I decide to order take-out and hop in the shower, hoping that the scalding water will burn her image from my mind. After a quick call down to the security desk to let them know that food is being delivered, I strip down and jump in the shower. Her big blue eyes are more vivid now than ever. Resting my forearms against the cold marble, I let the burn of the water wash over my head and down my body. Unfortunately, it doesn't rinse her memory away with it.

In fact, if the hardness of my dick is any indication, her memory is more alive now than ever before.

Ignoring the throbbing between my legs, I turn off the water. Maybe what I need tonight is a hard workout. Working out has proven to help distract me from whatever ails me. Maybe a little Metallica and an hour of heavy weights or a few miles on the treadmill is just what the doctor ordered.

After making a quick call downstairs with instructions to bring up the food and put it in the warmer, I slip on mesh shorts, an old t-shirt, and my running shoes. No one is in the building at this time of night, so I know that blasting heavy metal as loud as I can stand won't bother anyone. Though even if someone was still in the building, I don't think I'd give a shit about the volume of my music.

Two hours later, I'm dripping with sweat and exhausted. I opted for both lifting and running since my traitorous mind wouldn't stop replaying the scene from my office. There are so many different ways that the scene should have played out, so many things I should have said to her. Apparently, my subconscious is a cruel bastard, because two hours later and she's still all I can think about.

Even though my stomach is growling and I'm fatigued, I opt for another quick shower before dinner. The smell of Italian food fills the open kitchen as I stroll in butt naked. I never wear clothes at this point in the night. It's pointless. I'm either entertaining a guest where clothing isn't ideal, or I'm getting ready for bed, again where clothing isn't tolerable. I prefer to sleep in nothing but the soft sheet.

After inhaling whatever dish I ordered from the menu and chugging a bottle of water, I slip into my bedroom. The bedding has been changed thankfully, leaving the air clean and crisp. As I settle between the sheets, my mind goes right back to the subject I've been trying hard to forget tonight.

Why did Dani show up at my office? And why the fuck was I so rude to her? I know exactly why. I had just signed my life away, and her walking into my life changes everything. I panicked. I needed her gone so that I couldn't dwell on the fact that I just changed the direction of my life forever.

The company. Acquiring Bravado Resorts makes me one of the largest independent businessmen in North America. Between my properties and estate, and that of Bravado, it puts me at the very top of the list for net worth. And I just turned thirty. The sky is the limit for me and for Hunter Enterprises.

Yet, why do I feel like doing anything but celebrating?

Without even thinking, I grab my cell phone and summons the first speed dial.

"Yes?" Steven asks sleepily.

"How do I find her?"

"She's already found, Reid. Her name is Dani Whitley."

I take my first real breath since she walked into my office this afternoon. Dani Whitley. I finally know her name. Now I just need to find her.

Chapter Five – Unexpected Visitors

Dani

"He basically told you to leave?" Trysta asks from her seat across the table from me.

After my crying spell, I made it home just as Trysta was serving Ryan dinner. I know she could tell instantly that the meeting had gone horribly wrong, but once I reassured her that we would speak about it later, she let the subject go. There was no way I was talking about this in front of Ryan.

Now it's later, and she's anything but letting the subject go.

"Pretty much. I mean, I know I interrupted his workday and that he was probably busy, but I wasn't expecting him to be so upset to see me. I don't know what I expected, Trysta, but him dismissing me wasn't even a thought."

"How did you expect it to go?" she asks, concern filling her gorgeous features.

"I guess I thought he'd be happier to see me. Maybe it would have hurt less if he hadn't remembered my name. But when I walked into his office and he said my name, it gave me hope that we'd be able to reconnect for Ryan."

I take several calming breaths before continuing. "When I sat down, his face practically transformed right before my eyes. He was shocked, sure, but he was softer at first. Then, suddenly, he turned hard and brash, and basically told me that we had nothing to talk about."

"So you didn't tell him the reason for your visit?"

"Of course I didn't, Trysta. How could I? He didn't want me there anymore than he wanted to visit the dentist to have a tooth pulled." Except I'm sure Reid Hunter has never had to visit such a doctor to have any sort of work done. The man is a walking God; all trim and lean with hard lines and tight muscles. Even though he was in a suit, I could tell that the years have been good to him.

"So what's next?" she asks before taking a sip of her red wine.

"I wish I knew. I guess we go on the way it has always been. I've survived eight years without Reid or his help, I'm sure I can manage the rest of my life."

"But what about Ryan? You don't think he deserves to know his father?"

I wish I had the magic answer to her question. "Of course I think he deserves that, Tryst. I just want his father to be worthy of the kind of love Ryan will offer. I want him to know how rare and wonderful that kind of love is, and give it back to him willingly. After seeing Reid today, I don't think he's capable of the kind of love Ryan deserves."

And that thought breaks my heart.

"When Ryan is older, I'll tell him who is father is. I'll let him make the choice of whether he wants to meet him or not. He can choose to contact Reid, and I'll support his decision one hundred percent."

"If that's what you think is best," Trysta says.

"I do." Especially after the way he treated me today. Again, I didn't expect him to welcome me with open arms, but I did hope he'd be a little receptive as to my reason for being there. Hell, I thought for sure he'd be a little curious at least.

After checking on Ryan, I slip into my own room and get ready for bed. What an emotional day today was. I'm drained from the roller coaster ride I was taken on. But as I snuggle between my sheets, sleep doesn't find me. My mind tosses and turns as it recounts the events of today: learning that Reid is in Vegas, deciding to go visit him to tell him about his son, and being dismissed out of his office without so much as a backwards glance.

Sleep definitely isn't my friend tonight. I just pray that exhaustion eventually sets in enough to pull me into a welcomed slumber.

* * *

"We're going to have a test tomorrow morning, so don't forget to review your math facts tonight," I tell my students as they gather up their backpacks and schoolwork. As soon as the bell sounds, they erupt into chaos as they file out of the classroom and out of the school.

Wednesday is my day for morning duty, so I'm free to enjoy the post-school quiet without having to go outside and make sure everyone gets to their designated rides home. I leave my door partially open so that Ryan can get in easily when he's done saying goodbye to his teacher and friends. It's hard to believe that he's going to be in the same grade that I teach next school year.

Erasing today's notes from the chalkboard, a heavy knock pulls my attention towards the door. I'm stunned speechless as Reid Hunter hesitantly walks into my classroom. The air around me crackles with awareness unlike anything I've ever experienced before. Even after all this time, my body still hums to life when I see him.

"Uh, hi. I hope you don't mind me stopping by," he says as he takes a few steps closer.

"How did you find me?" I ask as I watch him stroll towards me. My feet are rooted in place, and I'm sure my mouth is gaping open in a very un-lady-like fashion.

86

"It wasn't that hard, Dani," he says with a smile. The smile that I remember. This smile reaches his eyes, and gently touches my soul. This is the smile that I've been dreaming about for most of my adult life.

"Wh-what are you doing here?" I ask, suddenly a little panicked with the realization that Reid Hunter is standing in my classroom.

"I felt bad for the way I treated you yesterday. I wanted to apologize."

Okay. I wasn't expecting that one.

"There's no need to apologize, Reid. It's been a long time. I shouldn't have just stopped by like that," I state. His eyes draw me in like a moth to a flame, and all I can do is stand there and wait for the burn.

"No, you didn't deserve to be treated so poorly like that. I'm sorry for the way I reacted to you," he says. We both stare at each other for several seconds while my heartbeat pounds relentlessly in my chest.

"It's okay," I respond finally.

"I see you finished school and became a teacher," he says with a smile. "You said that you really wanted to teach. What grade is this?"

"Third. It's the perfect age for me. Not too young, but not old enough to have completely horrible attitudes and manners," I reply with a chuckle, recalling the time I was a student teacher for sixth graders.

His smile practically lights up the room. Perfectly straight, white teeth shine back at me through those full lips. Lips that my body remembers if the shudder raking through me is any indication.

Reid seems to notice my sudden reaction to his presence. His smile turns serious and his eyes seem to dilate into black orbs of night. My eyes are glued to his Adam's apple as I watch his throat, which appears to be working overtime just to swallow. Abruptly, the air in the room seems to crackle with sexual tension that only Reid seems to be able to create. Without even realizing what is happening, we're both taking steps towards each other. My body is reacting entirely on its own since my paralyzed mind seems to have forgotten how to send any sort of signals to my extremities.

When we're standing close enough to touch, Reid slowly lifts his hand towards my face. "Dani -" Reid starts, but is cut off when the door to my classroom flies the rest of the way open and bangs off the wall.

"Mom, guess what Jason said to Mr. Foster," Ryan yells as he runs into the room at Mach Ten.

"Ryan!" I exclaim; jumping back from Reid as if I was a teenager just busted by my parents with a boy in my bedroom.

"You have a son?" Reid asks at the exact same time that Ryan asks, "Who's that?"

My mind goes completely numb. Even if I were able, I wouldn't know whose question to answer first. Reid's steel gray eyes bore into me so intently that I suddenly lose my ability to breathe. I gape widely as my eyes volley back and forth between my son and his father. The connection neither of them realize.

The resemblance is uncanny. Ryan is tall for his age with a lean build that screams basketball player. His gray eyes and dark brown hair match that of the man who stands next to him. His chin has the slightest cleft, and his cheekbones are well defined and strong. The only semblance that our son has to me would be the few sprinkled freckles on his nose. He's Reid's mini-me, and I've never been more blown away at the likeness than I am right now, at this moment, as they stand next to each other, sizing the other one up.

"Ryan, why don't you run down to the gym and see if Mr. Phillips is still here. I bet he'd let you shoot a few hoops while I talk to my friend," I tell my son.

Ryan appears leery to leave for several moments. I can see the questions in his eyes as he looks Reid up and down and then back up again. He opens his mouth to possibly argue with me, but I shut him down before he has the opportunity to speak up. "I'll only be a few minutes. I need to speak with Mr. Hunter about something really important. When we're done, we'll order a pizza, okay?" I say to my seven-year-old. I know it's the easy way out, but offering to order pizza for dinner is a sure-fire way to get Ryan to do what I need him to do.

And right now, I need him to leave my classroom.

"Okay," Ryan says before heading towards the door. Before he leaves though, he turns around and looks once more at Reid. Ryan's little eyebrows are furrowed in a look of concentration. My little man is thinking awfully hard about something. "Bye," Ryan says to Reid.

I stare at the doorway that my son just departed through. Once again, I'm left completely unprepared and confused about the conversation I'm about to have. Do I just blurt it out? Is there even a way to ease into the blow I'm about to deal Reid?

"You have a son?" he repeats, drawing my attention back to him and away from the empty doorway.

"Yes," I tell him quietly, wringing my hands together in front of my stomach.

Reid finally turns his attention to me and away from the entrance. His eyes are blazing with something. What? I'm not sure. I watch as his eyes drop down to my hands. He searches them fiercely as if looking for the answer to an unheard question. A wedding ring, I'm assuming.

"I don't even know how to start this conversation," I finally say out loud, though I didn't mean to actually say it.

Reid walks over and stands directly in front of me. His eyes blaze with fire. His stare is almost my complete undoing. "How old is he?" he croaks out, as if his throat is dry.

"He's seven. He'll be eight in a few weeks," I confirm, raising my chin up a little.

Reid's legs seem to wobble as he reaches forward and places his hands on my desk next to me. I can hear him struggle to catch his breath as he drops his head to his chest. After a few tense minutes, he lifts his head and pins me with a look. "He's mine?" he asks, though if Reid got a good enough look at Ryan, he already knows the answer to that one.

"Yes," I whisper.

Reid pushes off my desk and starts to pace around like a caged animal. The anger rolling off him is enough to keep me from stepping any closer. "And this is why you came by to see me yesterday?" he asks, the hardness evident in his voice.

"Yes," I confirm again.

Reid stops pacing and glares at me. "And you just thought that *now* was the time to share that little piece of information with me, Dani?"

He's clearly angry with me for the live grenade I just dropped in his lap, but surely he can see what choice I had. My own anger starts to rise as I consider his assumption. "How, Reid? I didn't know your name! I didn't know where you were from. I had no clue how to find you," I seethe back at the man in front of me.

Closing my eyes and taking a few calming deep breaths, a technique I perfected when Ryan was only a toddler, I take a moment before continuing. "Look, Reid, I understand this is shocking to you. I wasn't trying to disrupt your life or anything, but for the first time in eight years, I found out your last name. I always told myself that if I had the chance to find you, I'd tell you about Ryan."

My heart is beating right out of my chest. Reid's gaze is so fierce that I'm afraid he can see everything in my soul—my fears, my hopes, my dreams. I don't know if I should continue or give him a moment to process.

"I have to go," he finally says, breaking the quiet and answering my question.

"Go?" I ask when I realize he's about to bolt out of the door.

"Yes, I have to go," Reid says as he turns and heads towards the door with purpose.

He hesitates when he gets to the threshold, but doesn't turn around. Instead, he walks right out the door.

Right out of our life.

Again.

After giving myself about ten minutes to calm down my racing heart and my labored breathing, I gather up my bag and lock up my classroom. At least Ryan wasn't in the classroom when his father found out about him…and then walked out the door.

* * *

"Hey, Mom! Watch this shot," Ryan exclaims as he tries a jump shot from the corner of the free throw line.

"Great try, Ry," I holler as I watch it teeter around the rim and bounce off without going through the hoop.

"Is Aunt Trysta going to eat pizza with us?" Ryan asks after he returns the basketball to the ball bin at the back of the gymnasium.

"Maybe. I think she's working tonight," I tell him, ruffling the dark brown locks atop his head.

"Can we get black olives and bacon on the pizza?" he asks, his entire face lighting up. I can't help but laugh at his choice combination of toppings. I'm not sure where he came up with that combination because I'm more of a plain sausage kinda girl.

"Are you prepared to listen to her complain?" I ask with a smile.

"She got her gross veggie pizza last time and made me eat it. This time, I'm getting extra bacon and tons of olives," he says as he throws his backpack over his shoulder. "Can we invite Grandpa?"

"I'll send him a text message when we get out to the car and ask him," I say as I lead him towards the doors of the gym.

"Mom?" Ryan stops and turns those gray eyes towards me.

"Yeah?"

"Who was that guy in your classroom?"

I exhale deeply and look up at the Warriors mascot painted up on the wall of the gym. My heart aches for my son. He has no idea how close he was to the man who gave him his rugged good looks and his athletic ability. "He was just someone I knew back in college. I haven't seen him in a very long time."

"What did he want?" He asks, his eyes full of question.

"Just to say hello." My heart is beating a rapid-fire pattern in my chest. I don't want to lie to my son, but I can't tell him what just transpired in my classroom, not until he's old enough to understand everything.

Ryan looks like he has more questions, but he doesn't ask them. I watch as he gazes up at the painted mascot on the wall. The best thing I can do is reassure him of my love for him; to show him every day that he's the most important person in my life. Seven years ago, I took on the job of both a mother and a father. I am two people rolled into one, and I'll do everything I can to not let him down.

"Come on," I say as I throw my arm over my son's shoulder. "Let's go order us a pizza."

Chapter Six – Well, If That Ain't A Kick In The Ass

Reid

I have no clue how I make it to my car. I climb into my vintage Aston Martin and just sit there, staring off into the late afternoon sun.

Fuck me, I have a kid.

The ache in my skull is intense as I replay the scene again and again. Dani looked so beautiful standing in her classroom. The way she wore her plain black pants and ivory top turned me on more than the last woman who warmed my bed wearing thousand-dollar lingerie ever did. Her hair was down today, those soft honey locks framing perfectly around her stunning face. At first glance, my dick was hard and I longed to kiss those damn bee-stung lips of hers.

And then the boy walked in.

How in the hell did I go from wanting a woman so bad, I was ready to sell my soul to the devil himself, to finding out that I have a son? And not just any son, but a son with the one woman I haven't stopped thinking about in eight years.

Then the panic set in.

I knew as soon as I saw him that I was his father. How could you miss it? The kid looks just like me. Sure, I should probably order a DNA test. With my net worth, I'd be a fucking fool not to. Dani wouldn't be the first woman to claim I fathered her child. But how can I deny it? Yeah, he looks like me, but it's more than that. I can feel it. The moment I laid my eyes on him, I knew. I knew he was my son.

Fuck!

When Dani confirmed it, I panicked and had to get the hell out of that room. The walls were closing in on me and I found the air stifling, making it impossible to breathe. I knew that if I didn't get out of that room that very instant, I would say something that I couldn't take back. Lashing out seems to be my first line of defense when it comes to her. The last thing I need or want is someone like Dani thinking they can change me; like somehow I'll suddenly grow a heart and care more about them than my company, my business. Well, that's not happening. I've always been a heartless bastard and that isn't about to change now.

Throwing my car in reverse, I dial up the first number on my cell phone. Steven's greeting fills the speakers, as I drive swiftly out of the parking lot. Even with the shit that just went down, I'm still mindful of the fact that I'm in a school zone.

"Where are you?" I all but yell into the phone.

"Just pulling out of the office to head home," Steven says, voice filled with concern.

"Head to my house," I bark.

"I'm on my way." Concern permeates through the speakers as he asks, "Are you alright?"

My mouth opens to answer him, but I just can't say the word. Am I alright? Fuck, it sure as hell doesn't feel like I'm alright, or that I ever will be again. Suddenly, being alright feels like an unobtainable destination. Like being lost in the desert and looking for water. You don't even know if it even really exists anymore. "No," I finally state before clicking off the phone.

I drive on autopilot from the pleasant neighborhood where Dani's school is located to my estate in a gated community in

Vegas. Pulling into the driveway, I punch the code into my security system. The gate slowly opens, granting access to my massive property. I pass the Town Car that Steven drives for me parked in front of the front door. Pulling into the garage, which is more like a small car museum, I park the Aston Martin next to a Mercedes SUV and take a deep breath.

I slowly make my way into the house as if my shoes were filled with concrete. My head is throbbing with a headache and my mind is clouded with every scenario and "what-if" I could come up with. Stopping at the cabinet in the back of my home office, I fill two fingers of Scotch into a tumbler. Then I add two more for good measure.

I throw back half of the glass before I even turn and face Steven. When my eyes find his, he's watching me intently, gauging my behavior and cataloging my mood. Steven sits in the leather wing-backed chair across from my desk, waiting on me to make my move.

"I went to see Dani," I tell him as I sit down in the chair next to him. Right now, I need Steven as a friend, not an employee.

"Good for you," he tells me.

I take a few deep breaths before tipping my glass back and finishing off the liquid. "Do you remember when I told you about the time I met Dani?" I ask, knowing he'll remember every detail of the encounter that I shared with him. I don't even glance over to see his acknowledgement; I know he's nodding his head.

"That night when I told you about meeting her, I left out one very big piece of information." I long to get up and refill my glass, but I'm afraid that if I don't get this out right this instant, I might fucking burst. My emotions are all over the damn place, and I don't want to prolong this admission any longer than I have to.

Steven still doesn't talk. I watch him out of the corner of my eye. His leg is casually crossed atop his knee and his body screams relaxed. Yet, I know Steven well enough to know that he's anything but relaxed. He's listening intently, waiting to either react to something physically or verbally. It's the verbal reaction that I fear. And not because I'm afraid of Steven in any way, but because saying these words out loud will be an admission to my faults from that night eight years ago. Once I say it, it's out there, floating around the universe, and I can't take it back. I can't hide it or look it away. I have to live with it and what that admission means.

"The night I spent with Dani, I didn't use protection," I state, looking over at my driver, my confidant. His eyebrow arches in comprehension, but he still doesn't speak. It's starting to piss me the hell off and makes me squirm a little in my seat. Steven is the only man who can unearth me with just a single glance. He knows too much, and knows me too well, the bastard.

"I went to see her today to apologize for my behavior yesterday. When I was talking to her, a little boy walked in." I give him a few moments to absorb what I'm telling him. He continues to stare at me with those intense blue eyes. I shift in my seat, but he won't take his eyes off me.

"She says he's my son."

Fuck. Saying those words almost make me choke on the emotions I'm feeling. Anger. Confusion. Fear. More Anger. Pride. That last one is the one I wasn't expecting, and the one that scares me the most.

"Congratulations," Steven says with a slight grin. I don't know why, but hearing him say that word suddenly makes it feel real. I have a kid. A son.

"I'm scared to death," I whisper.

"Reid, a child isn't the end of the world," he says.

"Maybe not for the average man, but I'm not that man. I don't want kids, Steven. You know that. I don't know anything about being a father."

"Most men don't know anything about being a father. At first. It's something you have to learn, Reid. Like riding a bike."

"But you can't fuck up a bike for the rest of its life because you don't know what the fuck you're doing," I state blatantly.

"Sure you can. Have you ever wrecked a bike and then tried to ride it again with a bent wheel?" he asks with a grin. I don't know why, but his comment makes me laugh. And, damn, does it feel good to laugh. "My point is, that it might be bent, but the bike is still a bike. It just needs a little TLC."

"Can I ask you something?" he asks after a few silent minutes. Giving him a head nod, he continues. "Are you sure he's yours? I mean, I'm not trying to be an jerk, but this girl wouldn't be the first woman to claim she is the mother of the elusive Hunter Enterprise heir."

"I saw him, Steven. There's no denying that he's my son."

"Then, congratulations again. What's his name?"

"Ryan. He's gonna be eight next month."

After several more long minutes of silence filled with tension and question, Steven finally speaks again. "So, what's next?"

"I wish I knew. I kinda left without getting any more information out of her," I say, squirming again in my damn seat. Damn it, why do I feel like a child sitting in front of the principal?

"What does that mean?" he asks.

"When she told me that he was my son, I sort of left without saying much. I was shocked and freaked the hell out. I can't be a dad, Steven. I'm not built that way."

"Bullshit," he thunders at me, making me look into his eyes. "Yeah, you heard me. I call bullshit. You can do anything you put your mind to. I see it every day at the office, Reid. You always have been able to. There's no reason for you to believe that you can't be this boy's father."

"Are you kidding me? You know my dad," I say back. The intensity level in the room just spiked to ten. Speaking of my dad rarely happens, but when it does, it usually ends badly.

"Yeah, I know your dad. He's an asshole and a lousy example. But, that's just it, Reid. He's not you. I know you think you'll turn out just like him, but you'd be wrong. You are nothing like your dad," he states with a pointed look. I try to argue with him, but he won't hear me out.

"What do I do now?" I ask after my heart rate drops as close to normal as possible. "I have no idea what to do, Steven. Tell me what to do."

"I can't do that, Reid. You just have to follow your heart and do what you think is best for that boy, because if anything, he has to be a priority of yours from here on out. If you want him to be, that is."

Do I want him to be?

I could still walk away. I could financially support Dani and Ryan for the rest of their lives without blinking an eye. I could set him up with a trust fund of some sort, ensuring that he'll always have everything he could possibly need. I don't ever have to see him again, as long as the money always appears in their accounts. Though, they've clearly managed just fine without me for the past eight years.

Or I can get to know him....and what? I had a piss-poor excuse for a father. What the hell do I know about raising kids? And an eight-year-old? What the hell does an almost-eight year old eat, anyway? They're not still drinking out of a bottle, I'm pretty sure, but shit.

I can't do this.

"Well?" Steven asks.

"I don't know. The easiest thing to do would be to just walk away and set them up financially. I just signed the Bravado deal yesterday, Steven. A kid doesn't fit into that scenario."

"You're probably right, but only you can decide that. Think about it tonight, sleep on it, and see where your mind is tomorrow. She isn't going anywhere, so you don't have to decide your entire future right now."

That's the thing: my future's already decided.

And Ryan doesn't fit into it.

Chapter Seven – Movie Night

Dani

Ryan could tell something was up with me all night. If there's one thing I've learned from teaching, it's that the intuition of a child is powerful. They can pick up on your body language and your mannerisms with their little radars, pecking at you until you either give in or snap.

Ryan remained quite all through dinner, even when Trysta picked her olives off her slice of pizza and threw them at him. The smile he gave was forced and distant.

And it mirrored my own.

"Are you going to tell me why you're in such a funk tonight?" Trysta catches me in the kitchen while filling the dishwasher.

I turn towards the sound of my sister's voice. She's ready for work even though she's wearing yoga pants and a tank top. Her platinum blond hair is teased and sprayed, not a hair out of place, while her makeup looks like it was professionally done. Inside the bag that she drops on the floor is stuffed with tonight's uniform. The short black skirt and black and white corset are offset by the four-inch stiletto heels in the bottom of the bag.

"I don't even know where to start, Tryst." Pushing a few buttons so that the cycle starts, I turn towards her. "Reid came to see me today," I whisper. Saying it out loud is that slap in the face reminder of Reid's arrival…and departure today at school.

"Oh my God," she starts before walking over and sitting at the table. "What happened?" she asks.

"He showed up right after school let out. He did the craziest thing. He apologized."

"And that surprises you, why?" she asks with a small smile.

"I get the impression that Reid isn't the type of man to apologize about anything," I say. "He's…well, he just has this aura about him. It's all authority and power."

"I bet you wouldn't mind him showing you a little bit of his power," she says with a giggle and a suggestive eyebrow wiggle.

"Geesh, Trysta. Get your mind out of the gutter."

"When was the last time your mind was anywhere near the gutter, Dani?"

"That doesn't matter," I tell her. And it didn't matter to me. But for the record, it's been a damn long time since I was close to the gutter. "What matters is that while we were talking, Ryan showed up in the classroom."

"Seriously? What did he do?"

"He took one look at Ryan and knew. He didn't give anything away, but I could tell. There was tension in the air that hadn't been there before. As soon as Ryan left to go shoot hoops in the gym, Reid asked me about him."

"And you told him," Trysta states.

"Yeah," I choke out. "And he walked away." The image of Reid turning and all but running out the door like a fire-breathing dragon was nipping at his heels is so vivid and real that it's like it just happened moments ago, not hours. I can see the wrinkles at the elbows of his white dress shirt from the day's wear. I can see the way his Adam's apple worked overtime to swallow. I can still see the way his entire body commanded my classroom, and maybe a little bit of my body.

"He walked out? He just left?"

"Yeah," I tell her. "He just left. He asked me a couple of questions, but then his demeanor changed, and he just disappeared as quickly as possible. He said he had to go, turned around, and walked out of the classroom."

"Now what?" she whispers. I don't look up at her–I can't. The emotions of the past thirty-six hours are so raw and so close to bubbling up to the surface, that if I were to look up and see the pity in her face, I know my carefully constructed façade would crack wide open. I would shed the tears that I've been fighting all night. And I don't want to cry. Not over someone who owned all of my tears all those years ago. Tears that he didn't even know I shed.

"Now, nothing. I go on with my life, raising Ryan and doing everything I can to ensure he has the best life possible," I say while standing back up and grabbing a bottle of water from the fridge.

"Yeah, but you're entitled to support, you know. Reid has to support Ryan financially, even if he doesn't want to be his father."

"I don't want his money, Trysta. I've made it this far without a dime, and I'm not about to ask for it now. I just have to keep saving everything I can for Ryan's future. I've been working on his college savings, and I'll continue to do so with my own salary."

Trysta just looks at me with those wide blue eyes filled with so much sadness and sympathy. I hate that look. I don't want it. I don't want her–or anyone–to feel like they need to pity me and this life I've been living, the hand I've been dealt. I've been fine thus far, and I'm not about to let the fact that Reid chose to not be a part of his son's life affect me. Or Ryan.

But that still doesn't mean that I won't mourn the "what could have been." What could have happened if Reid was more understanding and accepting of the situation? The fact that my son could have had a father in his life will never be a mere memory. It will always be right there; front and center, in my mind, fluttering like a butterfly taking flight.

I won't let this affect us. I can't. I have been his mother and his father for almost eight years, and I will continue for as long as I live.

It's the only choice I have.

* * *

Friday night brings movie night. Trysta always works the weekends when the tips are lucrative, so Ryan and I decided to veg-out in the living room with a movie and popcorn. While I pop a bag of extra butter instant popcorn, Ryan goes through his movies to decide which one we'll be watching tonight.

"How about *Planes*? We haven't seen that one in a while," Ryan says from the kitchen doorway.

"That sounds good. I love that movie," I reply with a smile. I wouldn't trade these moments with him for anything in the world. I know the day is coming where Mom won't be as cool, so I'm holding on to these moments as tight as I possibly can.

Once the buttery popcorn is divided into two bowls, I join my son in the living room. He already has the movie in the DVD player, and is waiting for the cue to push play. After changing into some comfy sleep shorts and a tank top, we finally settle down and start the movie.

An hour into it, a knock sounds at the door. Knowing that my dad would use his key to let himself in the back door, I slowly make my way to the door, wishing I had a sweatshirt or something to throw over my tank.

When I get to the door and take a look through the peephole, I almost choke on the air in my lungs. Reid Hunter is standing on my front steps. Displeasure is the first emotion to set in as I realize that Reid is showing up at my house on a Friday night after eight o'clock. The next emotion is confusion. Why is he here? Finally, embarrassment rears its ugly head. Of course he would show up on a night where I'm already in my pajamas and scrubbed free of any makeup. Awesome.

The second knock, which comes louder and with more force, startles a little yelp out of me. Easing the lock until it releases, but keeping the chain secured, I slowly open the door. Reid stands there in snug dark jeans and a striped polo shirt that does nothing to mask the muscles in his upper arms and chest. If anything, the tight material only magnifies them. His feet are stuffed into a pair of nice brown loafers, and the watch on his wrist probably cost more than a half-month of my salary. For as put together as he appears on the outside, the lines around his eyes and the creases in his forehead tell a different story. His hair is mussed as if he's run his fingers through it repeatedly, and his eyes appear weary and lifeless. It's as if he's carrying the weight of the world on his shoulders.

"Can I talk to you?" he finally asks when I offer no greeting. I'm still so completely shocked that he's standing at my doorway that I've lost my manners. My eyes return to his for a few seconds before I close the door, remove the chain, and grant him access.

As Reid steps through the door, his eyes instantly drop to my chest. The intensity of his gaze is like a sucker punch, as his greedy eyes look their fill. As if I couldn't feel the moment my nipples harden under his scrutiny, the audible hiss that comes from his lips would have been a dead giveaway.

Upset at the reaction my traitorous body has to his mere presence, I cross my arms over my tank top, shielding myself from any further embarrassment. At least, I pray that's the outcome.

"Uh, do you want to go put on another shirt?" Reid asks, those steel gray eyes bearing into me so fiercely that I can feel it clear down to my toes.

Nope, nothing could save me from the embarrassment. Apparently, Reid would prefer I cover up my excitement caused by his gaze. Maybe it wasn't a lustful eyeful that he was drinking in like water. Maybe it was disgust and I read this entire scene wrong. Kill. Me. Now.

"What are you doing here, Reid?" I ask, trying to get my mind back to the problem at hand: Reid Hunter is in my house.

"I, uh -" he starts, but is cut off when Ryan runs into the foyer.

"Mom, you're missing the best part," he announces happily before he catches sight of the man by the front door. His gray eyes stare up at the man in front of him. God, looking at the two of them together is almost physically painful. The similarities are uncanny, and frankly, it freaks me the hell out a little.

"Ryan, do you remember Mr. Hunter?" I ask my son, dropping my arms from my chest to walk over to him. His swift head nod is the only response that I receive. "Well, I'm going to take Mr. Hunter into the kitchen and have a word with him, okay? You stay in the living room and watch the movie. I'll be back in just a few minutes," I tell my son as I steer him back towards the couch. I don't have to turn around to know that Reid is following me. I can feel his presence in the room.

Giving Ryan a soft kiss on the forehead, I turn and head towards my kitchen with Reid hot on my heels. When we step inside, I turn to him. "I'm going to grab a sweatshirt. I'll be right back," I tell him before slipping out of the small space and all but running back to my room.

Grabbing the first hoodie I can find, I slam my arms through the sleeves while trying to calm my racing heart. What the hell is he doing here? Why would he show up *now* of all times? It's been days since our awkward and tense reunion in my classroom that ended with him walking away, so what brings him to my doorstep at eight o'clock on a Friday night?

There's only one way to find out.

Zipping up the front of the sweatshirt, I head back out towards the room where I left Ryan's father.

Chapter Eight – Face To Face

Reid

I know the moment she steps into the kitchen. Not only can I smell her clean, floral scent, but also something in the air changes. It's packed with awareness and this unspoken sizzle that only happens when I'm near Dani. It screams of sex and want.

I've been staring at a picture of Ryan and Dani since the moment I walked into the kitchen. Dani's wearing a bright blue and green striped bikini that makes my dick instantly hard. Her honey-colored hair is pulled up high atop her head, and her eyes are covered up with a pair of big, black sunglasses shielding her from the intense sun. The boy with his arms wrapped around her looks so much like me at that age, it's scary. If it weren't for the woman standing next to him, I'd think it was a photo taken from an album back at my childhood home. Their smiles are so happy and free that you can feel the love pouring through the image. And the scary part is, the only thing I can think of right now is wondering where I might fit into this picture.

"When was this taken?" I ask without taking my eyes off the photo.

"Last month," she responds after clearing her throat as if to push away the sudden dryness. Still, I stare at the picture. Her body is a little curvier, her tits a lot fuller, but she's still the same breathtaking woman who blew me away all those years ago.

When the silence in the room all but gobbles us up, she asks, "Do you want a drink?"

Finally, I turn towards her, my eyes instantly dropping down to her hoodie. It was the most painful thing I've ever had to do, suggesting she cover up her beautiful chest, but I knew that if she didn't, I'd be too distracted. I'd never have the conversation that I came here to have. I'd end up throwing her over my shoulder and carrying her off to her bedroom. I'd end up doing just what images my mind has conjured up over the past couple of nights in bed alone. Nights where I did nothing but remember the way she felt against me, under me, riding me. Her body is imbedded in my mind like an exotic tattoo.

"You wouldn't happen to have any scotch, would you?" I ask, the corner of my mouth rising up slightly into a small grin.

"Uh, no. But I might have a little white wine left," she tells me as she slips around me and goes to the fridge.

"Actually, water is probably best," I say with a solemn tone. Even though I'd love to drink a few fingers of something hard to help with this nervous energy I feel, I'm thankful that we're settling on something a little milder than hard liquor.

Grabbing two bottles of water from the fridge, Dani turns back and takes a seat at the modest-sized kitchen table, which takes up a big portion of the kitchen. I follow suit, taking one of the bottles of water and chugging half of it in one big gulp. I feel her eyes on me as my throat bobs in quick succession. My mind instantly going straight back to the night I caught her watching me drink the same way. Only that night, it was beer…and it was right before we removed each other's clothes.

"I'm sure you're wondering why I'm here," I start, gazing down at my half-full water bottle. "Honestly, I don't know what the hell I'm doing here. No clue whatsoever and that scares the shit out of me, Dani." My voice is firm, yet hushed. I don't want little ears to overhear the conversation, and her look is grateful.

"I never wanted to be a father. I don't want that lifestyle. I have my work, and that keeps me extremely busy. There's just no time for a kid to be thrown into the mix." I watch as her breathing becomes slightly shallow and her eyes turn glassy. My admission is honest and clearly scares the shit out of her as much as it does me. She can see my struggle.

"I was ready to just set it up to support you financially and then walk away," I start. "I don't need a blood test, because I can see he's my son. But what frightens me most of all is that I can feel it. I know he's my boy." I take another large gulp of the water. My throat feels drier than the Sahara right now, and no amount of water can quench this thirst.

"Reid, you have to know that I never planned to disrupt your life like this. I thought it was the right thing to do to tell you about Ryan. It's completely your choice if you want to be a part of his life or not. I don't want your money. I won't bother you, I promise. I'll sign anything you want that says I can't come back to you later for anything."

"Here's my problem," I interrupt. I make sure I'm looking her square in the eyes as I say this. Even though this is *nothing* like one of my business transactions, I have to treat it as if it were. Focused. Blunt. Determined. "I don't want to walk away. I don't want to support you financially and step aside while someone else fills my shoes. I never wanted this, but I can't walk away from it now. That's the hardest part for me to swallow. I don't know why, but I can't just disappear into the night." I watch as Dani's eyes fill with unshed tears. Tears scare the shit out of me. I've never been able to do tears. I can't decipher them as good or bad, and women have used them too many times in my life as a means to try to get what they want.

"Like Batman?" I hear behind me. Both Dani and I turn quickly and look over at the boy in the doorway.

110

"What?" Dani and I both ask at the same time. The boy before me is wearing Batman pajama shorts, and his hair is tousled and standing up at all angles. I fight the grin threatening to spread across my face; he looks just like me when I wake in the morning. Well, minus the youthful pajama shorts.

"Batman. He disappears into the night after he saves the day." Ryan looks back and forth between the two of us, his gray eyes like little laser beams shooting straight at my soul.

"Is he your favorite superhero?" I ask, turning my full attention to the boy before me.

"Yeah, he's so cool. He wears a cape like lots of other superheroes, but he has a utility belt that has all kinds of awesome gadgets! Plus, he flies. And don't forget about the Batmobile! That thing is awesome and can shoot missiles and fire out the back!" Ryan exclaims in practically one long, run-on sentence. Hell, I'm not even sure he took a breath. I find myself smiling a real smile for the first time in I don't know how long.

"Batman is pretty cool," I confirm.

"I think my dad is Batman," he adds quietly. "That's why he's my favorite." All air is sucked out of the room, and for damn sure, sucked out of my lungs. Apparently, if the way Dani gasped is any indication, she's having a hard time getting her lungs to function properly, too.

"Why do you say that?" I ask just as quietly as his statement.

Ryan's gray eyes turn solemn with a hint of sadness as he steps forward and stands before me. "Because my dad can't be here with me. My mom says that his work is very important to lots of people and that he's needed elsewhere. Superheroes have to help get all the bad guys and put them in jail, so that must be why he can't be here with me."

The sadness in his eyes is so intense that it practically knocks me on my ass. I wasn't expecting to feel any sort of emotion towards this boy, but suddenly, I'm overwhelmed with it. Emotion that I haven't felt since I was a boy and my life was turned upside down.

I'm suddenly angry. Angry at the sadness in this boy's eyes. Angry at the fact that I'm the reason I see it. Instantly, I want to pull him into my arms and confess who I am. I want to promise him that he'll never be without his dad again. I want to vow that he'll never feel sadness and experience heartbreak again.

The problem is they're all vows and promises that I can't make.

It's not my place to tell him who I am at this moment. Dani and I have tons of shit to figure out, and the last thing I want to do is tell him before we're ready. Even though part of me is dying to confess, I know that it has to be the right time, and that's something that Dani and I need to discuss. So for now, I'll bite my tongue. Plus, there's the fact that I have no fucking clue how to respond to him. I'm so far into uncharted waters that I'm afraid I might never get out alive. Everywhere I look, I am surrounded by dark, murky water. It makes me want to get the hell out of dodge, and go back to Plan A where I send a check every month.

There's no way I can do this.

And then I look up at Dani and see the sadness in her smile. Suddenly, I want to punch myself in the fucking face for even thinking about walking away from them. The unexpected urge to protect them from any more hurt and hardship is so strong, it practically knocks me to the ground. It's a damn good thing that I'm sitting right now, because standing would be nearly impossible with the way my legs are shaking.

"Ryan, it's past bedtime. Why don't you go brush your teeth and get ready for bed," Dani states.

"Okay," Ryan replies and turns around. Before he vacates the room, he turns back around and says, "Good night, Mr. Hunter. It was nice to see you again." His eyes hold me captive with their uncertainty and fatigue.

"Good night, Ryan. I'll see you again soon," I tell the boy in a voice that I don't recognize.

His smile is natural and easy. His eyes instantly fill with something...hope, maybe? "Night, Mom," he hollers over his shoulder as he turns and runs out of the room.

And it's right there, in that moment, that I realize I've lost my heart forever.

Chapter Nine – Decisions, Decisions

Dani

I watch as Ryan runs out of the room. My throat is constricted so tight from the emotions I've been fighting that it's painful. I blink so rapidly that I'm sure Reid will think there's something wrong with me.

"He's a great kid," Reid says as he turns to look at me.

"Yeah, he is."

"Listen, Dani, I won't keep you. I didn't mean to just show up unannounced and disrupt your evening, but I just needed to see you for a moment. I needed to tell you that I'm not going anywhere. I don't know what exactly that means yet, and we definitely have some things to work out, but I can't walk away. Not now."

"Reid, I know that you have a lot of stuff to work out and that all of this is a huge shock for you. But you have to understand that protecting him is my first priority. I have to know without a shadow of a doubt that you are one hundred percent invested in this before I say anything to him. I can't–no, I won't–subject him to the possibility of having a father, and then have you flake out on him when you realize this isn't what you want."

"Can we meet and talk more soon, maybe dinner one night this week? I'd really like to talk with you more about Ryan," he says. Dinner with Reid is probably a really, *really* bad idea if I want to keep a clear head, but he has always been my one weakness.

"Reid, I don't know -" I start, but he cuts me off.

"Just dinner. We have a lot of stuff to discuss, and I don't want to do it here where little ears can overhear," he says, knowing that with that one little statement, he has me on the line. I'm sure he can see the question in my eyes and feel the resistance rolling off me in huge waves, but I'm sure he also knows that I'll do anything for my son.

Our son.

"Fine. My sister is off Tuesday night so I could do it then," I say, crossing my arms protectively over my chest. The action only reminds me of how I must have looked when I opened the door earlier. Right before he asked me to put on more clothes...

"I'll call you with details. I have a late afternoon meeting, but should be free around six-thirty," he tells me as he digs out a business card from his wallet. Retrieving the ink pen lying on the counter, he jots down something on the back of the card before handing me the card. "Call me if you need me," he adds.

I glance down at the ten numbers on the back of the business card. Following behind Reid as he walks towards the front door, something keeps nagging at me. Something's off and I can't quite put my finger on it.

Turning around after he opens the door, Reid says, "Call me anytime, Dani. I'm serious." His eyes are darker suddenly, like black orbs pulling me into the depths of his soul.

"Thank you," I mumble as I reach for the nob, but instead of touching the cool metal, I touch warm skin. Reid's hand turns, enveloping mine, causing fireworks to erupt in the pit of my stomach and my blood to zing through my veins.

I'm sucked into his expressive eyes so quickly that I don't even realize what's happening. I'm right back at that night, in the little blue tent on the small, overcrowded campground. I'm suddenly wrapped up in his arms, sweating and panting from exertion. I'm instantly wet and needy.

Before either of us can do anything that we'll regret–or not regret, depending on who you're asking–Reid leans in and gives me a small peck on the cheek. His warm breath kisses my over-sensitive skin, heating me up clear down to my core. His lips feel soft and damp against my cheek, and I feel myself swaying just a little towards his touch.

But before anything further can happen, he pulls away.

"Lock up," he whispers as he slips out the front door.

I watch him head down the steps and take the walk towards his car. When he reaches the driver's side, it suddenly hits me. Earlier in the kitchen, there was something that was bugging me, and now I know what it was. "Reid," I holler before he can slip inside the car. When he pauses and turns to me, I ask, "Why didn't you ask me for my phone number?"

"I already have it, sweet Dani," he says. The grin he offers me starts small enough, but eventually transforms into something entirely different. Something dirtier. Wolfish. The kind of smile that makes panties burst into flames. Oh, I can feel the heat, all right.

I just pray I'm strong enough to resist it so that I don't get burned.

* * *

"Cannonball!" Ryan exclaims moments before a tsunami of waves splash angrily onto the pool deck where I'm lying.

"Ryan!" My hollers go unheard over the sounds of my dad and son's squeals of joy. As angry as I try to be at the move, I have to admit that the water feels amazing against my sun kissed skin.

"Laugh now, Misters, but I'll have the last laugh when you're eating peanut butter and jelly tonight while I'm eating my steak off the grill," I quip, trying to hide my grin.

"Let's not splash your mother again, Ry. I've been looking forward to that steak all afternoon," my dad says. The grin he offers me says he probably wasn't an innocent bystander in the quest to drown me.

Deciding to take a quick dip in the pool before I light up the grill, I stand up and remove my ear buds. I had been listening to a steamy romance novel by one of my favorite authors; a luxury I only indulge in when I have my dad here to watch Ryan in the pool. My cell phone on the table next to me signals an incoming text message.

Unknown number.

Reid: *If I were a betting man, I'd wager a bet that you probably didn't add my number into your phone. So, this is just a reminder to add me. Reid*

Is it wrong that my heart skipped a little beat when I read his message?

Me: *I have no doubts that you are a betting man. Anyone in your line of work must be.*

Reid: *Did I win the bet?*

Me: *Yes. I'm adding you now.*

Reid: *Ha!*

After a few seconds, another text comes through.

Reid: *What are you doing today?*

Instead of replying with words, I snap a quick picture of our son swimming in the pool. He's laughing at something my dad said, head thrown back as he treads water. It's a great picture. Before I can talk myself out of it, I hit send. It takes several minutes before I get a reply.

Reid: ☺

Me: *You?*

A few moments later, a photo arrives of Reid's desk. Several file folders litter his workspace in an organized fashion. Reid is definitely someone who likes organization. Control.

Me: *On a Sunday?*

Reid: *Every day.*

Before I can reply, he sends me another message.

Reid: *Enjoy the afternoon. I'll see you Tuesday.*

Me: *You too. Do you know where I'm meeting you yet?*

Reid: *Later. I'll text you later.*

I can't help the way my lips curl upward at the thought. Knowing that Reid is going to text me again later only puts a little pep in my step as I make my way towards the water. It actually ticks me off a little that I'm reacting to him this way. I have no business getting excited about the prospect of talking to him. No business smiling at the idea of having dinner with him Tuesday night. No. What I need to do is steel myself against his intoxicating eyes and his lush lips. I need to focus on Ryan and determining if a relationship with Reid is possible.

Slipping into the pool, I let the cool water wash over me as I dip my head below the water. I've always loved swimming, and am thankful that Ryan has acquired my love for the water. He swims like a fish thanks to the extensive training he went through a few summers ago.

"A penny for your thoughts?" my dad asks as he walks over to where I'm floating at the far end of the pool.

I exhale deeply as I gaze up into his matching blue eyes. "Oh, Dad, I wish I knew where to begin."

"Does this have anything to do with the young man who was here the other night?"

I shouldn't be surprised that my dad is aware of Reid's visit, but I am. Trysta wasn't here and I have yet to mention it to her because of her work schedule, so there's only one way he could have found out.

"What did he say?" I ask as casually as possible.

"Just that a man named Mr. Hunter was here and also in your classroom. He said he was tall. Like Batman," Dad says with a chuckle. Only the mention of Ryan's favorite superhero isn't lost on me.

I look over my shoulder and watch Ryan. He's walking around the outer edge of the pool where it's a bit more shallow and he's able to touch better. "Mr. Hunter is Reid Hunter, Dad. I met him a long time ago."

"Does he have anything to do with that boy over there," he asks directly.

Turning to look back at the man who raised me, I answer him honestly. "Yes. How did you know?"

"Dani, I've always been able to read you like an open book. Your sister? Now she gave me more sleepless nights than I care to recount, but you? You wear your emotions on your sleeve. Always have. I could always tell when you were hiding something because your face gave it away."

Good to know. I always wondered how my dad knew that I was the guilty party when I was growing up. I guess I never really thought that I wore my feelings like a favorite t-shirt.

"I'm meeting him for dinner on Tuesday to discuss what happens next."

"I take it he didn't know about you know who?" Dad asks as we continue to have our conversation at a whisper.

"No. I didn't know how to reach him," I confess. I wonder if my mortification at having this conversation with my dad is written clearly on my face right now.

"So, he wants to be involved?" Dad asks as he floats next to me, both of us watching Ryan play.

"That's what we're trying to determine. Reid says he never wanted kids, but he can't seem to walk away from Ryan. I'm afraid he's going to worm his way into our lives and then change his mind."

"Well, he wouldn't be the first man–or woman–who decides they're not cut out for parenthood," my dad says without looking at me, but I know instantly that he's thinking about my mother. A woman who decided she didn't want to be a mom anymore.

"I know, and that terrifies me. I don't want that for Ryan."

"You can't control it, Dani. Because if he is who you say he is, then he has the right to be a part of that boy's life."

"And I want that, Dad, really. But I can't fathom the thought of him seeing Ryan, spending time with him, making Ryan fall in love with him, and then walking away." The thought makes me sick to my stomach.

"Again, that's out of your control. Right now, the only thing you need to concern yourself with is getting to know Reid and making sure you both are on the same page where Ryan is concerned." My dad has a way of speaking right to the heart of me. I've always been close with my dad, but when it comes to matters pertaining to Reid, I've always chosen to have those conversations with Trysta.

"Thank you, Dad," I tell him as I wrap my wet arms around him and kiss his aged cheek.

Swimming over towards Ryan, I give him a playful splash and get ready to dunk him. I never do it without giving him a look or the opportunity to prepare himself. There's nothing worse than being dunked unexpectedly, coming up spitting and coughing up pool water, chlorine burning your nose and lungs.

"Hey, Mom," he says as he comes up from the dunk. "I guess you owed me that one, huh?" he says with a big, toothy grin. It melts my heart instantly.

"Yeah, I owed you that one. I'm going to run up and start the grill, okay?"

"Okay," Ryan says, as he takes off towards my dad, no doubt hell bent on dunking his grandpa.

I watch as he swims gracefully towards my father, splashing and playing the entire way. His happiness is contagious, electrifying. I fear that I'm about to put more on him than his young mind can handle. What if he doesn't accept Reid? What if he becomes angry with me for hiding his father's identity from him? What if they don't get along?

But what if they do?

What if Ryan and Reid form an indestructible bond that carries him through the rest of his life?

What if he finally has everything I've ever wanted for him.

I'd be a fool not to try to give him that life. If making nice with Reid and working out a mutual agreement for the sake of our son is what I have to do, so be it. I'll do whatever it takes to ensure my son's happiness.

Chapter Ten – Dinner For Two

Reid

Tuesday. I've thought of nothing but tonight all damn day. I half listened in the meeting this afternoon with the owner of a singular casino on the outskirts of the Vegas Strip. It isn't my choice of property to consider, but Jon seems to think it's a great opportunity. Thankfully, he caught on to my lack of focal ability and led the meeting with grace. Fuck, that never happens. I never let someone else take over my meetings. I never need help in running my company. It's my company for a reason.

That was before Dani Whitley worked her way back into the forefront of my mind. I've been held hostage by the memory of those crystal blue eyes since the moment she walked into my office a week ago.

"Do you need anything before I go, Mr. Hunter?" Carly asks from my office door.

"You can call me Reid, you know. It's after five. And, no, thank you. Did you make the reservations that I requested?" I ask.

"Yes, of course. Dinner for two tonight at The Garden," she replies with a knowing smile. "Seems a little more laid back than your normal requests for reservations," she adds with a wider smile.

Carly knows me pretty well, but I'm sure she is way off on this one. She expects me to be dining with a plastic Barbie doll primped to perfection in designer clothes. She has no clue that my date this evening is a schoolteacher or why I chose this particular restaurant. Besides being much smaller and casual, The Garden is known for its relaxed atmosphere where you're allowed to hold private conversations without fearing that those around you can hear and listen in.

"It's not a date," I tell her, more trying to speak the words out loud as a firm reminder to myself.

"Whatever you say. If you don't need anything else, I'm going to head out. Blake is supposed to be home tonight following a week in Atlanta," she says with a bright smile.

"Go. I'm about finished here," I tell her firmly.

"Goodnight, Mr. Hunter," she adds moments before slipping out of my office. I listen as Carly shuffles around her office, removing her purse from her desk drawer before making her way towards the bank of elevators. When the door shuts, I'm bathed in silence once again.

Glancing at the clock on my desk, I realize it's already five-thirty. That only gives me less than an hour to freshen up, change clothes, and get to the restaurant. After flipping off the lights in my office, I slip inside my private elevator, which whisks me up to the apartment above my office. On the ride up, I recall Dani's heated text exchanges from last night when I told her that I would be picking her up at quarter after. She insisted multiple times that it wasn't a date, therefore demanding that she meet me at the restaurant.

I can't wipe the smile off my face as I slip into the bathroom for a quick shower, which in itself is a telltale sign of how this girl affects me. Dani is the only woman who has ever caused this sort of reaction. Sure, plenty of women have caused blood to flow quickly below my belt, but none cause it to stay there for long periods of time without any relief in sight. And don't get me started on how my heartbeat quickens whenever I think of her. For a coldblooded, heartless bastard, that reaction is the one that terrifies me the most.

Hopping in the Aston Martin, I speed off towards The Garden. Traffic is heavy for a Tuesday night so it takes me longer to get there than I planned. I usually have Steven drive me to dinner meetings, but this isn't a typical dinner meeting. The last thing I want is to undergo one of his famous inquisitions on the ride home. Especially when I'm not sure I'll know the answers.

I'm surprisingly nervous when I pull into the parking lot next to the restaurant. That's the first clue that this isn't a normal business deal. This is my life. This is something that I never wanted. This is brand new, uncharted territory and I have not one fucking clue how to navigate it. Wiping my palms on my thighs, I lock up my car and head towards the front of the restaurant.

Inside, the place is lively for a Tuesday evening. A nicely dressed hostess stands at a wooden stand just off to the right. My eyes bypass her long, curly blond hair and are instantly drawn to the inches of cleavage bursting forth from the top of her white button down shirt. Red, plump lips smile widely over straight, white teeth as she takes in my khaki pants and blue button-up. When she licks her lips, I can practically hear the unspoken offer. Unfortunately for her, an appreciative eyeful is all I have to offer this evening as I think about the woman who is about to meet me here any moment.

"Good evening. May I help you?" she offers suggestively, again with that fuck-me smile. I'd be a lying ass if I said this was the first time I was practically propositioned for something dirty with a beautiful stranger. Fuck, it wasn't that long ago that I would have taken Miss Perky Tits into a backroom somewhere and fucked her senseless.

Not tonight. Tonight, I have other plans.

"I'm meeting someone here. Reservation under Hunter," I say politely but with a disconnected tone.

"Oh, yes, Mr. Hunter. We have your table ready for you. Follow me," she offers as she steps into the dining room.

Activity and laughter fills the small space. The lighting isn't bright, but it doesn't have that romantic, low glow either. It perfectly matches the cream and burgundy décor and dark walnut woodwork.

As the hostess, with a little extra swing in her hips, leads me towards the table in back, I realize that my dinner companion is already seated. Dani sits in a chair with her back to me, staring out the glass window. The sun is still high in the sky, casting a warm glow over the glass buildings in the background and the dog park just off to the right. But the way the sun reflects off of Dani's hair is the most breathtaking sight of all. I steal several unabolished moments of categorizing her beautiful features. I'd memorized them that night years ago while she slept naked against my skin, wrapped up in the sleeping bag. Those memories have kept me company many nights since then.

"Is there anything else you need, Mr. Hunter?" the hostess asks with a smile. Dani turns and faces me. She's stunning in her plain black maxi dress with black flats.

"No, thank you," I offer without looking away from the woman sitting before me.

I ignore the hostess as I slip into my chair. "Sorry I'm late," I tell Dani as I grab the menu. "Traffic was heavier than expected."

"It's okay. I was only waiting a few minutes," she says politely. Still I can't pull my eyes away from her.

After ordering glasses of red wine, we both sit in uncomfortable silence. Not knowing how in the hell to start this conversation, I opt to study Dani as she twists her wine glass between her fingers. Her nails are trimmed neatly with not a drop of polish on them. I watch her fingers spin the delicate glass; my mind instantly going back to the night where those fingers caused so much pleasure. Fuck, what I wouldn't do to get lost in her touch once more.

Adjusting my rapidly growing erection and shaking my head to eradicate those dirty images that have no business planting in my mind, I decide to get down to the reason we're here. "I know you don't know me, Dani. I know you're taking a huge leap of faith in me, and I appreciate that. I can't promise you that I won't mess up. I can't promise you that I won't say something that I shouldn't or do something that is wrong. I can't promise you that I won't piss you off, probably more than once. But I want to try, Dani. I want to try for you and for Ryan."

I take another deep breath before continuing. "This is one of the only times in my life I feel truly out of control and I fucking hate it. Sorry," I mumble and give her a sheepish grin. She rewards me with another smile as she waves her hand as if to excuse my foul language. "I'm always in control. It's my job to maintain every ounce of control I possess. It's what makes me good at what I do. But this? This makes me feel reckless. I have no clue what's about to happen and that doesn't sit well with me," I confess.

Amazing how much lighter I feel saying those things out loud. It's as if saying them relieves me of the burden I've felt carrying around the weight of my stress. No, not stress. Stress I can handle. I handle it every day, and damn well. This? This is something different. Something fearful on the verge of chaos, and it terrifies me.

"Reid, I have no idea what happens next. I'm scared that you're going to worm your way into our lives and then leave when you realize this isn't the life you want. You've said it yourself that you don't want this life. I'm terrified that you're going to walk away and leave me with the mess of a little boy with a broken heart."

"What if I promise you not to walk away?" I ask instantaneously, without thinking at all. It's the first thing that comes to mind.

"You can't promise that," she says.

"I can. I can't promise you a lot of things, but I can promise you that. I won't abandon him, Dani. I don't know how, but that little boy has already burrowed his way into my life. I knew it the moment I saw him standing next to me in your classroom that from that moment on, nothing would ever be the same. I want to be his father. I won't–no, I *can't* walk away. *That* I promise," I tell her, sucking in greedy gulps of air while my heartbeat races a rapid pace in my chest.

I can see her heartbeat in the pulse point in her neck. Hers is beating a hundred miles a minute like mine. The steady beat reminds me of that night. I long to lean forward and trace that point, down to her collarbone, with my tongue. My cock drums heavily in my pants, a sign that it agrees wholeheartedly with my big head.

"Okay," Dani whispers. That one word of agreement sealing my fate forever. "When do we tell him?" she asks, her light blue eyes burning holes into me.

"As soon as possible," I say. I don't want to wait. I've missed seven, almost eight years of Ryan's life and I'm not about to let any more time slip by.

"What about this weekend? You can come over for a cookout and we can tell him then," she says with a nervous look.

"Perfect. I'll clear my schedule for the entire weekend," I say without so much as batting an eye. I *never* clear my schedule. I can almost see Carly's shocked reaction in my mind when I tell her.

"Okay," she says again.

After ordering our food, I steer the conversation towards another topic that leaves me curious and edgy as hell. "Can I ask you something?"

"Sure," she says as she picks at her salad.

"Is there a boyfriend I need to worry about?" I ask casually, throwing in a cocky little smile at the end to fluster her. The result is exactly as I had hoped as she fidgets uncomfortably in her chair.

"That's none of your business," she defends with a huff.

"Actually, it is. If someone is going to be around my son, I want to know." My tone is curt and my focus direct. No, I'm not trying to be an ass, but I know I'm coming off that way.

"Ryan is, and always will be, my first priority. I don't bring strange men around him. He's never met anyone that I've gone out with. In fact, I've barely dated since I had him, and I don't plan on it now. So don't go acting like I'm some kind of harlot with a swinging front door who invites anyone with a dick to stop by her place, you jackass," she seethes through gritted teeth.

And there it is. The admission I'd hoped for. Hell, I wasn't exactly sure what she'd say when I egged her on, but I never imagined it would be that sweet. It was better than anything she could have ever said. Dani hasn't dated. There's no one in her life. Her confession sends my heart racing and my blood pumping.

"Why are you smiling?" she harshly whispers.

"Because I'm damn happy."

"What about that could possibly make you happy, Reid?"

"The fact that I don't have to get some Tom out of my way, Dani. The fact that you don't share your bed with some Joe. Or maybe it's the fact that you haven't filled *my* spot in your life. Take your pick," I say through my smile.

"You...I...I don't even..." she starts, but can't seem to find the right words. "Ryan. This is about Ryan, Reid. Don't go inserting yourself into my life like you belong in it. You belong in Ryan's life," she says fiercely.

"Yes, I do. But you're a part of Ryan's life. In fact, you're the most important person in it. Therefore, I'll be inserted into your life as well." I take a huge drink of my wine. "Besides, I needed to know if I had to get rid of anyone because I will, Dani. There will be no one else in your life, sweetheart. I'll be there. If anyone is going to warm your bed or keep you up all night, it's going to be me. *That* is another promise," I tell her, leaning forward and giving her a direct look to drive my point home.

I know I'm fighting dirty, but I don't give a shit. Ever since she walked back into my life, I've wanted her. I want Dani now as much as I wanted her that night eight plus years ago. It's time I let her know it. I won't let her go this time without a fight.

I don't exactly know what this all means, but I know that she's always been more in the back of my mind. She's not just one of the women I fuck to satisfy my urges. She's not just a piece of arm candy that I can take to fundraisers and dinner meetings. From the moment I met her, she's always been something bigger, something deeper, and something truer. I'm not getting rid of that; believe me, I've tried. So, the only option I have right now is to embrace it and see where it leads.

"Don't say anything," I tell her. "I can see your brain working overtime. It's practically smoking. Just know this. I'm not going to rush anything with you, but I'm not going away. I'm in your life forever now. I want you, Dani. I've wanted you from the moment you stepped off my elevator and walked into my office. And I always get what I want. Always," I say confidently.

"Now, let's enjoy dinner and figure out how we're going to tell our son that I'm his father," I say casually as if I didn't just confess my desires and intentions. More shocking is the fact that saying those words was so easy and natural; like breathing or walking.

Dani stares at me with wide blue eyes. Her beautiful mouth is hanging open from shock, I assume. I give her a little wink before cutting into my steak that the waitress just deposited in front of me.

"Mmmmm, this is good. You should try it," I say as I chew slowly, giving her a closed-mouth smile and another wink.

"I'm suddenly not hungry," she mumbles, dropping her eyes down to her plate with a huff in defeat.

Oh, my little Dani. You haven't seen nothing yet.

Chapter Eleven – Confessions

Dani

I'm a nervous wreck as I check the clock on the wall for the tenth time in just under an hour. I swear the clock is intentionally moving at a snail's pace. I woke up this morning well before my alarm. Sleep barely came to me at all last night as I've fretted and worried about what I'm going to say to Ryan today.

Reid should be here any minute. The plan that we came up with is to spend the day in the backyard swimming and getting to know each other. Then at dinner tonight, we're going to drop the bomb on him. I just pray that the impact doesn't destroy him.

"Mom, are you ready to go outside?" Ryan hollers from the back door.

"Almost ready, buddy," I tell him as I grab the sunscreen and the towels.

Just as we step outside, I hear a vehicle pulling into the driveway. I told Reid to come around back when he arrives, so I head back to the pool area to prep it for Ryan. Setting the towels down on the lounger next to mine, I hear the gate open and the heavy footfalls that can only be Reid's.

"Mr. Hunter," Ryan exclaims, happy to have a new swimming partner for the afternoon.

When I told him last night that Reid was going to come over and swim and cook out with us, he was instantly ecstatic. He talked for twenty minutes, asking tons of questions that I wasn't able to answer like what is his favorite food and what sport did he play in school. I'm sure he's anxious to start his inquisition the moment Reid walks into the backyard.

"Hi, Ryan. And call me Reid, okay?" he says casually with a smile.

Ryan looks over at me for confirmation. I have always instilled the best manners I could in Ryan, teaching him that you always call someone by Mister or Miss until instructed otherwise. I give him a polite nod, granting him permission to call Reid by his first name.

"Are you ready to swim?" Ryan asks, standing at the water's edge, eagerly awaiting the cue to jump in.

"I'm ready," Reid says. "Let me put my stuff down."

Walking over to where I'm standing, Reid says, "Good afternoon."

I turn my attention towards him for the first time since his arrival. He's wearing a pair of blue and red board shorts that hang low on his hips. When he removes his t-shirt, I'm treated to a mouth-watering view of his marvelous physique. Younger Reid had an amazing body, but older Reid? Panty-wetting. Nuclear. Adult Reid is a Greek God. His chest matted with a sprinkle of dark hair is defined and toned to perfection, but what holds my attention now is the way the V of his hips drops dangerously low into his shorts. A thin trail of dark hair disappears into the top of those shorts, making me wish I were a world explorer, eager to discover where that path leads.

"Stop sexually assaulting me with your eyes or I'm never going to make it through this afternoon without tasting you," he whispers against my ear, his breath tickling the shell of my ear. I inhale a deep breath and shiver uncontrollably, noticing the way my core throbs with awareness.

This is going to be the longest afternoon of my life.

"Sorry," I whisper, returning my eyes up to his. His eyes are practically black with something dark and dirty. Need. Desire. It's all right there, written across his face like some ancient proverb.

"Don't be sorry. Just don't do it when I'm about to swim with our son and have hours to go before I can touch you," he bites out in a tone laced with pure sex.

I swallow the lump in my throat and turn back to rearranging the towels; anything to keep my hands busy. Without thinking, I unzip my cover-up and slip it over my body. My body immediately becomes aware of Reid's presence as my nipples pucker beneath my black and pink bikini. Reid hisses as my eyes slam back into his. The stare down is erotic and all-consuming.

"Are you coming in, Reid?" Ryan asks from the side of the pool. He's watching us, waiting to jump in, oblivious to the sexual tension buzzing around like bees at a picnic.

"Go ahead and get in, Ry. Reid will be there in a second," I say taking a step back, away from Reid's sexual pull. Without so much as a glance in our direction, Ryan turns and jumps into the water.

"Come on, Reid," Ryan yells as he starts to swim out towards the middle where a water noodle floats.

"I better hurry, huh? I don't want to keep him waiting," Reid says with another wink and an award-winning smile. Seriously, Oscar speeches are delivered with less charm and charisma than what I'm receiving right now.

All afternoon, I watch as Reid and Ryan swim, play, and talk. Occasionally, I'm pulled into their conversation, but for the most part, I listen, trying to step back and let father and son get to know each other; even if son isn't aware of father.

Feeling the heat of the afternoon sun, I decide to cool myself down in the pool before I get ready to grill dinner. I stopped by the store yesterday and grabbed the makings for kabobs with a variety of fresh vegetables, plus a dozen ears of sweet corn that I will throw on the grill as well.

As I step over to the side of the pool, I can't help but smile as Ryan uses his hands to drive home his point as to why Batman is the far superior superhero. In the eyes of this child, Spiderman, Thor, Superman, or any other superhero doesn't stand a chance.

"Hey, Mom," Ryan exclaims as he chases the floating basketball and swims in to go for the dunk.

Treading water, I feel Reid's presence moments before his touch. Big, warm hands slide effortlessly over my back, wrapping around my stomach. Even through the water, I feel the trail of heat.

"This bikini is doing bad things to me, Dani. Very bad things," he says moments before I feel his erection pressed into the crease of my ass. It takes every ounce of self-control I possess to not push back and grind against it like a virgin at the *Magic Mike* premiere. It feels just as big and glorious as I remember. Biting my bottom lip, I do everything within my power to keep the moan from slipping from my lips.

"We can't do this," I whisper hoarsely in a voice that isn't my own.

"No?" he asks as he lightly strokes his hand over my stomach, angling it down towards the junction of my legs.

"No," I say so hoarsely that it doesn't come out as a word; just a deep exhale of quickened air.

"You're probably right. I shouldn't do this," he whispers against my ear, snaking his tongue out to trace the shell of my ear, while his hand glides down to my sex. Even through the material of my bikini bottoms, I can feel the warmth of his hand, the firmness of his fingers, and the wetness in my response to both.

"Reid, let's shoot more hoops," Ryan exclaims, breaking the moment like a mirror. I jump away from Reid's touch so quickly that I slip and almost swallow water. The sounds of his chuckles as he swims towards Ryan are the only thing I hear over the sound of my racing heart.

I quickly get out of the water, suddenly anxious to dry off and start the grill. Anything to put distance between Reid and myself. Grabbing the towel on top, I wrap it around my body, covering as much of myself as possible, as if wrapping myself in some sort of protective sexual tension force field. Without even thinking, I turn and glance at Reid. The smile he offers almost drops me to my knees.

My force field failed.

An hour later, I've finished setting up the patio table for dinner. I set four place settings knowing that Trysta should be making her appearance any minute. She's been sleeping all afternoon, but I received a text a little bit ago saying that she was getting ready for work and would grab food on her way out.

Ryan and Reid got out of the pool as soon as I geared up to place the food on the grill. Reid quickly took over as Grill Master, manning the grill with ease and efficiency. Ryan, on the other hand, hovered next to where Reid stood, drinking in every movement he made. His game of ten thousand questions continued up until the moment I sent him in the house to wash up for dinner.

"These look great," I say to Reid as he brings the platter of food to the table. Pieces of chicken and steak are mixed with slices of onion, green peppers, mushrooms, and butternut squash. The cornhusks are toasted to a golden brown, the corn on the inside juicy and tender.

"They smell great, too. You put together a mean kabob," Reid says as he sets the platter in the middle of the table. Taking in the fourth place setting, he adds, "Are we expecting someone else?"

"My sister is inside getting ready for work. She'll probably grab a bite to eat before heading out," I tell him as Ryan bounces down the back steps and heads straight towards us.

"I'm starving," he exclaims as he pulls out the seat next to where Reid is standing. I take that as a good sign that he has enjoyed his time this afternoon. It makes me hopeful for the blow we're about to deal him. "You sit next to me," Ryan adds with a wide grin.

Pulling out the empty chair, Reid sits down next to Ryan. They both immediately start to fill up their plates with kabobs. I'm rooted where I stand as I watch Reid butter up Ryan's ear of corn as if he's done it a hundred times before. The Nevada air is suddenly thicker and headier than ever before.

"Cat got your tongue?" Trysta whispers in my ear.

I spin around, startled by my sister's closeness. How did I not realize she was behind me? Apparently I was lost in the picture that Reid and Ryan painted. "Holy shit, you scared me," I murmur harshly.

"Maybe if you weren't eye-fucking the man in front of you, you would have heard me talking to you as I walked up," she sasses back.

"Whatever. I wasn't eye-fucking him. I was watching him with Ryan," I confide in her.

"He's pretty good with him, I take it?" she asks, her blue eyes searching my face.

"He has been wonderful," I say, turning back to the table, taking my seat.

"Reid, this is my sister, Trysta. Tryst, this is Reid Hunter."

"Ah, yes, Reid Hunter. I actually met you, unofficially, a few weeks back. You were playing cards at the Mirage where I work, though we weren't introduced." Trysta gives him a quick once-over without making it too obvious that she's appreciating Reid's very gorgeous assets. It causes my heart to stop beating in my chest. Even though I know Trysta wouldn't do anything to cause me any harm–including anything with Ryan's father–it still causes a bit of worry deep in my chest.

"Of course," he says. "I was playing cards that night with my friend, Jon. I believe I went home with quite a bit of the casino's money," he adds with a chuckle.

"It's nice to finally meet you," Trysta says while extending her hand towards Reid.

"Very nice to officially meet you, too."

I watch as Reid shakes the hand of my older, model thin sister. I hold my breath as I wait for his reaction to my beautiful sister. He wouldn't be the first man to pass me over in favor of Trysta's voluptuous curves and perky double D's. But Reid keeps his eyes on her face, his body language polite. I smile inwardly and breathe a sigh of relief when he immediately starts to talk to Ryan again. The spike of jealousy and doubt was real, even if completely unfounded.

"So, how has today gone?" Trysta asks with a knowing smile.

"Good," Reid says at the same time Ryan proclaims, "Awesome!"

Trysta's raised eyebrow is the only way she asks the burning question. I answer her with the shake of my head. No, we haven't told him yet.

"Well, Reid, it was nice to meet you. I've got to get to work, so I'm going to take some food to go," she says as she stands up and removes the goodies off two kabob sticks, depositing them on a plate.

Saying her goodbyes to everyone, Trysta slips out the back gate and heads towards her car. Even though the food is delicious, my appetite has vanished. Are we doing the right thing by telling him? Is it too soon? How will he react? So many questions.

Realizing that I'm surrounded by silence, I glance up and see Reid watching me intently. There are little crinkles around his eyes and his face is as serious as ever, giving off the appearance that he's older than his thirty years. It's as if laughter is a luxury he can't afford to have. I realize the seriousness is his way to prepare himself for the conversation we're about to partake.

"Ryan, I need to talk with you about something, okay?" I ask my little guy as he finishes up his dinner.

"Okay," he says, looking over at Reid.

"If it's okay with you, I want Reid to stay for this conversation. It has to do with him," I say to my son. His head nod is the only reaction I get.

"I know you've been wondering a lot lately about your dad. I told you he has a really, really important job, and that's true," I start, though I'm not really sure buying and selling corporations, especially casinos, is what I'd classify as an 'important' job. "Well, what if I told you that your dad was here?"

Holding my breath, I wait for some sort of reaction. The way Ryan's eyes light up and he smiles bigger than the Hoover Dam, I know that this news could possibly be the best thing he's ever heard. God I hope so…

"What do you mean?" Ryan asks, looking back and forth between me and Reid, who has remained quiet up to this point.

"What if we told you that I am your dad?" Reid says quickly. Like pulling off the Band Aid. Not exactly how I was planning to say it, that's for sure. My plan was to ease into it a little more, make sure that his delicate little mind can process everything we're saying. Then Reid goes and just blurts it out.

"You're my dad?" Ryan asks, confusion written all over his young little face.

"Yeah," Reid says so confidently that it chokes me up instantly. "I'm your dad, Ryan."

I hold my breath until I feel myself starting to get lightheaded. Ryan glances between Reid and myself, then back again, giving away nothing. Suddenly, his chair flies backwards, falling behind him onto the concrete. I gasp as I prepare for him to bolt, but what he does next floors me. Ryan throws himself onto Reid's lap, hugging him so fiercely that I can tell Reid isn't able to suck in oxygen.

Tears threaten to spill from my eyes as I watch the scene unfold like the dramatically beautiful ending of a romance movie. Reid holds on tightly to Ryan as if he's afraid he'll disappear unexpectedly.

"You're really my dad? Like really, *really?* I knew you'd come back for me, I knew it! I bet you were someplace really cool that's just like Gotham City. I bet you can't tell me where, though, cause it's a big secret. Maybe someday when I'm older and can be your sidekick, you'll tell me where you've been," Ryan says, pulling back to gaze happily up at his dad.

"Someday," Reid whispers as he gives Ryan a small smile and a wink.

"Mom, did you know my dad is a real superhero? I knew it, Mom. He can't tell me, but I've always known it. And now he's back!" Ryan rejoices from Reid's lap.

"He's back," I confirm to my son, offering them both the best smile I can to convey happiness and excitement. But, underneath my smile, I'm full of worry and uncertainty. I just pray we did the right thing by telling Ryan so quickly.

And most of all, I pray that Reid keeps his promise about always being there for Ryan. Because ready or not, there's no turning back now.

Chapter Twelve – Down and Dirty

Reid

I watch through the small window on the back of the house as Dani washes up the few dishes from dinner. She slipped inside to clean up the mess about fifteen minutes ago, giving Ryan and I another opportunity to visit and play.

Telling Ryan that I am his father is something I'll never forget. I'm sure Dani wasn't ready for me to just blurt it out the way I did, but I couldn't contain myself any longer. I've always been the talker, the negotiator, in business. I talk, you listen. Listening to Dani talk to Ryan made it crystal clear that she had no clue how to say the words she was trying to get out. That's why I stepped in. Rip off the Band Aid.

I never knew it could feel this good to say those words. I'm not going to lie and say that I wasn't scared to fucking death, because I was. But, I was more afraid of never telling him. More fearful of him never knowing who I am to him. And that thought gutted me to the core. This little boy is quickly thawing my frozen heart faster than an ice cube in the Sahara Desert.

"Come on, Ryan. It's time for your bath," Dani says from the back door.

"But I was telling Reid what I want for my birthday next month," Ryan whines.

"No arguing, Mister. You know it's already well after bedtime. You'll be able to see Reid again soon," Dani says as she steps out onto the porch.

"When?" Ryan asks, turning his eager eyes back to me.

"How about tomorrow? Maybe we can go to the park or something?" I offer. The park. I haven't been to a park since I was ten years old.

"Yes!" Ryan exclaims as he gets up and throws his arms around my neck. "Will you still be here when I get done in the bathtub?" he asks. How in the fuck am I supposed to say no to those big doe eyes? It's official. I can't.

"I'll hang around until you're done to say goodnight. But then it's off to bed," I tell him, amazed at how well the fatherly tone rolls off my tongue.

"Deal!" he shouts before turning and running into the house.

"You're welcome to step inside and hang out while I help him with his bath," Dani says from the doorway. She doesn't have to tell me twice. I quickly stand up and follow her inside. "I'll be right back. Make yourself at home," she says as she slips down the hallway towards the bathroom.

My attention is instantly pulled towards the refrigerator. That picture of Ryan and Dani wearing the same bikini that she was wearing today is secured to the fridge with magnets. I continue to gaze at the picture. I'm drawn to it tonight much as I was a little over a week ago when I showed up at their house uninvited. There's something so beautiful about the way she looks. Sure, she's a gorgeous woman, but there's something more, something meaningful. Love. It's written all over her face, in the way she stands with her arm wrapped around Ryan. And the look on his face shines his own adoration for his mother.

The photo reminds me of the way my own mother looked in photos of my childhood. There weren't many since Mom usually the photo taker, but I can recall a few. Photos of family vacations, birthday parties, and holidays. Me and Tara…and Reagan. Dad was rarely in the pictures. He was usually too busy working to waste his time on creating family memories. Maybe that's why most of my memories are tainted.

Removing the photo from its place on the fridge, I run my fingers along the delicate lines of her face. She is without a doubt, the most breathtaking woman I've ever known. If I never knew anything more about the woman and child in this photo, I would know that they are happy and loved. For that, as a father, that's more than I could ever wish for.

A father. How in the hell did that happen? Well, I know exactly how it happened. I've relived that night so many times in my dreams that I could recite it backwards, while drunk. It could have only happened that one night. Before then, I had made damn sure that it wouldn't happen, making sure I always had my own condoms. I knew my days were numbered the moment I woke up in that tent and realized we never used protection. All three times. I never wanted this. I still don't know if I can handle it. But I know that turning around and walking away will be the greatest mistake of my life. Slipping the photo into the cargo pocket on the khaki shorts that I changed into after spending the afternoon swimming, I take a seat at the kitchen table and wait for Dani and Ryan to finish up.

Ten minutes later, Ryan runs into the kitchen wearing another pair of Batman pajama shorts. Man, does this kid like Batman. "Mom says I have to go to bed now, but we're still going to hang out tomorrow, right?" Ryan says with fervent, shining eyes.

"We sure are, Ryan," I tell him with a smile. Moments later, he throws his arms around my neck, squeezing me with everything he has. "Reid?" Ryan says, turning those big steely eyes on me.

"Yeah?" I ask, still holding him within my arms.

"Can I call you Dad now?" he asks quietly. The world stops spinning with that one simple question. Yet, there's nothing simple about it. My chest tightens so taut that I fear I'll never be able to breathe properly again. My eyes burn with unwanted emotion as I stare into the eyes that match mine.

"You can call me whatever you want," I tell him huskily. The smile I'm given could bring a cease fire in an active warzone. It's at that exact moment that the heart I didn't know I still had starts to beat again. And it doesn't just beat. For the first time in as long as I can remember, my heart is alive, tap dancing in my fucking chest.

"Okay, then I'm going to call you Dad," Ryan says through his cheeky grin.

"I would love that." And I would. Hearing that one word out of his mouth gives me hope. It gives me life.

"Good night, Dad," Ryan proclaims as he slips out of my arms and heads out of the kitchen. Dani barely has enough time to move aside before he runs her over in the wake of his excitement.

When my eyes find hers, I see the unshed tears. Without a thought, I stand up and go to her, pulling her smaller body flush against my larger one. She grabs on to the back of my shirt, holding on for dear life as her tears fall. Dani in my arms is heaven and hell all at the same time. Hell only because I know this touch will only make me want her more.

Her body is firmly plastered to my own from head to knees so that I no longer know where I end and she begins. I inhale the scent of her shampoo mixed with chlorine, and it instantly reminds me of our afternoon together. I had fun. Fun like I've never had before. A different kind of fun that I've never really experienced before; at least not in my adult life.

"Please don't hurt him," she whispers against my chest, and the words rip me wide open.

"I won't," I vow, closing my eyes in silent prayer that it's a promise I never have to break.

* * *

Later that night, sleep evades me. I'm haunted by the words that Ryan said moments before he darted off to bed. Every time I close my eyes, I see Dani's exotic baby blues looking up at me while I held her in the kitchen. Those eyes filled with so much trust and worry. And I don't have to mention the way my body remembers the feel of hers pressed against me.

It took every single grain of self-control I could muster to walk away from her tonight with a mere kiss on the cheek. Fuck, if I didn't want to throw her over my shoulder and fuck that worry away from her. But, if I'm going to make a lasting impression on Dani, it needs to be focused on Ryan. Not what could happen in bed, closet, or anywhere else I could get my hands on her.

Though that image is damn welcome, right now.

I've tossed and turned for the better part of an hour. I tried a workout first to eradicate the dirty images in my mind, but when that didn't work, I tried scotch. The only thing that did was get me half-drunk with a raging hard-on.

Evicting her from my mind is a lost cause, I know it. Recalling how my dick felt so snuggly between her ass cheeks is enough to make me take my dick in my hand. Finally. This is usually the moment where I'd call up any of the numbers in my cell phone and invite her to meet me at the apartment, but the idea of anyone satisfying this intense desire doesn't sit well. In fact, I'm pretty sure no one else will be able to satisfy me.

Only Dani.

It doesn't take me long and I'm panting and moaning. It might be my hand that's doing the work, but in my mind, it's Dani's hand wrapped around my engorged cock. It's her touch that brings me closer and closer to release. I imagine everything that her sweet little mouth would do to me: her tongue, her lips, her teeth. Back then we never got to enjoy anything like this. With the exception of the way I brought her to orgasm with my mouth and fingers, we were both hell bent on getting me buried deep inside her. Each of the three times, we never got around to any serious foreplay.

I'm so close that I know it's only a matter of seconds before I blow. Keeping my eyes closed, I think of only Dani and the night we shared as my balls tighten and my cock releases warmth on my stomach. It's a juvenile move, jacking off in bed, but I don't give a fuck. There's no way my body could wait until we're finally at that place to take things to the next level. In fact, if the way my dick is already half-hard and ready to go another round is an indication, I'm not sure I'll ever be able to completely quench my thirst for her. Being inside her is the only way to sate this desire.

I fear that I'll be jacking off nightly.

Finally, exhaustion starts to set in. Whether it's from the workout, the scotch, or the intense round of bed hockey for one, I'm not sure. Probably a combination of all three. My eyelids are heavy as I clean myself up and find a comfortable position in bed. I only wish I were sharing my bed with a certain blond with long, tan legs and a great rack. Motherhood hasn't done anything to squash my desire for Dani. If anything, it has only intensified it.

She's nothing like any of the women I've ever known. They're darkness to her light, evil to her good. Even back then, there was something about her that made her different. Maybe that's why I've never had the desire to bring any of the other women to my home. I keep them away from my private sanctuary by inviting them only to the apartment, and even then, they're not allowed to stay the night. The only night I've ever experienced wrapped up in someone's arms have been hers.

It's a heady, yet troubling realization as I slowly drift to sleep.

145

Chapter Thirteen – What A Difference A Day Can Make

Dani

Reid pulls up in his slick, black SUV at exactly eleven o'clock on Sunday morning, ready to start our day of adventure. He's all smiles as he comes through the back door like he's done it a million times. He looks excited and refreshed as he strolls in wearing a plaid pair of shorts and a matching gray polo shirt. It's the look that I will always associate as Reid's 'casual' look.

I wish I could say sleep was easy last night, but that's far from the case. Reid shows up all energized and well rested, while I'm on my second pot of coffee just to get me through the morning. Every time I closed my eyes, I kept replaying the moment where Ryan asked Reid if he could call him Dad. The moment I heard that one word come from Ryan's mouth, I about lost it. My chest was so tight and my lungs burned as I did everything I could not to cry.

Then, when Reid wrapped his arms around me, I lost it. I cried equally in happiness and in fear. I was putting my faith and my trust in him. I didn't feel alone for the first time since I peed on that stick. Even though I've always had my dad and sister, I've always felt like I was taking this journey solo. In that moment, when Ryan called Reid Dad, I knew I would never be alone again.

At least where Ryan is concerned.

The jury's still out on my love life.

"Dad!" Ryan hollers from just inside the door. He barely lets Reid step inside before he throws himself into his arms. Fortunately for Reid, he's already braced for impact with a smile on his face.

"Hey, Ry. You ready to go?" Reid asks, glancing over Ryan's head and looking at me. He scans me from my face all the way down to my sandals, and then back up again. The appreciative way he looks at me is a reminder of the connection we have.

"Where are we going?" Ryan asks without letting go of Reid.

"I thought we'd go have lunch at Mandalay Bay and then go to Shark Reef," Reid says with a wide smile.

"Yes! I've only been there once and I was little," Ryan says as he dives into his tale of visiting Shark Reef a few years back.

"Hold on, little buddy. Let's get ready to go and you can tell me all about it in the car," Reid says, winking at me over Ryan's head.

"Okay," Ryan proclaims as he slips outside and heads towards Reid's waiting SUV.

"Good morning," Reid says moments before he places a kiss on my cheek. His lips are warm and inviting, and I long to turn just enough so that his lips are planted firmly on my lips.

"Hi," I reply.

Before either of us can say anything more, a loud, steady horn honks in the driveway. "We better go before he decides to drive himself," Reid says with a cheeky smile.

Thirty minutes later, we're seated at a table inside Sports Book Grill, the restaurant Ryan chose inside Mandalay Bay. Ryan is practically bouncing in his seat–partially from the excitement of seeing Shark Reef, but also from the thrill of sitting next to his father. He's talking a mile a minute with animated arms, while Reid looks on with affection and glee in his eyes. A look I don't think I've ever really seen before. Gone is his seriousness and foreboding. Gone are the intensity and the shadows. His entire face radiates light and laughter in this moment. And when he winks at me before turning his attention back to our son, I know in my heart that I'm witnessing a truly unique and treasured moment.

But just as fast as the snap of my fingers, I see that look fade away.

Reid tenses, the arm resting on the back of Ryan's chair dropping down to his lap as he suddenly sits up so straight, you'd think a rod was placed in his back. His gray eyes follow the line just over my back. When I turn around, I see only a handsomely dressed man and a young woman walking our way. Something about the man looks vaguely familiar…

"Well, well, well, if it isn't Reid Hunter. I have to say, my friend, I am very surprised to find you here on a Sunday. I thought you worked seven days a week," the man says with a hearty chuckle and a wide smile.

"I do get out of the office every now and again, Jon. You know that." Reid's eyes are serious, but they lack tension. Obviously, Reid knows this man. His reaction appears more out of surprise than apprehension.

"Excuse me," the man says as he turns to me. "Where are my manners? This is Monica," he adds as he turns back to the elegantly dressed woman next to him. Her burgundy wrap dress hits just above the knees, is form fitting, and gives off an elegant, yet daring view of cleavage. Her hair is in a simple up-do that clearly came from a stylist, and her entire appearance speaks of grace and style. But it doesn't match her smile. Dark red lips stretch across blinding white teeth. I can't stop looking at her smile. It looks fake. Viperish. Possessive.

And I have no clue why.

"Monica, nice to meet you," Reid says casually without extending his hand. "This is Dani and Ryan. Dani, meet my right hand man, Jon."

Jon. That name rings a bell, and if the way he's smiling at me is any indication, he clearly knows me, too. His smile holds secrets and mischief.

"Nice to meet you," I say, placing my hand inside of his extended one.

"Dani. That name rings a bell," he says with a knowing smile. The moment his lips touch the top of my hand, I all but come out of my skin. I glance over at Reid who looks like he's about to jump over the table, throw me over his shoulder, and stalk out of the restaurant.

"What brings you to Sports Book?" Reid asks, not even acknowledging Jon's unsaid question.

"Monica and I were just passing through on our way to lunch when I thought I spotted you. I told her it surely couldn't be *my* Reid, the man who is holed up in his office, trying to plot his next move in world domination." Jon continues to smile. What the hell is going on here?

"Yes, well, everyone has to eat," Reid says casually, dropping his eyes back down to the drawing Ryan is making on the back of the paper on the table.

Jon's eyes follow Reid's. "That they do, buddy," Jon says.

The silence at the table is plausible. You could cut the tension with the steak knife sitting at my place setting. Jon and Reid continue to have words with only their eyes, and it frankly starting to drive me crazy. Clearly, they both know something that I don't know. And when you throw in Monica, she seems more interested in sneaking a peek at Reid's crotch than anything; and she isn't even trying to hide it.

"Mom, look. I drew a picture of me and Dad," Ryan says, holding up a drawing of two stick figures, one shorter one and one taller one wearing a cape.

"That's great, Ry. We'll have to take it home and put it on the fridge," I say to my son.

"No, I want Dad to take it home and put it on his fridge," Ryan says innocently before handing the picture to Reid.

The gasp I hear next to me is so loud it draws attention from the tables surrounding us. Jon's eyes are practically bugging out of his head as his eyes bounce between Reid and Ryan. Monica appears to be all ears now as she inches closer to the table, waiting to get the scoop. Apparently, Reid hasn't mentioned the fact that he's a father to even his right hand man. Interesting.

"Did I just hear what I think I heard?" Jon asks; his eyes focused solely on Reid's steel gray ones.

"We'll talk about this Monday," Reid says in a harsher, hushed tone.

Ryan's eyes sweep over his dad's flushed features, and I know instantly what he's thinking. He's afraid he did something wrong. His eyes start to shine, but it isn't from excitement anymore. No, it's from unshed tears. And if the way his throat is bobbing is any indication, I'd say it's safe to say that he's fighting to keep his emotions under control.

"Will you excuse us a moment," I say as I extend my hand towards Ryan. I don't even look at Reid as I quickly usher my little boy away from the table.

When we reach the back of the restaurant where the restroom is located, I kneel down and turn to my son. "What's wrong?" I ask Ryan.

"Dad didn't say he liked my picture," he whispers just as a tear streaks down his face. "And he seemed mad that I gave it to him," he adds just as he unleashes a sob that rips my heart from my chest.

"Hey, hey. No. Your dad loves your picture, Ryan. And he wasn't mad that you gave it to him," I start but stop when I'm all but picked up and moved aside. Stunned, I can only stare as Reid bends and gets down to Ryan's level.

"Hey, champ. Is everything okay?" Reid asks full of concern.

"You didn't like my picture," Ryan whales through big crocodile tears.

"Are you kidding me? I loved your picture. I can't wait to go home and put it on my fridge," Reid says with a smile.

"Then why did you look so mad?" Ryan asks innocently.

Reid takes a few seconds to collect himself, looking up and over at me for help. *There's nothing I can do to help, buddy. You dug this hole, now you climb out.*

"That was my friend, Jon. I work with him, and I hadn't gotten around to tell him that I was having lunch with you and your mom. So he was really surprised when he saw us," Reid says. "I, in no way, was mad at you for that picture. I love it. Thank you so much," Reid adds before leaning in and placing a kiss on the top of Ryan's forehead.

His apology seems to be enough to suffice Ryan's need for clarification, because the next thing I know, Ryan throws himself into Reid's arms. Their hug is tight, the sniffles of my son's earlier crying fit a distant memory.

"Ready to have lunch and go see the aquarium?" Reid asks, those gray eyes full of light again.

"Yep!"

Ryan takes off towards our table, Reid and I slowly bringing up the rear. "I have no idea what just happened, but I know I messed up," Reid says quietly.

"He thought you were mad at him for giving you the picture. He could feel your reaction to his statement, Reid. Little kids are like sponges. They absorb everything. I know you weren't mad at him, but he thought you were," I tell him as we approach our table, Jon and Monica nowhere in sight.

"I wasn't mad at him, I just hadn't said anything to Jon yet. This wasn't how I wanted to tell him about Ryan," Reid says.

"I figured that much out. But you need to remember that this is not just new to you, but new to Ryan too. He's feeding off of our reactions and your words, using them as guidance."

"God, I have so much to learn," Reid mumbles, and I can't help the small bubble of laughter that erupts.

"Yeah, you're about to get a crash course in Parenting 101," I say as he holds my seat out for me.

The rest of the lunch goes off without a hitch. Ryan reverts right back to his happy mood, scarfing down most of a cheeseburger and order of fries. My chicken sandwich, on the other hand, hit my stomach like a piece of lead. I can't stop thinking about how Monica's eyes and smile appeared to assess me quickly and find me lacking. I know I'm not the typical type of woman Reid surely goes for, and honestly, it's not like he's *going for* me now. We share a son.

That thought brings my mind crashing back to another realization. Reid is going to date. Reid is going to have strange women around my son. He's going to find someone and settle down with them, and where does that leave us? I feel that Reid's in this for the long haul, but what if the little woman isn't? What if she treats my son badly or tries to replace him with kids of her own?

"What just happened there?" Reid asks, his eyes assessing me intently as he slips his credit card out of the small folder on the table and signs the slip inside.

"What?" I ask, stunned.

"You just went somewhere in your mind. I could see it. And I'm guessing it wasn't a happy place," he says with those eyes of coal holding me hostage.

Instead of answering him, I turn to Ryan. "You ready to go?" There's no way I can tell Reid where my mind went. At least not right now.

Reid doesn't say a word as he follows behind Ryan and me. Ryan's doing all he can to keep our slower pace, but I can tell his desire to run ahead is strong. When we reach the entrance to Shark Reef, Reid pulls out his wallet immediately and pays the fees. Swiftly, we're granted access into the giant aquarium.

As Ryan bounces up to the first wall of glass we see, I feel Reid's eyes on me. I try to ignore his gaze, but like two magnets, I'm pulled towards him, uncontrollably. "Talk to me."

"What are you talking about?" I ask, trying to play coy, but knowing that I fail miserably.

"What were you thinking about back at lunch?" he asks. Stopping and glancing over at Ryan where he's plastered to the glass, watching sea turtles, he turns to face me. Reid places both hands on my shoulders, essentially holding me in place and making sure I can't turn away.

I could try to blow him off and come up with some other story, but something tells me that Reid will see through it. Huffing out a deep breath, I look up into his eyes, trying to put on my 'casual' face. "Look, Reid. This is none of my business, but I realize that you're going to date women. I know that you'll have people in and out of your life. What you need to understand is that Ryan hasn't had that before. He's used to having my every bit of attention focused on him.

"And now he's going to want that with you. So, the only thing I ask is that you remember that when you introduce him to women," I say, that last word all but biting my tongue.

"You're afraid I'm going to traipse women through my house like the Macy's Parade at Thanksgiving?" he asks, his eyebrows wrinkled and his eyes crinkling with laughter.

"Don't laugh. I know you will," I say before quickly adding, "And not that I care or anything, but just remember that Ryan should be your main focus when he's around." I huff on emotions that I didn't realize I had. The thought of Reid wrapping his arms around someone else all but drops me to my knees. I have no idea where that came from. Reid and I shared one night–one amazingly perfect night–but besides Ryan, I've had no hold on him since.

"Dani," Reid says as he steps closer, invading my personal space, his arms still firmly holding my shoulders. When he runs his big hands down my arms, I shudder at the unexpected desire coursing through my body.

"Dani, I don't want to parade women in front of our son. You need to know that I'm a very private man. My personal life and business life rarely collide. What may or may not happen after hours in the privacy of my place will never affect Ryan. Ever. You have my word."

His words do help soothe the rapid beat of my heart, even though it does nothing to soothe another ache I suddenly feel. I know Reid hasn't been a monk since our night together. I know there have been women–and since my mind is a ruthless bitch, I imagine there have been lots of women. But I can't get over the thought of Reid sharing the same intensity, the same passion, the same hunger that we shared that night all those years ago.

"And for the record," Reid starts, pulling my attention back to him. "I don't want just *any* woman filling my bed. I don't want *any* woman to scream out my name when I'm buried deep inside her. I want *you.* And if there's one thing you'll learn about me, Dani, it's that I *always* get what I want. Always, baby," he whispers moments before his lips take mine.

His kiss is like gas to my already burning libido. Suddenly, I'm wishing we weren't in the middle of an aquarium, surrounded by families and little eyes. Instantly, I wish we were alone where we could rediscover each other's bodies.

But we can't. Not right now.

I pull back quickly, wobbling on my own two legs. Before either of us can say anything, a voice calls out to us. "Mom, Dad, come look at this crocodile," Ryan says, his voice clearing away the lust-filled haze.

"Dani, you need to know that I don't date. And even if I did, I just found out I have a son who's going to be eight years old. That is what I am going to focus on right now. But I will also tell you this," Reid starts as he steps close again. "*If* something happens, it will be with my son's mother. There's an underlying current that pulls me to her–always has. So, while we're not putting labels on anything at the moment, know that I'm interested in exploring this intense chemistry that I know you feel too. Know that I'm coming for you, Dani. I'll wait until you're ready, but I can guarantee that it'll be soon. Very, very soon.

"Now, let's go see the crocodile with *our* son." Reid casually places a firm kiss in the middle of my forehead, reaches down and grabs my hand, and pulls me off towards Ryan.

My heart never stood a chance.

Chapter Fourteen – RSVP

Reid

"Legal is delayed on the Riviera contracts because their Board of Directors are no longer backing the President of the Board's decision to sell," Carly says in the background. Hell, she's been talking for the last ten minutes and I haven't a clue what the fuck she's said.

"Reid!" she exclaims as she slams her hand down on my desktop. "What the hell is wrong with you?" she asks, concern written all over her beautiful face.

"Nothing," I respond automatically, clearing my throat as I look down at the latest financial report on the Riviera property.

"Reid Hunter, that's the biggest crock of crap I've ever heard. I could have just told you there was an elephant in the room and you wouldn't have blinked an eye," Carly says.

I look around the room instantly as if I were going to see some magic elephant sitting in the corner somewhere.

"Just distracted, I guess."

Distracted? What's more distracted than distracted? That's where the fuck my mind is. Dani. Ryan. I can't get them out of my head. It's been over a week since our trip to Shark Reef, and I've spent almost every night at their house–leaving to go home to my empty house when Ryan goes to bed.

I haven't worked past six o'clock in the past eight days and the result is a pile of work anchoring down my desk, filling up my email. But I can't seem to stay away from them. The one night I wasn't able to go over to their place, I was miserable and thinking about them the whole night. A dinner meeting with the President of the Board for Riviera had been in the works for weeks. Hell, months. But the entire time I sat there listening to the man drone on and on about how their profits have been falling and investors are pulling, all I could think about was whether or not Dani was asleep yet and whether Ryan brushed his teeth before bed. But knowing Dani as well as I do now, I know that she made sure he did before bed.

It took every ounce of control that I had to not excuse myself and leave the meeting. Jon kept giving me that look, like he knew exactly where the fuck my mind was. Oh, he knew that I wasn't mentally present at that meeting. If it wasn't written all over my face, it surely was a dead giveaway when I missed important details of the conversations and he had to speak on my behalf.

The Monday after our lunch and visit to Shark Reef, I knew I'd have my best friend in my office before my first cup of coffee. What I wasn't expecting was for him to beat me in. Jon was already sitting in one of the leather chairs across from my desk when I stepped off the elevator, well before seven o'clock.

I barely had my briefcase deposited on my desk before the Great Inquisition began. When I told him I hadn't taken a paternity test, I thought he was going to leap across the table at me.

"You're a fucking idiot if you think someone–even someone like Dani–won't take advantage of you the first chance they get. Screw your fucking head on, Hunter. It's one little fucking test."

"I will not let you speak about Dani in any other manner than respectful. Do you hear me?" I seethe at my best friend. *"I know. I KNOW, Jon, that that boy is my son. I feel it right here,"* I yell as I pound on my chest, just over the location where my frozen heart once sat dormant. A heart that only truly started beating again in the time I've spent with Dani and Ryan.

"Reid, I'm not suggesting that Dani's like the others," Jon starts before I cut him off.

"She's nothing like the others," I reply directly, looking so deeply into his eyes that I can practically see his brain. "Nothing."

"What about Bravado?" he asks, his eyes wild with concern.

I look across the desk at my best friend. It's the first time that I've thought about that deal since I signed on the dotted line. There's no backing out. By the end of the year, I'll own that company, and he'll own my soul. "The deal is done."

It had taken us a good ten minutes to cool down from the heated exchange. Jon was adamant about getting the blood test, but I stand by my decision to omit it. I don't need some stupid piece of paper to confirm what I already know. It's a moot point, and I won't subject Ryan to any sort of unnecessary testing.

It's been a little tense with Jon since that Monday morning blow up. I'm just glad it didn't come to fists. Not that I would have backed down from him, but I would have been unhappy to walk away from a ten-year friendship. And I would have walked away. In the end, if I had to choose between Jon or Dani and Ryan, I'm one hundred percent sure that the only thing my best friend would have seen was my back as I turned the other direction.

"Did you hear anything I just said?" Carly huffs, her annoyance crystal clear.

"Sorry. What were you saying?" I ask, adjusting myself in my seat.

"The wedding. It's next weekend. RSVP's were due last week so I put you down for one. Your suits will all be hanging in your closet upstairs -" Carly starts, but I cut her off.

"Two."

"What?" she asks, confused as ever.

"RSVP for two," I tell her. Her big brown eyes just stare at me.

"Reid, I don't want to be rude here -" she starts, but again, I cut her off.

"You called me Reid," I say with a smile.

"Yes, I did," she says with a fluster. "Anyway, I don't want to be rude, but I really don't want you bringing one of your money-hungry floozies to my wedding."

It takes me a moment to absorb her words, and when I do, I can't help but bust up laughing. After a few seconds, I look over at her shocked face and only laugh harder.

"What's so funny?" she asks.

"You," I say through my laughter.

"What did I say?" she asks, clearly dumbfounded.

"Money-hungry floozies?" I ask, eyebrows sky high as the smile spreads widely across my face.

"Well, they are, Reid. You may not be able to admit it, but I will. Every time I send some flashy little piece of jewelry to one of their houses, all I get is phone calls–phone calls that you clearly avoid–telling me how much they appreciate your generosity."

"Those are parting gifts," I tell her.

"Do they know that?" she asks.

"I never lie about my intentions, Carly. Never."

"So tell me why you're RSVP'ing for two," she asks.

"I'm bringing a date. And *NOT* a money-hungry floozy. I'm bringing someone that I'm sure you would approve of. She's a schoolteacher named Dani."

"You're shitting me. Does Tara know?" Carly asks, referring to my little sister and Carly's best friend.

"Why would my sister know? It's none of her business."

"I'm pretty sure she makes it her business," Carly quips with a grin.

"That she does. But to answer your question, no, Tara doesn't know her. Yet. You'll both meet her at the wedding."

"Wow. If you're bringing this woman to an event where your sister is going to be there, I'd say this could be serious," she adds.

Is it serious? The thought of being without Dani causes panic to set in. My days are spent thinking about her and my nights spent dreaming of her and only her. So is this serious? I'd say it's pretty fucking serious.

"Anyway, there's something else you need to know," I say.

"Besides the fact that you're bringing a date to my wedding? Or maybe the fact that I've heard you laugh more in the last fifteen minutes than I ever have in the five years I've known you? What else could there possibly be?" she asks with a smile.

"Brat," I mumble as I think about the laughter that I've given so freely the past week. It's all because of Dani and Ryan. I've laughed more in the past few days than I have *ever* in my life. Again, that's all them.

"I have a son," I tell her easily.

The look on her face is almost comical. It goes from confusion to excitement to shock and then right back to confusion again. "Wait, what?" she whispers.

"I. Have. A. Son. His name is Ryan and he's going to be eight at the end of the month."

"Is it April Fool's Day?" Carly asks while flipping through her day planner as if to verify the date.

"No, it's not, and it's not a joke. I met Dani eight, almost nine years ago on a trip down to Arizona. It was right before I started working for my father," I tell her. When I look up at her, I find her watching me intently, hanging on my every word. "Anyway, one thing led to another and we slept together. I realized the next morning when she was gone that we didn't use protection. I didn't know her last name, only that her name was Dani and she lived there in Phoenix.

"Fast forward a few weeks ago, Steven shows up in my office with Dani in tow. To say I was surprised to see her here was an understatement. That initial meeting didn't go well, so I had to track her down. When I did, I discovered she had a son. He's the spitting image of me."

"Holy shit," she whispers. "Reid Hunter is a father? I think the world just shifted on its axis." Carly continues to stare at me. I'm sure my little sister has told her all about my lack of desire to become a father.

"Well, I am. And he's a great kid."

"Well, congratulations," Carly says with a genuine smile. That's the thing about Carly; all of her smiles are warm and genuine. "And I assume Tara doesn't know yet because my phone hasn't been ringing off the hook."

"No, she doesn't. I'm meeting her for lunch this afternoon so I will fill her in then."

"Well, then I'll let you get to it before your lunch," Dani says as she stands up, gathering all of her files and documents. "Oh, and Reid?" she says, stopping at the doorway. "I really am happy for you. You seem…different lately. Happy almost." Her smile is direct, and it shoots straight to my chest.

I am happy. For the first time in my adult life, I feel lighter and freer. Happy is only the start of it.

* * *

I watch as Dani comes back outside and joins me on the deck. I helped her get Ryan to bed thirty minutes ago while she went upstairs to tend to her sister. I'm not sure what's going on with Trysta, but it's dramatic and full of female emotions.

"Everything okay?" I ask as she slips into the chair next to me and takes my half-full bottle of beer from the table. There's nothing sexier than a woman drinking your beer, her plump lips touching the cool glass in the exact same place yours just touched. Just the thought of those lips has my dick hard enough to break concrete.

I adjust myself in the chair as I wait for her to answer. "Yeah, she's fine. Guy trouble," she says without really saying anything at all. And that's fine. I'm pretty sure I don't want to fucking know anyway.

"So, next weekend, my assistant is getting married," I start, shooting for casual, but knowing that I miss the mark. I can hear my own nervousness in my voice. Fuck. I've never asked a woman to attend something like this with me. Somewhere where my friends and family are going to be.

"Alright," she says, those stunning blue eyes with reflections of the pool lights staring up at me.

"And I was hoping you'd go with me." There. Said it.

"As in a date?"

"Yes," I say immediately. No hesitation. "Carly has been my assistant for a couple of years, but I've known her a little longer than that. She's my sister's best friend."

"And will your sister be there?" she asks curiously.

I nod my head, waiting on her answer. I try to gauge which answer I'm about to receive, but her face doesn't give anything away. It's a rare occasion since Dani usually wears her emotions plainly on her face.

"Okay," she whispers as relief courses through me. "I'll call my dad and see if he can watch Ryan for me."

"All night," I whisper as I lean forward, moving to the edge of my seat.

"All night?" she whispers in return, her breath fanning against my face.

"Yeah, I want you to stay with me next weekend. At my house." Her eyes widen as she absorbs the meaning of my words. I want her to stay with me–all night. Hell, I'd take her back with me right this moment if she'd agree to it.

"Okay," she answers again with a small smile. But that little smile means more than just her decision to be my date for next weekend. That smile gives me something to look forward to. And I'm hoping it's something dirty.

"Ryan asleep?" I whisper as I wrap my hands around her neck, trailing my fingers across the delicate tanned skin.

"Yes," she whispers breathlessly.

"Trysta?" I ask, bringing my second hand up and weaving it into her long, honey-colored hair.

"Watching a movie in her bedroom," she adds moments before I claim her lips with my own. I've been dying to kiss these lips all night. Taking this slow and trying to keep my hands to myself has been practically impossible, but the last thing I wanted to do was push Dani too far. I've been getting to know my son, spending as much time with him as possible. That doesn't mean I haven't been longing to spend some alone time with his mother as well.

"Come swimming with me," I whisper against her swollen lips. Her eyes hold a little extra twinkle tonight. Maybe it's from the kisses we just shared or maybe from the thought of going for a midnight swim. Either way, I want to see how much sparkle I can put in those beautiful fuck-me eyes.

"Now?" she asks, pulling back and looking over her shoulder.

"You said it yourself. Ryan's passed out and your sister is in her room. Come swimming with me," I say moments before claiming her lips once again. The least amount of time I can give her to talk herself out of this, the better. Maybe if she's so wrapped up in my kisses, in the way she feels when I'm touching her, then she'll live a little and jump in the pool with me.

Fuck knows I could use a cool down right now.

Even though I plan to heat things up well before either of us have the chance to cool down.

"Come swimming with me," I say a third time as I stand up and extend my hand down to Dani.

"I'm not wearing a swimming suit," she says wearily, standing before me.

"Neither am I," I reply, claiming those lush lips once again.

My hands dive back into her hair, angling her head upward and allowing me perfect access to her mouth. My tongue dives in, tasting and licking every part of her hot mouth. When her tongue slides against mine, I practically erupt in my pants. Fuck, do I want this woman. Bad.

Keeping my lips firmly locked on hers, I start to walk us backwards towards the water. Pulling back ever so slightly, I reach for the hem of her shirt and start to pull it skyward. Dani shivers as the night air kisses her abdomen. *Oh, don't worry, sweet Dani. I'll be warming you up real soon.*

As quickly as I remove her shirt, I pull mine up and over my head even quicker, tossing it somewhere into the darkness surrounding us. I caress the tender skin of her cheek before running my hands down to her chest to the glorious satin covered mounds I recall from my dreams. Her nipples are already pebbled through the material, and I waste no time in pushing both cups to the sides and freeing them from their confines.

I bend down and latch onto one perfect little nipple. Her moans fill the night around us, ensuring that my dick is harder than it has ever been. Sliding my hands down her sides, I slowly lower her shorts without removing my mouth from her nipple. As the shorts slide down her legs, I already have my hands on my belt, unbuckling it with as much hurry and awkwardness as a teenaged boy. Smooth.

As we both stand on the cool concrete next to the pool, I free us of our other clothes except undergarments. Our lips continually meet, our tongues dance, and our hands touch any and all available skin possible. When I feel her soft fingers glide down my chest and dip into my boxers, lightly grazing the head of my cock, I almost drop to my knees and start singing Hallelujah. Her touch is my undoing. It's my drug.

Knowing that I won't last long if she continues to touch me, I back up until we're at the water's edge. Dani looks over her shoulder one last time, as if to confirm that we're still alone. She stands before me wearing nothing but her bra and panties set. Even in the darkness, I can see the moisture glistening through the thin material from between her thighs.

God, I want to bury myself between her legs.

But I won't.

At least not tonight.

"Come on," I say, releasing her and slipping down into the water. You'd think the shock of the cool water would kill the raging hard-on I'm sporting in my boxers, but hell no. Nothing seems to relieve the ache down there. Nothing but Dani.

When she first sits on the edge of the pool, then slips down into the water, I waste no time grabbing ahold of her. Goose bumps pepper her entire body–from the water or from my touch, I don't know. I prop myself back against the pool's edge, and pull Dani through the water until she's flush against me. Her back to my front. I know there's no way she can miss the massive hard-on pressed between her ass cheeks, but when she gasps, I have all the confirmation that I need.

Suddenly in a frenzied hurry to taste her skin, I dive into the deliciousness of her neck. I've been dying to kiss her all night, and I'll be damned if I'm not going to get lost in the silkiness of her smooth neck once again. She tastes just as I remember. Running my tongue from the shell of her ear down to her collarbone sends my blood roaring in my ears. It's so loud I almost miss the sounds of her moans.

Dani's hands wrap around my thighs as she grinds her ass into my cock. The breath I'm trying to intake lodges firmly in my throat causing my brain to short circuit further. Wrapping my arms firmly around her, my hand travels down to the junction of her legs. The satin material is soaked and it has nothing to do with the fact that we're in a pool.

I quickly slide my fingers underneath the elastic. I can feel the heat radiating off her body before I even touch her. I'm not gentle as I take her swollen clit between my fingers. I lick and suck on her neck, and she grinds herself back against me. I'm so close to losing my mind that I have to think of anything other than the sweet ass rubbing me into oblivion. Periodic Table of Elements. Dates of every major US war. Fuck, even reciting the State capitols has to do something. But, no. My body won't be denied; my mind won't be distracted.

Slowly, I slide one finger into her ready body. Water makes a horrible lubricant, but with the extent of her wetness, I slid with ease. She's warm and tight as I push my finger in as far as I can. This angle gives me a perfect position to caress her swollen nub with my palm. As I slowly pull the finger out, her female juices mixing with the water, I slip a second one in. Dani gasps as her body tries to adjust to the girth of two of my fingers. She's so fucking tight.

Her beautiful heart-shaped ass continues to rub against me, instinctively seeking relief the only way her body knows how. It takes more self-control than a starving man facing a buffet to keep myself from slamming my dick into her. But I won't push her tonight.

"Let go, baby," I whisper against her ear as I pump my fingers ruthlessly into her body, all while grinding my palm against her clit. I can feel the moment her body starts to tense in sweet release. Her legs go ridged and her internal muscles clamp down tighter than a vise on my fingers. My free hand snakes up to pinch her nipples, while firmly holding her hostage against my body and the assault with my fingers.

The sounds of her release fill the night sky. It's loud and consuming, so I grab her chin and turn her head, swallowing the sounds of her orgasm with a deep kiss. I continue to kiss the fuck out of this woman long after the aftershocks of her release subside. With each nip of my teeth and flick of my tongue, I feel myself slipping further and further into unknown territory. Territory that I never wanted to explore. Yet, with my arms wrapped firmly around Dani's body, the fear of the unknown doesn't look so scary.

"Wow," she whispers against my lips.

"That was the most beautiful thing I've ever witnessed," I tell her honestly as I continue to rain gentle kisses on her well-kissed lips.

"I can't believe I just did that in the pool," she says, her words clearly laced with guilt.

"That's why it has chlorine," I remind her.

"Yeah, but I still feel like I need to drain and refill it before Ryan swims tomorrow," she says.

I slowly remove my fingers from her warm body. As much as I'd love to carry her off into the house and have my wicked way with her, I know that it isn't the right time. I'm not about to let our first time together after an almost nine-year absence be in a pool with our son sleeping just inside the house.

"I'm going to head home," I tell her as I spin her around. Saying those words is almost painful. Her long legs wrap around my back, her pussy rubbing through the material of our underwear. My dick throbs, all but begging for release. It's a painful reminder that I need to get the hell out of here before I'm unable to do the honorable thing and leave.

"Wait, what about you?" she asks, her voice a whisper in the night.

"What about me?" I ask, knowing damn good and well what she's talking about. My dick slams itself against my stomach, as if to say, "*Right here, asshole. Remember me?*"

"You're just going to pleasure me with your fingers and leave yourself hanging like that?" Her face is full of concern, but I also see something else. I see a hint of mischief.

"I'm not going to let it happen in a pool. When I take you for the first time again, it'll be in a bed. It'll be where no one can hear you. It'll be when we have nothing to do but make each other scream for hours. Not here. Not like this," I tell her, those blue eyes sparkling in the darkness.

"Sit on the edge of the pool," she demands as she pulls back from my body. I shiver at the loss of her body heat, which, honestly, shocks the shit out of me. I've never felt the need to pull a woman's body against me. The desire to pull her back is so strong, it almost drowns me.

I look up at those smiling blue eyes, the smile on her face so wide you can almost see all of her teeth. She licks her lips instinctively, and it's right then that I know. I know what my little vixen is thinking. Part of me wants to hop up on the edge of the pool and let her go to town on my dick. The other part of me wants to put a stop to this. I don't want her to feel like she has to, because she doesn't. I had planned on taking a long, long shower when I get home.

"Dani, you don't have to do this," I tell her.

"Reid, you don't know how badly I want to do this," she replies, our eyes locked on each other's.

After the world's longest stare down, which is probably only about five seconds in reality, I turn and hoist myself up and onto the edge of the pool. The air is cold against my wet body, but I know I'll warm up very quickly. I'm stuck staring at Dani as she swims towards me, eyes focused solely on the bulge between my legs.

Dani stands up at the edge of the pool and slips comfortably between my legs. Her nipples are pebbled, displayed perfectly over the top of the satin bra, which makes my dick thicken even more. I have no clue how that's even possible.

Her eyes are focused on my face as her hands wrap around the hem of my boxers. Using my hands as leverage, I lift up and give her the access she needs to remove my boxers. My balls are so damn tight, I'm afraid they might permanently suck up into my body. Between the combination of excitement and the wet, cold air, they're as blue as a crayon, and the tightness and heaviness isn't going away anytime soon.

I stare down at her beautiful face as she licks her lips once more. The action causes a stirring in my groin and my breath to pant in anticipation. But when she lowers her head, I can no longer fight the desire coursing through me. Her mouth consumes me–mind, body, and soul–and all I can do is sit back and enjoy the ride.

I've died and gone to heaven.

Chapter Fifteen – Sisterly Advice

Dani

The past week has been much of the same. I get up, go to work, bring Ryan home where we get his homework done while I start dinner, and Reid comes over. He spends time with Ryan helping with any lingering homework, reading at bedtime, and generally bonding with him. After Ryan's in bed, I usually find myself wrapped up in Reid's strong arms while he showers me with hot kisses and promises of what's to come when I spend the weekend with him. While watching him leave at the end of each night is difficult, I understand why it has to be that way. I find myself being drawn closer and closer to him, and the thought scares me a little.

A night here or there, Reid has to work late. I get the impression that his cutting out early so that he can come to my house is something that didn't happen before. I've learned that Reid is a workaholic to a fault, so knowing that he's leaving work at a decent time to come hang out with Ryan and me is a heady feeling.

"Are you ready for tomorrow night?" Trysta asks as she helps me clean up from dinner.

Reid took the entire weekend off from work for the wedding and my impending visit to his house, so he had some things to wrap up this evening. While he called between meetings earlier, I don't expect to hear from him until tomorrow afternoon when he picks me up for his assistant's wedding.

"I think so," I mumble, recalling the dress hanging in my closet. The navy blue chiffon t-length dress is a stunner with a high neckline in front, and virtually no back. It's not something I would *ever* feel comfortable wearing, but after trying it on, Trysta assured me that it was the only dress that would do. When I looked at myself in the mirror, I had to admit that she might have been right. The dress is stunning, and I can't wait for Reid to see it.

"Are you nervous?" she asks with a chuckle.

"Nervous? Why would I be nervous?" I ask nervously.

"Oh, maybe it's the fact that you're about to meet the sister of the man you're going to be boinking later that evening. Or maybe it's the fact that you haven't been boinking at all and you're going to boink with a man you boinked with over eight years ago and got knocked up," she says.

"Stop saying boink," I insist as I turn to rinse the final dish.

"So which is it? Are you nervous about meeting the family or about the boinking?"

I exhale deeply knowing that she isn't going to let this one ride. "I guess a little of both," I tell her honestly and turn around.

"Well, the family I can see. It's not every day that you meet the family of the elusive Reid Hunter."

"It's just his sister, Tryst. He doesn't ever talk about anyone else," I say.

"Okay, so you meet the sister. Big deal. You have a way with people, Dani. That's why you're the teacher, and I serve the drinks. She's going to love you just because you're you," she says with that big smile filled with sisterly love that I latch onto when I need it. "Let's talk about the sex, because I can't understand why you'd be nervous about that. It's not like you haven't already done it," she says with a humorous little glint in her eyes.

I can't help but smile. "I know. But when we did *that* before it was a long time ago. We were just young kids and we had consumed a bit of alcohol," I recall. "Now, I don't know, he's all...manly."

There's no hiding the blush I feel creep up my neck and spread across my cheeks.

"You ain't kidding, sister. That man is 100% pure raw sex in a suit. He's about as manly as they come," Trysta says with a decisive head nod. I'm sure the blush is a beautiful shade of oh-my-god red.

But's she's right. Reid is powerful and dynamic in his suit. When he walks into the room, he owns it, commands it. It's in his nature. Even when he's casual in his khakis and polo, he still oozes authority and sex appeal. The man is walking sex.

"But it's been so long since I've been there, Trysta," I whisper, knowing she'll know exactly what I'm talking about. Trysta is well aware that I have only had sex once since Reid, and even then, I was too drunk to remember it.

When we moved here from Arizona and I purchased this house, Trysta convinced me to go out and do a little celebrating. She had just secured her job at the casino, and when the night manager wanted to make a good impression on her, he gave her vouchers for a night of fun: dinner, drinks, dancing, and a hotel room. Not just any hotel room, but a suite.

Dinner started off well, even though it was interrupted a hundred times by Trysta's new co-workers stopping by to say 'hello.' When we moved the party to the dance club on the top floor, that's when the real fun started. Tequila. Endless amounts of tequila.

I found myself on the dance floor the entire time, first with Trysta, then with an off-duty bartender named Blade. Next thing I know, I woke up with a splitting headache next to Blade's very naked body in the smaller of the two rooms of the suite. While Blade's muscles had muscles, he wasn't the typical guy I usually go for. In fact, he was as far from the safe route as they possibly come. Even now, I can still recall the way he looked with his tattoos and his rock hard ass cheeks staring up at me from where he was lying on top of the sheets in the middle of that bed. Unfortunately, that's all I can remember of my night of debauchery. When the shock wore off, I grabbed my clothes and slipped out the door as quietly as humanly possible, anxious to get out of the hotel room before he woke up.

And that was the last time I saw Blade. And tequila.

"Don't worry about that part, Dani. It'll all come back to you, I'm sure. It's not exactly something you can forget how to do," she says with another smile.

"You're right, I'm being ridiculous," I say with a shake of my head.

"Seriously, Dani, just have fun. You and Reid have this crazy, monkey-sex chemistry that I can practically feel the moment I'm in the same room as you two. You have nothing to worry about. Reid wants you. I can see it each and every time that man comes over. Just sit back and enjoy the ride, baby. Because if Reid Hunter is anything like how I picture him, then you're in for one hell of a joyride," she says with a huge smile.

Yeah, if Now-Reid is anything like Then-Reid, then I'm in for the ride of my life.

"Hey, shouldn't you be getting ready for work?" I ask after glancing at the clock on the microwave.

"Yeah," she mumbles. Things with Trysta haven't been so hot on the work front. Ever since she caught Ryker–the pit boss she started seeing a few weeks back–with his arms around another cocktail waitress and his dick between her legs, she's been in a funk.

I wish I knew how to cheer her up. Trysta's problem is that she goes for the wrong kinda man. She always gravitates towards the tall, dark, and handsome type. The type that isn't looking for anything other than a few rolls between the sheets. And Trysta has always seemed okay with that, but lately something is different. I can't pinpoint what exactly it is, but I'm determined to get to the bottom of it.

"Hey, you know I'm here for you if you need to talk, right?" I ask with a solemn face.

She looks at me for several heartbeats before offering me the smallest of smiles. "Yeah, I know. I'm okay, Dani. I just wish I didn't keep falling for douche bags," she says before walking out of the room.

Trysta's latest dilemma weighs heavily on my mind all night, well after she has left for work. With Ryan in bed and Reid working tonight, I take full advantage of enjoying a quick night swim, followed by a long, hot bubble bath. But even when I try to relax, my mind keeps trailing back to the sadness in Trysta's eyes. Something has happened to dim her light. Something that she isn't quite ready to share with me. But if I know my sister well at all, I know that eventually, she will. She'll fill me in on what has been bothering her. That's what best friends do.

But until then, I guess I just sit back and wait.

Chapter Sixteen – Dinner Meeting

From Hell

Reid

Steven drops Jon and me off in front of a little Italian restaurant off the strip. This place is well known by the locals for its exquisite entrees and fun atmosphere. Leo, the owner, is an acquaintance of mine, and whenever I need to have a dinner meeting, I always prefer Leo's place.

"Your party is waiting. This way," the hot, young hostess says to me and Jon. The way her greedy little eyes devour our bodies tells me she's much more interested in showing us something other than to our seats.

Jon's eyes remain glued to her ass the entire time we follow her towards the table. The smile she gives him is inviting as she sets our menus down at the two remaining chairs. She doesn't even bat an eye at the way he's practically eye-fucking her in the middle of the restaurant. In fact, the way she smiles at him tells me that they're already making plans to meet up afterwards.

Pulling my eyes away from the scene next to me, I take in my tablemates. Douglas Cruz stands up and extends his hand towards me. I barely even register the faces of the other men around the table. I don't even notice their existence any longer when my eyes slam into the heavily made-up face of Cynthia Cruz.

"Gentlemen, you remember my CFO, Anthony Forrester, and second in command, Joshua Harkins," Cruz says, drawing my attention towards the two men seated at his right. "Also joining us is Cole Jacobs and Roger Peterman," Cruz adds, gesturing with his hand towards the men directly seated in front of us.

"And of course, I'm sure you both remember my daughter, Cynthia," Cruz says with a wide, wolfish grin. My gut tightens as he says her name. Cynthia. Or Cyn as she prefers to be called.

"Reid, darling, it's so good to see you again," Cynthia says as she saunters around the table and approaches me. Placing her manicured hands on my forearm, she presents her cheek.

Cynthia is dressed in a fitted dress that displays ample cleavage and miles of long, tan legs. But her tan looks fake. Like the kind you get from too much time in a sunbed, not from spending time outside by a pool like Dani.

Dani. Just the idea of Cynthia being here, touching my arm, and gazing up at me like I hung the moon and the fucking stars is enough to turn my stomach. I slowly step backwards a bit, doing everything in my power not to draw attention to the fact that I want her away from me. I know the deal to acquire Bravado is signed and sealed, but that doesn't mean I want to ruffle any feathers right now before the ink is officially dry. Douglas Cruz and his team will still be very much involved—even though in a much smaller capacity—with Bravado. My acquisition of the multi-million-dollar enterprise comes in tiers, only the first one of retaining a few of Cruz's key players being fulfilled at this point.

It's the next tier that has my blood pressure near stroke level.

I try to take the empty seat farthest from Cynthia, but Jon pulls it back and slips in before I can take a seat. That leaves one chair left available: right next to Cynthia. Reluctantly, I take the seat. She immediately begins talking about something to do with a country club or some stupid shit about an inclusive spa. I couldn't care less. I listen to her drone on and on until the main entrees are served.

Finally, she shuts up long enough to eat the measly little portion of food on her plate.

"So, Hunter, I believe my team has fulfilled the first phase of the merger. It's time for the next portion," Cruz says after the dinner plates are removed from the table.

"I don't want to rush it. We have until the end of the year to complete the next phase," I say, looking at Cruz over his daughter's head. Cynthia offers me a wicked smile moments before I feel her hand on my knee and slide upward towards my thigh. I jump a little in my chair, slamming my knee into the underside of the table. Not wanting to draw any more attention, I gently grab her hand and move it towards my knee. I definitely don't want her hand anywhere near my junk.

"Why wait?" Cruz asks, clearly irritated with my desire to hold off.

"I told you it would be complete by the end of the year, and I will fulfill that. I'm not in any hurry," I reply with a stone face.

Cruz's loud laugh echoes through the restaurant. "Oh, Hunter, I'm well aware that you have until the end of the year, but I was hoping you'd humor an old man and take care of it now so that I can enjoy handing my company over to you. This *clause* is only delaying the inevitable. You want my company, you fulfill the contract," he says with a direct look.

I'm well aware of the fucking contract. The only way to ensure I walk away with Bravado is to fulfill the damn contract. It pisses me off that he's reminding me of the terms we negotiated for close to a year. A damn year of my life spent on securing this deal.

The entire time I sit here, chewing on his words, I think of Ryan and Dani. I had just signed this deal the day she blew back into my life like some torrential coastal wind. Now, the weight of this deal is bearing down on me. For the second time in my life, I regret a business deal.

A deal that I can't back out of.

A deal that will ultimately change everything.

* * *

When I pull into Dani's driveway, I park next to the older Chevy truck that belongs to her father, Robert. I met him for the first time earlier in the week when Dani invited him to join us for dinner. Ryan was thrilled to have what he considers his entire family at his house at once. He knows he has another aunt, Tara, and will meet her soon. It's been hard holding off my viper of a sister. She's as determined and anxious to meet Ry as he is to meet her.

When I told Tara about my son, I'm pretty sure she thought I was joking. Her laughter filled the small café as we enjoyed soup and sandwiches for lunch. It took her a few minutes to get her laughing fit under control; all while I just sat there and stared at her, waiting her out so that I could finish with my news.

When Tara realized I wasn't joking, that's when the shock set in. Wide-eyed and mouth gaping open, she gawked at me for several long, silent minutes as if I had sprouted a second head right before her eyes.

Her eyes continued to shine brightly with unshed tears as I told her an abbreviated version of my story with Dani and how Ryan suddenly appeared in my life. It felt good to tell it, and honestly, it was pretty easy to say. Each time I tell it, it's as if I didn't even freak the fuck out a few weeks ago at the prospect of becoming a father.

I filled Tara in on my reaction to the news. I wouldn't be able to hide it from her anyway. My little sister has some sort of radar when it comes to me and the shit I'm hiding. She's always been the one person who can see through the bullshit. Well, her and Steven. At the end of lunch, she hugged me and told me that she was anxious to meet her nephew.

It's been a bitch thus far holding her off. Soon. She'll meet him soon.

I don't even have to knock on the door. As soon as I come through the back gate, the back door flies open and my little buddy runs out, meeting me at the top of the stairs. Without even realizing it, my arms are open and Ryan is launching himself at me. I hate hugging. Hugging is nothing more than an awkward attempt to connect with someone intimately. But when he hugs me–and damn does that kid hug me a lot–I find myself hugging him back. Heart beating wildly, arms wrapped up tightly, holding on for as long as I can, hugging.

"Guess what, Dad? Grandpa bought us Battleship! We're going to play tonight. I bet I can sink all of his boats before he can sink mine," Ryan all but yells at me a few inches from my face.

"That sounds like an awesome time, buddy. Are you all packed up and ready to go?" I ask, setting him down as we make our way into the house.

Robert is standing in the kitchen leaning against the counter, talking to Trysta who looks like she just got home from an all-nighter. I know her job keeps her up all night, but there's something about her today.

Trysta is a beautiful woman. I'd be blind not to see it. Her long blond hair is lighter than Dani's, but that's about the end of the physical differences. They do have the same blue eyes and facial structure. I imagine Robert had his hands full when these two girls were younger. One of the other main differences between the girls is personality. Trysta is loud and bubbly, while Dani is meek and shy.

While both girls are gorgeous, Dani is the only one I see. She's breathtaking.

And when she walks around the corner wearing a navy blue dress and silver strappy heels, I lose every ounce of air I have in my lungs.

The room is suddenly silent as I take in the woman before me. She is without a doubt the most beautiful woman in the world. Her long, tan legs extend for miles and miles, hypnotizing me as she walks into the room. Her arms are bare and the neckline hits right at her collarbones. The dress is stunning in a slightly conservative way.

My legs are moving without even realizing it. As I step closer, nearing her personal space, I can smell the intoxicating combination of her shampoo and perfume. I almost audibly groan when I catch a whiff of her scent. But as heady as that sensation is, nothing prepares me for when I wrap my arms around her and meet nothing but bare skin. Soft, alluring, sexy as fuck bare skin.

Suddenly my dick is so hard, I could break glass. As I pull her flush against me, my hands slide effortlessly along her back. I feel every bump of her spine. Each one shooting a hard jolt of lust straight to my groin. This time, I can't fight the groan. It slips out loudly, urgency and need clearly evident in the animalistic sound.

Dani's eyes widen. My dick is practically knocking on her stomach, begging to come out and play. My hands continue to explore her back like Christopher fucking Columbus as my mouth claims hers. I forget everything. I forget about the wedding that we're attending, I forget about our son and her family standing in the room behind me, I forget about the deal that has been causing sleepless nights. I forget it all and just feel. I feel her hot skin against my hand. I feel the way her body molds to mine as if it were made specifically for me. I feel the way our bodies fire to life. But most importantly, I feel the way my heart skips a beat and then speeds up quickly. It's a terrifying feeling, but one that I can't miss. One that I don't want to miss.

A throat clears somewhere behind me. I pull my lips away from Dani's, but continue to look down into her blue eyes. They're heavily lidded and shine with her own lust, and it takes everything I have not to throw her over my shoulder and run straight back to her bedroom–caveman style.

"They're just kissing, Grandpa. That's what mommies and daddies do," Ryan says so matter-of-factly that it makes everyone laugh. It is what mommies and daddies do, and it's exactly what this daddy wants to do with that mommy.

"You look gorgeous," I mumble as I kiss her lips once more.

"Thank you," she replies with a slight blush creeping up her cheeks. "You look pretty handsome yourself," she adds, taking in my gray suit and navy blue tie. It wasn't even planned, but we match pretty well. Twinkies, as Tara and Carly would say.

God, did I just say Twinkies?

World, here's my man card.

"Dad, do you have everything that I set aside for you?" Dani asks, glancing around me. Dani walks over and begins double checking Ryan's overnight bag, while I keep my back to the room and pretend to look at something on the counter, silently willing my hard-on to subside before I turn around.

"Dad, will you walk out with me to the car?" Ryan asks. That does it. Knowing that he's right there behind me essentially kills any wood I'm sporting.

"Sure thing, buddy," I say as I turn and take the overnight bag from Dani's hand.

"You be a good boy for Grandpa," Dani says as she bends over and kisses our son on the cheek. "Make sure you brush your teeth before bed," she adds, unable to control the mother in her.

"I will, Mom," he replies with a smile. I can't help my own smile that spreads widely across my face.

"Dad, I'll see you tomorrow. Maybe we can go get a Battleship game and I can show you how to play," Ryan offers with serious eyes.

"You got it," I tell him before bending down and ruffling his hair. Ryan wastes no time at throwing his arms around my shoulders and squeezing me hard. I return the hug fiercely, letting the joy of holding him wash through me.

I'm surprised to find that I'm going to miss him tonight. I miss him every night after I leave their house, but tonight, knowing that Dani's going to be at my place and Ryan isn't, well, it's a sadness that I unexpectedly feel deep down in my gut. I make a mental note to have him over as soon as possible. That big ol' house could use the sounds of his laughter and him running through the halls.

We watch them pull out of the driveway before Trysta excuses herself to go get ready for work. Glancing over at Dani, I can see the love and sadness at Ryan's departure. While this is a new sensation for me, I'm sure she feels this way every time he leaves. It's as if a piece of your heart left you–even if it's only gone for a little bit.

It's at that moment that I realize a piece of my heart just drove away for the weekend, too.

It's a humbling feeling just to know that I have that piece to lose.

Chapter Seventeen – White Wedding

Dani

I can feel Reid's eyes on me. I know he's watching me, waiting for my reaction to Ryan leaving. Even though he's only away for the weekend, and it's with my dad, I still feel that uncontrollable sadness when he's gone.

"You are stunning," Reid says again, pulling me out of my funk and straight into his arms. My only response is to kiss his lips. This is one of those moments where words aren't needed. Everything I want to say to him I can say with a kiss.

"We should go before I decide that we're not leaving at all," Reid says, his lust-filled words so full of life and meaning.

"Let me grab my wrap and clutch," I say as I step out of his arms and slip back inside. I feel the void of his warmth immediately.

I slide into the passenger seat of a sleek, silver BMW. The ride still holds that new car smell as I take in the black and chrome interior. My entire body practically melts into the buttery-soft leather seats. I can't help but touch the sporty dash and the smooth door panels as Reid shuts the door, enclosing me in luxurious comfort. Now, this is a car.

Reid sets my overnight bag behind the driver's seat before slipping inside himself. Neither of us really speaks as we make our way towards the small church where the wedding ceremony will take place. My nerves are practically pulsating through the car the closer we get to our destination.

"What's the matter?" Reid asks, taking his eyes off the road for a moment to check on me.

"Oh, nothing," I tell him with a quick little smile.

"No, don't do that. I can tell something is going on in that big, beautiful brain of yours," he says as he signals to turn into the parking lot of the church.

"I guess I'm just nervous," I whisper.

Reid doesn't say anything as he pulls into the first available parking spot, and I start to think he didn't hear me. As soon as the car is off, he is out and walks around to my side. Without saying a word, he opens the door, removes my seatbelt, and helps me stand up. Then his lips come crashing down on mine. I feel the warmth of his breath fanning across my face as his tongue darts into my mouth, licking and sliding against my own. He tastes like mint as his amazingly talented tongue caresses mine.

Breaking the kiss but keeping his lips a whisper away from my own, Reid says, "Don't be nervous. I promise that everything is going to be fine."

Offering him only a slight head nod, I gaze into his steely gray eyes and know that he's right. Everything tonight is going to be just fine. I have the father of my son, the man I've come to care a great deal for in the past few weeks, with me. Hell, if I wanted to dive into it further, I'd wager a bet that says I'm falling in love with him.

But I won't get into that tonight. There's no room for those emotions to start poking around, stirring up questions that I don't have the answers to.

Questions that I'm pretty sure I won't like the answers to.

So tonight, I'm going to enjoy the man I'm with.

Tomorrow, I can deal with these uncertain feelings that tonight is suddenly rousing up.

* * *

The wedding of Carly and Blake was beautiful. There's no other word to describe it. The handsome groom stood at the front of the chapel wearing a striking black tuxedo against his tanned skin. He's every bit as tall as Reid is, but where Reid is lean with hard muscles, Blake looks like he eats children and young adults for breakfast. He's as wide as a football player, and screams power in a military sort of way as his corded muscles stretch underneath his tux.

The bride was stunning, plain and simple. Her designer ivory dress hung perfectly against her smooth caramel skin, her raven hair in the sleek updo. The smile on her face didn't waiver the entire ceremony, and you couldn't help but tear up the way those two looked at each other while they recited their vows, their love and adoration shining brighter than the lights of the Vegas strip.

While Reid and I waited for the ceremony to start, he filled me in a bit on their relationship. Carly has been his assistant for three years. She met Blake at a bar the night before he was to go undercover for his job as an FBI agent.

Little did either of them know, their paths would be crossing again in a very unconventional way. Carly's birth father happened to be the man Blake was working for. The criminal he was trying to take down. When Blake and Carly found each other again, it was in the midst of a major federal case of auto theft and crime. It was also then that Blake learned he had fathered a baby girl with Carly. Natalia is an adorable little two-year-old. Her midnight hair is the same as her mother's, while her green eyes are clearly her father's.

It was a hard road for Blake and Carly to travel down, especially when the bust happened, which essentially took Roman Hernandez off the streets and locked him up behind bars for the rest of his life.

But Blake and Carly battled through it, and now they're husband and wife.

"So you are the mysterious Dani," a tall blond woman says as she approaches our table. Even if I didn't know the maid of honor at today's wedding was Reid's sister, Tara, I would have known instantly when she approached. The resemblance is uncanny.

"Hello," I say, standing up and extending my hand.

"Oh, none of that," she says as she grabs my arm and pulls me into a hug.

"Don't suffocate her, Tara," Reid says behind me.

As Tara lets go, I can see the love shining in her beautiful gray eyes as she gazes up at her brother. "It's good to see you," she says as she steps into his arms.

"Good to see you, too," he replies before kissing her cheek. "I thought you said you were bringing a date," Reid adds, looking over her shoulder.

"Oh, he's here…somewhere," Tara says with a dismissive wave of her manicured hand. "So tell me all about yourself."

I take the seat I was just in, right next to a beaming Tara Hunter. "Uh, well…"

"Tara, calm yourself. You'll have plenty of time to get to know Dani," Reid says with a stern voice. But the way his eyes sparkle, I can tell there's no heat behind his words.

"Oh, big brother, why don't you run along and get me a glass of white wine. Dani and I are going to partake in a little girl talk," she says with a sweet smile.

Reid exhales deeply before standing up and looking at me. "Can I get you another glass?"

"Sure," I say with a look of awe. I can see it as plain as day. Tara Hunter not only has her big brother wrapped around her finger, she has him wrapped around her entire hand. The big, stern, scary businessman I've heard all about–and witnessed firsthand that day in his office–just took off to get his sister a drink without even batting his eye.

"He's a big teddy bear," Tara whispers as Reid walks away, heading towards the expansive bar in the back of the room.

I blush a little at her comment, recalling the way his arms wrapped around me while his fingers did dirty things to my body in the pool. "Oh, I can tell by the way you're blushing that you've already seen his teddy bear side," she adds with a smile.

I decide not to tell her that it's his animalistic side that caused my skin to heat like the room suddenly turned into a sauna. "Tell me about my nephew. I've been dying to meet him but Reid keeps putting me off."

Finally, a subject I can talk about. "He's amazing. He's about to turn eight at the end of the month and actually looks just like your brother," I say with a smile.

"He told me. And he also told me how you two met," she whispers.

Again with the damn blush. I glance over and watch as several guests shake Reid's hand, engaging and pulling him into their conversations, no doubt centered around money and business. Reid is a powerful man in this town, even at the ripe ol' age of thirty.

"Don't be embarrassed. I'm happy that you both found each other again. Reid...well, Reid's passion is his work. He's aggressive when needed and oozes more dominating power than any single person I know. But he's not happy. He hasn't been happy in a very long time," Tara says as she watches her brother start to make his way back to our table. I want to question her on the cryptic comment, but I'm out of time. Reid gently sets a glass of wine down before both of us, as well as his own glass of dark, amber liquid.

"So what have you ladies been talking about in my absence?" he asks.

"I was just telling Dani all about how you used to play Barbies with me when we were little, even though I didn't have a Ken doll. And that you had a stuffed bear named Pookie," Tara says while sweetly smiling and sipping her wine.

"If we weren't in a room full of people, I would kill you right now," Reid playfully thunders across the table; though I can tell there's no punch behind his words.

Tara laughs as a skinny, nerdy man approaches our table. "There you are," he says as he bends down and places a kiss on her cheek.

"Guys, this is Eddie. He works in my office. Eddie, my brother, Reid, and his girlfriend, Dani," Tara says so casually. But I don't miss the way I choke a little on my breath when she says the word *girlfriend.*

"It's Edmond, actually," Eddie says with a look towards Tara. I can't decipher it exactly, but if the mischief evident in her eyes is any indication, I'd say this is a game they've played before. "Oh, wow. Reid Hunter. It's an honor to meet you, sir," Edmond says with starstruck eyes beneath dark, heavy glasses.

"And it's good to meet you, Edmond," Reid says without really glancing his direction. Instead of looking at the newcomer at our table, Reid's dark eyes are focused entirely on me. His gaze consumes me like a wildfire devours a dry forest.

I'm lost in those steel gray eyes while we continue to ignore all conversation around us. When they announce that dinner is being served, we pull our eyes away from each other. A delicious smelling plate is placed before me, but my mind won't calm down enough to even enjoy it. I keep thinking about those all-consuming, carnal eyes and the unspoken words they said to me. Like a deer in a field with a lone wolf, I know that my time is limited. I'm about to be devoured. Consumed.

And the food in front of me is the last thing on my mind.

"Eat," he whispers against my ear. "You're going to need your energy."

I swear my sharp inhale can be felt by everyone in the room, and certainly heard. But when I look up, all conversations and dining around me seems to continue. Risking a quick glance over at Reid, I watch as he slowly moves a piece of steak towards his mouth. Using his teeth, he gently pulls the meat from his fork in the most erotic display of eating I've ever witnessed. My body shivers with anticipation as goose bumps pepper my heated skin. Reid does nothing to hide the smirk on his lips as he slowly chews his food.

I practically orgasm in my seat.

"Eat," he whispers heatedly with a wink, that knowing smirk still plastered on his face.

I have no idea how I make it through the meal. Food appears to be missing from my plate, so I know I've consumed some, I just don't recall it. Tara is doing everything in her power to ruffle her date's feathers, including calling him *Eddie* every chance she gets. Edmond, annoyed with Tara's antics, draws Reid into as many conversations as he possibly can throughout the entire dinner, but I have no clue what they actually talk about. Every time I look at the man next to me, his intense gaze makes my brain go all fuzzy and my mind completely blank. I'm like a girl with a crush who just discovered her raging hormones.

Enjoying my glass of wine, we sit back and watch as the new Mr. and Mrs. take to the dance floor for their first dance. Blake's smile is impossible to miss as he twirls his new wife around the floor, whispering something every few seconds. And if the way she keeps gasping is any indication, I'd wager a bet that it's something dirty.

After a few more songs, I feel Reid's warm breath feather lightly against my ear as he says, "Dance with me, beautiful." Before I can even reply, he stands up and offers me a hand. Taking a quick breath, I place my small hand in his much larger one.

As we start to make our way towards the dance floor, I hear Tara say behind me, "Dance with me, Eddie." I can almost picture the look he gives her while she grins down at him sheepishly.

I watch wordlessly as Tara and Edmond join us on the dance floor. They stand as close as necessary to dance, but it lacks any sort of sexual connection. The way they dance looks more like Reid and Tara dancing. There's no way her *date* is any more than just a couple of friends enjoying the evening together.

And then I see it.

Tara looks over Edmond's shoulder, silently watching a man on the other side of the room. He's sitting at a table in back with a leggy brunette in a skintight black dress. The man laughs at something the brunette says, but his eyes lack the heat that one would associate with a man who's doting on the woman he wants.

And then he turns and glances at the dance floor.

His eyes darken as he zeros in his gaze on Tara. He watches as Edmond spins her around the floor, laughing and carrying on as if they have not a care in the world. Suddenly I feel like I'm watching some crazy game of cat and mouse, though I'm not sure who is the cat and who is the mouse.

"You've been awfully quiet tonight," Reid says as he pulls my body against his, our bodies touching from chest to thighs. When his warm hand fans out across my bare back, I shiver uncontrollably. "Is that because you keep thinking about later tonight? I can see it in your eyes, Dani. Every time I look at you, I can picture the thoughts in your head. It's written all over your beautiful face. I can see the need and want written right here," he says as one hand traces the soft lines of my cheek and my eyes.

I let out a little gasp as his hand runs down my cheek and lands on my lips. His finger outlines my lips as his eyes stare down, his desire to kiss me as evident as the soft lights. "Do you want me to kiss you?" he whispers, leaning in another fraction of an inch.

I mumble something incoherent as I nod my head. At least, I think I nod my head. His lips devour mine in a mind numbing mating of mouths. Reid wastes no time sliding his tongue inside my mouth, licking and slashing at my own in the most erotic kiss of my life. His thick erection is snug between my stomach and his. I move in closer, desperate to feel his hard length against me, like a hussy in heat.

"Get a room, you two. This is a family affair," Tara says close to our faces, breaking the lust-filled spell.

"I plan to," Reid mumbles, barely pulling away from my lips.

We dance another slow song, but I have a feeling it has more to do with the fact that Reid's sporting a hard-on the size of a baseball bat than the fact that he wants to be dancing. When I'm not lost in the feel of his arms wrapped around me, and the way his hand keeps dipping lower and lower on my bare back, I'm watching Tara.

"What has you so distracted?" Reid asks.

"Who is that man?" I ask nodding towards the mystery man in the back of the room.

"Which one?" he asks, turning us both so we can admire the room.

"The one at the bar with the brunette with the fake Double D's," I say.

Reid's chuckle is like music to my ears. "That's Scott Dixon from Legal," he says. "You actually met him a long time ago. He's a buddy of mine that I went to school with, and when he graduated from law school, I brought him on as the head of my legal department. Why?"

I don't know if I should say anything to Reid about the glances I keep catching between Scott and Tara. The last thing I need is for Reid to go all protective big brother on her, especially when I haven't talked to Tara about it. What if I'm wrong? "Nothing. I just thought he looked familiar," I go with.

Reid keeps his eyes on his friend as Scott practically ignores his date in favor of watching Tara across the dance floor. I can't miss the sexual desire in his eyes, and apparently, I'm not the only one. Reid growls as he follows the direction of Scott's eyes, which land directly on his sister. Uh oh.

"Are you ready to get out of here?" Reid asks a few moments later.

"Yes," I whisper, his hand flexing against my back.

Apparently, Reid Hunter doesn't have to be told twice. He all but drags me off the dance floor so fast that I have no clue how my heel-covered feet can keep up. His strides are long and powerful as we walk hastily towards our table to retrieve my wrap and clutch.

It takes us another thirty minutes to get to the main entrance of the reception hall. We were stopped by no less than a dozen men, all anxious to shake hands with Reid and try to engage him in conversation. Jon and Monica were in the mix as well as Scott and the brunette I now know as Brittney. Monica continued to devour my date with her eyes while Reid, Jon, and Scott discussed something work-related. Brittney, on the other hand, appeared to be bored out of her freaking mind, if the eye rolls and huffs of frustration were any indication.

Finally, after saying goodbye to the bride and groom and offering another round of congratulations, we make it to the door.

Reid keeps his hand firmly around mine as we step outside and walk towards the valet stand. A few sexually tense minutes later, Reid's BMW pulls up to the sidewalk. With a firm handshake laced with tip money, Reid escorts me towards his waiting ride.

Neither of us speaks on the drive towards his house. I watch as streetlights and buildings pass. Eventually, Reid steers us towards a residential area. The houses are massive and the lawns pristine, even for living in the middle of a damn desert.

When we pull into a gated driveway, my heart rate kicks up, and considering it was beating at stroke level the entire ride, that's saying something. Reid casually keys in his code, which grants us access to his home. And holy shit is it a home! The massive white house can only be described as an exquisite mansion.

Evidently, I must make some noise to clue Reid into my shock. "It's just a house, sweetheart," he says as he drives his car into the biggest garage I've ever seen. There are four individual bays but the cars are two deep. As I take in the amount of wheels in this room, I'm not too much of a girl to realize that the back row consists of rare, expensive cars.

"Just a house," I repeat as Reid opens the passenger door. His garage is bigger than my entire house.

"This way," Reid says, placing his warm hand on my lower back. I notice as we head towards the entryway that he's carrying my overnight bag. Good thing he remembered, because my nerves are so frayed, I completely forgot about retrieving my bag.

Reid opens the door, motioning for me to enter. This is it. There's no turning back now, not that I have ever thought about turning back.

I want this.

I've wanted this since I dragged myself out of that tent in the early morning light all those years ago. The morning I knew that my

193

life would never be the same again. In that morning light, I knew. I knew Reid was different than every single boy, guy, or man I've ever known. He left his imprint on my life and deep in my heart, and not entirely because of the child we created together.

I lost a bit of my heart to Reid Hunter that night in the desert, and if I'm not careful, I'm going to find myself in the same situation again. Only this time, there'll be no getting it back. There'll be no turning around and walking away. Reid Hunter will own me completely.

The scary part is, he might already.

Chapter Eighteen – Didn't Even Make It Past The Stairs

Reid

I'm nervous. Fucking nervous. I'm standing in the middle of my kitchen wiping my clammy hands on the outside of my gray slacks. I can only remember being this nervous one other time and that was the night Dani and I created our son.

Dani turns in a complete three-sixty taking in the expansive kitchen. The appliances shine like brand new, and that's because they practically are. I rarely use my kitchen. Most meals are enjoyed in a restaurant with a business associate or at the apartment. I glance around the room, taking it all in as if it were the first time, seeing the room through Dani's eyes.

"Would you like a drink?" I offer, dropping her overnight bag down on the island.

"No, thank you," she whispers quietly. My little vixen is as nervous as I am. The thought is invigorating and intoxicating all at the same time.

Without giving either of us time to think, I walk towards her like I'm stalking my prey.

Pulling her against my body, we clash in a frenzy of needy mouths and grabby hands. I waste no time diving my fingers into her hair. Bobby pins rain on the imported tile with satisfying little pings as I dig and tug at the strands, freeing the long, lush locks of golden

195

blond tresses. The moan she breathes into my mouth lights me up so fiercely that I'm afraid my desire for her will never be sated.

"God, you were so fucking beautiful tonight," I tell her honestly. "Every man in that room wanted to know who you were. All eyes were on you all night, sweetheart. Everywhere I looked, those assholes were undressing you with their eyes, wanting to see what only I get to see. Only. Me." I'm practically growling my words at this point. They sound foreign and animalistic, and I barely recognize them as my own.

Her lips are already swollen from my kisses, marked by me and only me. Those baby blues shine brightly with lust, her breath little pants of excitement. I waste no time in removing my suit coat, tossing it somewhere into the kitchen. With the extra layer gone, I pull her into my arms again, picking her up and walking towards the staircase. The entire way, I consume Dani's mouth with my own, loving the way her mouth molds to mine.

Halfway up the stairs, I stop and set her down. A combination of her sexy as sin silver heels and the fact that she's a step above me, we line up perfectly. Without breaking the connection of our mouths, I let my hands caress her body in a heated frenzy. The blue material of her dress sculpts perfectly to her luxurious body, hugging her curves and teasing my dick.

I *need* to see her body. Now.

Pulling back slightly so that I can see her eyes, I place my hands on her shoulders and slowly run them down her arms, goose bumps peppering her smooth flesh, pushing down the material of her dress as I go. As expected, Dani isn't wearing a bra. There's no way she was able to with the entire back of her dress missing. Her pert little nipples bud when exposed to the cool air, making my mouth water.

Dipping down, I take the first one, then the second one in my mouth. I lick, suck, and tease each one until they're standing at full attention, begging for more. Much like myself right now in my pants. Giving the material of her dress a little push over her hips, I watch as the beautiful dress finally lies in a pool of blue at her feet.

"Fuck me," I whisper, realizing that by her audible gasp, I actually said the words out loud.

Running my hands down the silky skin of her waist, I find my way to those black lace panties. Turning her around, I finally get my first glimpse at the back view of her gorgeous body. "That dress was the biggest cock tease all night. Every time I touched your back, I was picturing what it would look like without that dress covering your beautiful ass," I say, rubbing my hands down her back and over the globes of her rear. "If I knew what was hiding underneath that dress, we wouldn't have made it through the first course."

Dani's back is vibrating from her deep breaths, her legs slightly spread apart. The picture of her standing before me like this in her fuck-me heels is better than any photo in any of those magazines we used to jack off to in high school.

With one quick motion, I spin Dani back around and lower her onto the stairs. She deserves every bit of the two-thousand thread Egyptian cotton sheets on my California king sized bed, but I'll be damned if I'm going to pass up this opportunity to claim her on my staircase.

With her weight back on her elbows, I spread Dani out before me like some all-you-can-eat buffet. And I'm a starving man. I run my hands up the velvety skin of her thighs, heading upward and towards the junction of her legs. I feel Dani's eyes burn into my face as I trace the journey of my hands with my eyes.

Her panties are soaked. I can smell the intoxicating scent of her arousal. Hooking that little scrap of lace with my pointer finger, I gently move it aside and expose her core. Using a single finger, I run it from one end to the other, coating my finger in her juices. Dani's moans fill the entryway, hell, probably the entire lower level of the house. Her entire body quivers as I gently slide first one, then a second finger inside her wet heat.

I gaze up at her, drunk off the way her heavily lidded eyes watch my fingers move in and out of her body. Her internal muscles grip my fingers, pulling me in with each thrust. I can tell she's getting close. Her hips start to move in rhythm with my fingers, gyrating and rocking, and her breathing labored. Dani wraps her legs around my neck, the heels of her shoes biting and digging at my skin. But I couldn't care less.

Bending forward, I swipe my tongue along her swollen nub. Dani practically shoots off the stairs. I lay my free arm across her stomach to ensure that she can't get away from me. Keeping my fingers pumping deep inside her, I lick and suck at her clit, not letting up on either assault.

"Let go," I demand. And before too long, Dani goes crashing over the edge of the cliff. Her wetness coats my face, my lips, and my hand as she rides the waves of her orgasm. The entire time, I watch the euphoric effects of her release wash over her face, transforming her from stunning to the most spectacular creature I've ever seen. Watching her come is the most fucking gorgeous thing I've ever witnessed.

I don't even give Dani time to catch her breath. My need for her is too great. I make quick work at removing my tie, button-up shirt, and dress pants. My dick is throbbing in my pants, especially after witnessing the stunning display of her eruption just a few moments ago. Grabbing my wallet, I pull a condom from within and make quick work at sheathing my erection.

Dani bends forward and makes a move at eliminating her shoes. "Leave them on," I tell her as I help her stand. Her legs are shaky so I hold her hips steady the entire time.

Sitting down on the stairs, I guide her towards my lap. With one quick pull, that little scrap of material she calls panties is ripped from her body. Dani's long legs straddle my waist as she positions herself above me. Taking my dick in my hand, I rub it through her wetness, coating the protection in her dampness. "I have craved you for over eight years, Dani. Craved to feel your body ride mine like it did that night. Show me," I say without taking my eyes off hers.

Slowly, I feel her tightness envelop me. She's just as tight as I remember, maybe even more so now. Hissing a deep breath, I grab onto her hips while she places her palms on my chest to give herself leverage. When I'm buried balls deep, I feel her slowly start to slide up, taking every bit of my sanity as she goes. She feels so familiar, so right, that it's a struggle to breathe.

When she's relaxed enough to move a little more freely, she starts to pick up the pace. She crashed back down on my cock, hard, grinding and moving against the place we are joined. I've never felt something so incredible in my entire life. If I weren't focused on watching the ecstasy on her face, my eyes would have rolled up into the back of my head.

I can tell that she's starting to get winded, her pace starting to slow, so I take over. Gripping her hips, I push her body up and then slam it back down on my length. The pace is fast, bruising, but neither of us care. We both race full steam ahead towards a mutual release of epic proportions. I watch, hypnotized, as Dani reaches up and starts to rub her tits. "Fuck," I hiss, driving myself up and into her sweetness like a man possessed.

I know the instant her release takes hold. Her entire insides grip my dick and won't let go. Her screams fill the entire house, my name the only one on her lips. It's enough to push me flying over the edge with both feet. My balls tighten painfully as my release rips from my body, spilling everything I have into the confines of the protection. I continue to pump into her until there is nothing left but heavy breathing and rapidly beating hearts.

"Jesus," I mumble against the damp skin of her neck. Dani makes some sort of nonsensical statement before wrapping her arms tighter around me, her chest firmly against mine.

We stay like that for several minutes. I rub the damp skin of her back with my hand while placing soft, tender kisses on her shoulder. Neither of us speak. It should scare me how content I suddenly feel to have my arms firmly wrapped around a woman. But Dani has never been any woman. She's my woman. *The* woman.

And that's another thought that should scare the fuck out of me. But it doesn't.

Both are things I don't even care to get into right now. Right now, all I want to do is get this woman up to my bed so I can ravish her body all over again.

"Hold on, sweetheart," I tell her as I slowly start to stand. I feel like a sailor getting his sea legs for the first time. They're wobbly and foreign to my body.

I finish walking up the stairs, leaving our clothes for later. Hell, where we're going, clothing isn't allowed. I throw back the bedding and slowly deposit Dani onto the soft sheets before making my way to the in-suite bathroom to dispose of the condom. After quickly cleaning myself up, I head back inside the bedroom with a warm washcloth. Dani's so far out of it that she doesn't even stir as I clean her beautiful pussy. With a quick toss of the cloth towards the closet, I slip into my bed.

Dani moves towards me without even opening her eyes. Her body seeks mine out in sleep, much like my arms are doing as they pull her in tight. With a leg thrown over the top of mine, she sighs deeply against my chest. Her breath tickles me, as the enormity of this situation sets in.

I've never–*NEVER*–had a woman in this room. I've never wanted to, but the thought of Dani *not* being here almost turns my damn stomach. The thought of her *not* warming my bed, snuggling against my body, and gasping my name in pleasure is unthinkable. In just a few short weeks, she's wormed her way right back into that empty place in my chest where my heart should be.

Oh it's there, beating wildly with excitement and fear. A lot of fear. Never has a woman imbedded herself in my life and my soul the way Dani has. I'm unable to stop it. Hell, I don't want to stop it. Dani is right where she belongs, wrapped against my body.

In my arms.

And in my heart.

I only wish I was capable of giving it away.

Because when push comes to shove, I'm going to be the asshole who breaks her heart when I walk away.

* * *

"Can we get olives on our pizza, Dad?" Ryan asks from his position next to me in the red booth.

"Sure can," I tell my son, offering Dani a wink from across the table.

Following Carly and Blake's wedding, Dani and I spent the entire weekend in my bed, only slipping out long enough to fuel our exhausted bodies. I'm insatiable when it comes to her. I crave her morning, noon, and night, and have stopped at nothing to get her.

I've spent every night at her place since then. For one entire week, I've done nothing but put everything that used to be important to me aside and focus my attention on her and Ryan. We've swam, cooked meals together, and smiled together more than I thought was possible. It's still terrifying, but each day gets easier and easier. I don't want to run anywhere, unless I'm running towards her. And our son. I'll never get enough of his laughter.

Tonight is the first night Ryan is staying at my place. I'm damn excited to have him there, and even more ecstatic that I convinced Dani to come too. She's put up quite a fight in the past few days, insisting on staying in one of the spare bedrooms, but I'm not having it. The only place I want her is in my bed.

I won't bend on that one, and I always get my way.

"Get whatever you want on it, Ry. I'll eat anything," I tell my son as I ruffle his brown hair.

"Cool. What are we going to do when we get to your house tonight, Dad? Can we watch a movie? Play video games? Swim?"

"It'll be getting close to your bedtime, but we can see what kind of trouble we can get into tonight with your mom beforehand," I reply. Dani just sits there, watching us interact, with that gorgeous little smile on her face. She looks peaceful, relaxed. It's a natural look; one that suits her.

After Dani orders a large pizza, salad, and breadsticks, I watch Ryan as he draws a picture on the back of the paper placemat. "So what are you going to do this summer?" I ask.

"As soon as school lets out, I'll get to sleep in and swim every day!" Ryan exclaims.

"Sounds like a great summer."

"Yeah, it'll be fun. Until Mom makes me go to the library and read," he says, his displeasure at the prospect of reading during his summer break clearly evident.

"You don't like to read?" I ask, dipping my breadstick in nacho cheese sauce.

"No way. I want to play basketball. I get to do basketball camp with Mr. Phillips this year. It's only for eight and older, so I couldn't do it last year," Ryan says, looking up with twinkling gray eyes.

"You like basketball?" I ask, resulting in a quick head nod from my son. "I played in high school, and a little in college. Not anything too big, but I enjoyed the sport. We'll have to play sometime soon," I tell him. My statement earns an excited cheer from his seat next to me.

"But, here's the thing, Ry, you have to keep practicing your reading. It's very important later in life, even if you don't really want to do it. Did you know I read daily at work?" Ryan shakes his head, wide-eyed as if absorbing every ounce of attention I can give him. "Yep, I read lots and lots of papers every day. Reading is extremely important in the business world. So, while basketball is important and fun, you have to work hard on your school work, too."

I look over at Dani when I realize that her fork has stopped mid-air. She's staring at me with a look of awe on her face, and I'll be damn if it doesn't make me want to puff out my fucking chest. This whole parenting this is new to me, but when she smiles at me, I know I did something right, and it feels damn good.

I can't contain the smile I give back to her. "Okay, Dad. I'll go do my reading at the library this summer. Maybe you can come with me sometime," he adds with a hopeful look.

"I'll see what I can do," I reply. "The key is to find books that interest you. They have books on basketball and other sports. Find some of those, and you'll be all set."

"Thanks, Dad!" Ryan exclaims. I'll never get tired of hearing that word. For as scary as I always thought it would be to hear, it's nothing compared to the feeling I get deep in my chest when Ryan says it to me. I'm in awe over this kid, and I can't believe how good it feels knowing that he's mine.

We spend the rest of the dinner talking about Ryan's summer plans and anything else a little boy can think of. The topic of his birthday comes up often, and I'm genuinely excited to know that I'll be there for this one. My heart picks up a little faster beat when I think about all of the ones I've missed. Too damn many, that's for sure. Well, not again.

Never again.

Ryan is bouncing in the backseat as we drive towards my place. He's talking a mile a minute about everything we pass, and Dani just seems to take it in stride and smile. When I pull up to my gate, I have to stop Ryan from jumping out of the back of the car and running up the lane. The car is barely in park when he throws open the back door and jumps from the vehicle.

"Ryan, slow down," Dani chastises.

"Dad, do you have a dog?" Ryan hollers, clearly ignoring the warning from his mother.

"No I don't, buddy."

"You should get a dog. This yard is huge and a big dog would have so much fun here. Something big like a German Sheppard or a Lab. Then I can teach it tricks and fun stuff when I'm here with you. I bet we could even name him Rocco, and he would be my best friend in the whole world," Ryan says in practically one breath.

I never wanted a dog. I don't want the mess, the hair, the slobber, or the shit. But seeing how excited Ryan is about the prospect of a dog makes me want to run to the nearest shelter and get a damn dog.

Fuck, what is this boy doing to me?

"Ryan, a dog isn't something we're considering right now," Dani says as we walk towards the door in the garage. I instantly turn around and want to tell her that if Ryan wants a dog, we'll get him a fucking dog. But when my eyes connect with hers, I wisely keep my mouth shut.

For now.

"Let's take your bags upstairs, and then you can check the place out," I say over my shoulder as we head inside. They each have an overnight bag, which I'm gladly carrying, but I notice right away that Ryan's is surprisingly heavier than Dani's. I'll take that as a good sign that she didn't bring much in way of clothes with her.

That or he packed everything he owns.

"What's that smirk for?" she asks as we proceed through the kitchen and dining room and head towards the stairs.

"Your bag is lighter than Ryan's. I assume that's because you didn't bring many clothes. Fuck knows you won't need them," I whisper against her ear.

Dani instantly inhales, a slight blush creeping up the column of her neck. "See, this is why I want separate rooms. You're incorrigible and our son is here."

"No worries, sweetheart. I will be on my best behavior this weekend," I say as we climb the stairs, Ryan already running ahead to scope out the room I arranged for him. "But make no mistake about it, I *will* have you in my bed tonight. And I *will* have you in my shower in the morning. If you run, I will find you. I will carry you back to my room and tie your delectable ass to my bed. Do you understand me?" I ask, my voice low and laced with need.

Dani's blue eyes are bright as she gapes at me. Standing at the top of the stairs, it takes everything I have to not drop the bag, throw her over my shoulder, and have my way with her until she's crying uncle. The look she gives me mirrors my need for her, and that makes me so fucking happy I could cry.

"Dad, is this blue room mine?" Ryan asks down the hall.

"Sure is, buddy," I tell him as we slowly make our way towards our son.

The room I had set up for him was complete this past week. When I asked Carly before her wedding for the name of a decorator–fuck knows I can't use the one I used when I bought the place–she recommended a man by the name of Zachariah. Just knowing that it wasn't the same woman as before was enough for me saying *yes* before I even knew anything about him.

As we step into the room, I have to admit that Zachariah did a great job. He painted the walls alternating deep blue and white with everything a boy could imagine. Not knowing what exactly Ryan's into left a huge question mark in the decorating category. So, I left it up to Zachariah since he's the expert.

A tall full size bed sits in the middle of the room with green and blue bedding. A desk sits along the wall with the walk-in closet, which is already filled with plenty of clothes in his size. I didn't want to miss the chance of Ryan staying the night because he didn't have clothes. One call from Carly to my personal shopper, and the closet was filled with size eight clothes for every season and occasion by the end of that day.

And his isn't the only closet with new clothes hiding inside.

"Mom, look! It's the new Xbox system," Ryan exclaims as he looks with wonder at the big television and gaming system attached.

"Yeah, we'll talk about that," Dani mumbles under her breath loud enough so I can hear her. I thought all kids love gaming systems? What the fuck did I do wrong?

"Are these all mine?" Ryan asks from the depths of the closet before I can ask Dani about what she meant.

"They sure are, Ry."

"Mom, that means I can come here all the time and have plenty of clothes."

"It does," Dani says quietly. Glancing over at her, I can almost see the wheels inside that beautiful head of hers turning. Something is up, and I'll be getting to the bottom of that shortly.

"Ryan, why don't you get on a pair of pj's, brush your teeth, and get ready for bed?" Dani instructs from the entrance to Ryan's in-suite bathroom.

"Ah, Mom, do I have to?" he whines, and I'm unable to control my smile.

"Yes, you do. No arguing," Dani says with her arms firmly crossed over her chest. While the position is meant to show her authority to Ryan, the only thing it manages to do for me is stir my dick to life. Her beautiful tits are pressed upward, giving a lush view of creamy, smooth skin.

"Why don't you meet us downstairs, Ryan, and I'll show you the rest of the house before bed," I suggest, hoping I don't piss off Mama Bear again.

"Okay," Ryan mumbles begrudgingly.

I follow behind as Dani heads downstairs. I realize I'm like a puppy dog, trailing behind my master, waiting to see if I get a treat or not. Fuck, when did I become *that* guy?

"Are you going to tell me what I did wrong?" I ask as I round the corner and step into the family room.

"You didn't do anything wrong, Reid. I just wish you had asked before you bought all that stuff for Ryan. He doesn't need all of it," she says.

"That's what's wrong? I thought it was something bad. Dani, you can't fault me for wanting to buy things for my son. I have seven birthdays to make up for here. This money means nothing to me if I can't share it with the people I care about," I say as I pull her into my arms.

Dani comes willingly as I wrap my arms around her back. I find her lips instantly, giving her a slow, deep kiss. A kiss that hopefully displays all of my intentions for later this evening.

"Mom, did you see how big this TV is?" I was so busy kissing Dani that I didn't even hear Ryan come into the room, let alone stand right next to me.

"Yes," Dani says, jumping back and out of my arms. "It's a big TV."

"Show me the house, Dad."

Fifteen minutes later, Dani and I are tucking Ryan into his new bed. The mundane task seems so natural and easy as we both give him hugs before slipping out the door. Dani caved and is allowing him to watch a few minutes of cartoons before falling sleep since it is a Saturday night. Together, we walk out into the hallway before I pull the door closed behind me.

"What if he gets scared? It's a new place for him?" Dani asks nervously.

"He knows where my room is, Dani. If something bothers him, he'll come looking for us," I say moments before I claim her mouth with my own.

"And I don't want him to find me in a compromising position," Dani mumbles against my lips.

"I love your compromising positions."

"Reid," she starts.

"It'll be fine," I reply, again seeking out her lips with my own.

"But what if he -" she starts before my mouth cuts her off once more.

"The only thing I'm worried about is the fact that I'm clearly not doing a good enough job at distracting you," I tell her before I dive my hands into her hair, pull her body as close to mine as humanly possible while clothed, and plunge my tongue into her mouth. Her soft moan fills the hallway and essentially lights my body on fire.

There. That shut her up.

"Come to bed with me," I whisper, nipping at her bottom lip.

"Okay," she whispers.

I all but drag her into my bedroom. As soon as we cross the threshold, my hands are everywhere. Her hair, her back, her ass. I have grabby hands and I can't seem to do anything about it. Not that I want to.

"I've been waiting to get you back in my bed since last weekend," I say as I start to pull her shirt up and over her head. Dani is wearing a black lace bra, her rosebud nipples pebbling out through the material.

Unable to control myself any longer, I bend down and suck one nipple in my mouth. The course material feels rough against my tongue as I lick and taste the first one, then the second. Dani gasps and pushes her tits further into my mouth.

Sliding my hands down her hips, I quickly unbutton the front of her jeans and skim them down her long legs. The little scrap of lace material I find underneath is already soaked through. Her essence fills the room, and my mind. It's all aroused woman, mixed with something uniquely Dani. And it makes me hard as fucking stone.

"Stand right here," I tell her as I drop to my knees and prepare to worship the woman before me.

Nudging her legs apart, I run my tongue slowly up the inside of her thigh. I can feel her legs quiver beneath my touch. Grabbing ahold of her ass, I use my tongue to push her soaked panties to the side, giving me better access to the goods hiding underneath. Dani leans back against the door as I swipe my tongue through her folds, offering me that first taste of her sweetness that I crave.

I continue to suck and lick at her core. Dani's hands slide into my hair, gripping and tugging gently with each thrust of my tongue. Her breathing is labored, and she rides my face like a professional bull rider. Knowing that she's getting close to coming, I use two fingers and thrust them into her wetness. She starts to come violently against my fingers, while I continue to storm her clit with my mouth. I watch in awe as her eyes flutter closed and a small smile spreads across her face.

I'd be a fucking liar if I said that smile didn't do something to me. Some sort of caveman reaction that makes me want to pound on my chest and bellow a war cry loud enough to frighten furry woodland creatures.

Getting back up, I make quick work at removing every bit of clothing I'm wearing. I sheath myself in a condom before I move back towards Dani. She hasn't moved an inch from where I left her leaning back against the closed door. Flipping the lock, I grab ahold of her ass and hoist her up. She automatically wraps her legs around my waist, lining up her body with mine perfectly.

Using the door as leverage and keeping one arm planted firmly under her ass, I reach down and slide my dick through her wetness. Dani trembles as I pull back slightly and position the head of my dick at her entrance. Her heavily lidded eyes are locked on mine. Leaning forward, I place a kiss on her lips. It's a tender kiss, sweet and full of unspoken meaning, but it also doesn't take long before it turns carnal and hungry.

When I bite down just enough to sting her bottom lip, I slam home. A loud thump reverbs through the room as her body bangs into the door. I swallow her loud groans of pleasure as I pull back and do it again. Over and over again, I nail Dani against the door, eating her moans and loving her mouth with my own. I feel the glorious bite of her nails scoring my back, but I don't give a shit. If anything, that pain only fuels my pleasure.

I can tell by the movements of her body that she's ascending towards another orgasm. Her arms tighten around me, her insides grip my dick like a vise, and her legs scissor firmly around my back. And I don't let up for a second. Hell, I couldn't even if I wanted to. I'm too far gone. Possessed.

"You gotta be quiet, sweetheart," I warn her knowing that she's on the verge of screaming from the mountaintops.

"Can't," she mumbles, scratching at my back once more.

"Gotta try, baby," I say right before her internal muscles squeeze the ever loving shit out of my cock.

I feel the familiar tingling at the base of my spine and know that it's only a matter of seconds before I follow her over the edge. As the scream reaches the tip of her tongue, Dani latches her teeth down, biting the hard muscles of my shoulder. The pain sends me soaring into oblivion as I come harder than ever before.

My body is raked with aftershocks and my knees suddenly struggle to keep us in an upright, standing position. With her sated in my arms, I slide down to the floor, my body all but giving up after that workout. Dani leans her head against my chest, curling herself into a warm little ball. I'm still buried deep inside her with no sign of my erection going anywhere. Even after the marathon sex we just had, I'm ready to go another round with her as if my dick were Mike fucking Tyson.

Only her.

"Come on, sweetheart," I mumble against her head as I slowly pull my body from within hers. She tries to stand, but her legs are too weak.

Pulling her into my arms, I carry Dani the few feet to my bed, gently laying her down on the side I deemed as hers after the last weekend she stayed. She doesn't even open her eyes as she snuggles into the pillow, curls up on her side, and reaches for me. I lean down and give her a tender kiss before slipping into the bathroom to dispose of the condom.

After cleaning myself up, I stare at the man reflected back at me in the mirror. I have no clue who this man is. He's not the one I used to look at, day in and day out. Gone is the ruthless man whose heart stopped beating at such a young age. Gone is the man who fucks 'em and chucks 'em. Gone is the man who refuses to look into the future and see anything other than dollar signs.

Replacing that man is someone in love. I know it. I can't deny it and won't even try. The scary part is that I have absolutely no clue what to do with this foreign emotion. I've never willingly given love to another person who doesn't share my blood. I haven't said the words since I was a young boy and the woman I loved was ripped from my life. Even Tara doesn't hear those words. Not anymore.

This is the part where I'd usually run so fucking fast away from the house you'd think my ass was lit on fire. But the thought of running away from Dani makes me lightheaded. Not only does it seem wrong, but impossible. I don't want to run. I want to stay, and wrap my arms around the woman sleeping in my bed.

The woman I love.

So, for tonight, that's what I'm going to do.

Tomorrow, I'll start to figure out how I'm going to let her go.

Chapter Nineteen – Good Morning, Sunshine. Breakfast?

Dani

I wake up hotter than hell. My entire body feels like it's pressed against a furnace. As I crack open my eyes, I catch a glimpse at the morning sun rising out the vast amount of windows along the east wall. It's a breathtaking picture.

Speaking of picture, the next thing I notice is the framed photograph on the nightstand. It was easy to miss last night since the room was darkened when we arrived, and my attention was clearly diverted elsewhere.

The photograph is of Ryan and I at the pool and used to be on my fridge. I noticed it was gone, but didn't think too much about it at the time. Now, I smile at the prospect of Reid taking that photo, framing it, and displaying it prominently on his nightstand.

The next thing I notice is the very naked, very hard man sleeping next to me. I watch his even breathing as his chest rises and falls with each breath he takes. From this angle, he looks softer and gentler, like the world doesn't rest on his firm, wide shoulders. This is a different side of Reid, and I'll be honest, I like waking up next to him. And that begs the question, how can he be so calm in slumber and so hard beneath the sheet at the exact same time is beyond me?

"Stop staring at me before you start something you can't finish," Reid mumbles sleepily.

"Who says I can't finish it?" I ask with humor in my voice. The clock on the nightstand says six-thirty, which is a little after my usual wake up time. Something tells me that sleeping this late is a rare occurrence for Reid, as well. He seems more like the up by five, workout complete, shower fresh by six-thirty kind.

I reach over and run my hand down Reid's bare chest, heading straight down to that thick shaft I felt against my leg a moment ago.

"Mom!" Ryan exclaims from the hallway.

Grabbing the sheet, I yank it clear up to my chin in an attempt to hide every sliver of naked skin my body possesses. I internally chastise myself for sleeping nude. Though I'm usually up before Ryan, there's no way in hell I ever want to be caught sleeping naked, especially in the same bed as Reid where both of us are as naked as the day we were brought into this world.

"Settle down. The door's still locked," Reid says as he hops up and grabs a pair of running shorts. My eyes are glued to his firm ass as the material slides up his muscular legs and rests dangerously low on his trim hips.

"Mom? Dad?" Ryan asks before knocking on the door.

"Be right there, buddy. We'll start breakfast for your mom," Reid hollers before slipping into the bathroom. I listen as the water runs in the sink and the sounds of him brushing his teeth trickle into the room. I, on the other hand, am still rooted in the middle of the bed with the sheet pulled up to my pupils.

"We're going to start breakfast. Why don't you go take a shower and then come down?" Reid suggests. "Food should be ready by then," he says as he places a tender kiss on my lips. "I'll even have coffee."

Before I can even reply, Reid heads towards the door, releases the lock, and steps into the hallway. He's greeted by an anxious child, eager to help make breakfast.

"Come on, Ry. Let's go cook something good for Mom," Reid says as they continue down the hallway.

When I hear nothing but quiet for several minutes, I slowly slip out of Reid's bed and all but run to the bathroom. Inside, I find Reid had set my overnight bag down on the counter. Digging out my toothbrush, I quickly brush my teeth. The fixtures and counter tops are as sleek and shiny as I remember from last weekend. I'm sure Reid has a housekeeper that comes in regularly to clean his house. He's more of the pay to have it done kinda guy.

Inside the shower, I find body products that instantly grab my attention. They're...girly. Giving the lid a quick flip, the entire shower is filled with a subtle vanilla and lilac fragrance. Are these for me? They're clearly not for Reid since his expensive brand of body wash that I've only read about in fashion magazines is still on the shelf; right next to where this body wash sat. And not just body wash. There's an expensive brand of feminine shampoo and conditioner on the shelf as well. And right next to that, a pink razor and moisturizing shaving gel.

Reid must have purchased these products this week for me. I can't fight the smile that threatens to take over my face at the thought of him thinking far enough ahead to grab shower products. Was this purchase done with only this weekend in mind or maybe longer? Could he be anticipating more weekend visits in our future?

I dress quickly with a smile on my face and head down to join the boys in the kitchen. The first thing I hear when I reach the bottom of the stairs is the laughter spilling around the doorway. Whatever Reid is saying has Ryan in stitches. His laughter is contagious, I've always known that, but when I hear Reid laugh as well, the sound stops me in my tracks. I've seen Reid smile and I've heard his guarded laughter, but this is something different. Something deeper. Happier, even.

Free.

"What's so funny?" I ask as I round the corner. When I my eyes focus on the sight before me, my own laughter bubbles up from deep within my gut.

"Dad is messy, Mom," Ryan says with more laughter.

There isn't one surface in the kitchen not covered with something. Pans, utensils, milk, and waffle batter is everywhere. And I mean *everywhere.* How it can be dripping from the ceiling and smeared in Ryan's hair is beyond me.

"What happened in here?" I ask, incredulously.

"We're making waffles," Ryan says with a beaming smile.

"I see that. Why is there more batter on the ceiling than in the waffle maker?" I ask, afraid to take further steps into the room for fear that I'll bust my rear on the spilled ingredients.

"Dad thought it would go quicker if we used the mixer to stir the milk and the waffle mix. I turned it on high and then it started flying everywhere," Ryan says, while Reid looks on with a matching grin. The smudge of batter on his left cheek is downright adorable.

I slowly make my way forward, mindful of the slippery batter covering every available surface, and approach my boys. "Why don't you run into the bathroom and wash your face and hands, and I'll whip up another batch of batter? Looks like you don't have much left in this bowl," I tell Ryan when I notice his batter bowl is all but empty.

"But Dad and I wanted to surprise you with waffles," Ryan says.

"Oh, don't worry. I was definitely surprised," I reply through my laughter.

Stripping off Ryan's t-shirt, I watch as he carefully makes his way out of the kitchen and heads towards one of the downstairs bathrooms.

"So, clearly that didn't go the way I thought it would," Reid says behind me. Turning around, a burst of laughter slips from my lips. "This isn't funny," Reid says, fighting his own smile, and trying to give me a stern, bossy look.

"Oh, this is really funny."

Before I can say anymore, Reid grabs me and pulls me into his arms, slamming his lips down onto mine. Suddenly, the incident with the batter magically disappears from my mind. Reid's tongue slides against the crease of my lips, begging for admission. And what's a girl to do but oblige.

Reid runs his hands up my neck and grips the sides of my face. He angles me upward slightly, giving him better access to devour my mouth his with own. I grip the back of his t-shirt, hanging on for dear life, while this man consumes me like a chocolate sundae. I don't even care that Ryan could enter the room at any moment and find us making out like high schoolers. Right now, the only thing I can think about is the way this man makes me feel. Coveted. Captivated. Alive.

I finally pull back a bit to catch my breath. Reid's eyes are dark with want, his breathing labored and matching my own. It takes every ounce of control I possess not to hop up on the batter-covered counter and wrap my legs around his waist.

"You look beautiful with waffle batter smeared on your cheek," Reid says as he runs his thumb down my cheek and over my bottom lip. His touch causes an involuntary shutter to rake through my overheated body. Of course, the blush taking over my face doesn't help any either.

When Reid turns slightly to his right, I catch sight of white and start laughing all over again. "What's so funny?" he asks with his arms still wrapped around me.

"I don't know how to say this, but you have waffle batter in your ear." I try to keep a straight face, really I do, but I can't. Laughter erupts all the way from my toes and tears suddenly fill my eyes.

The corner of his mouth ticks just a bit, but he keeps a straight face. If it weren't for the mischief and twinkle that suddenly fills his eyes, I would think he was upset at me for laughing. But there's no anger when he attacks.

Reid grabs my arm with one hand, swipes as much batter as he can from the counter with his other hand, and effectively smears it all over my face and hair. I scream, but am unable to get away from his assault as his grip on my arm tightens. It's not painful, but it's clear that I'm not escaping him anytime soon.

"That was mean," I mumble.

"Now, you look edible," he says moments before he claims my lips once more.

"I need another shower," I whisper against his lips.

"What a coincidence. I happen to need a shower as well. Maybe we could save water and shower together," he says, running his batter-covered hands through my hair.

"You're incorrigible."

"Only for you, sweetheart," he whispers. Reid places another brief kiss on my lips before pulling me towards the entryway of the kitchen. "Come on. Let's wash all of this goo off of us and try for round two."

My eyebrows shoot skyward as I consider his words. "Not that kind of round two. Though, I like where your head is at, and that is definitely at the top of my list of favorite ways to enjoy round two. We need to try for round two of breakfast. Making a mess makes me hungry," he says with a wink.

He makes me hungry. Hungry for food, yes, but also for him. There's something so very hot about a man who takes the time to cook with his child, makes the biggest mess ever to where the kitchen is left looking like the refrigerator exploded, and still looks adorable afterwards.

This is just another one of those little moments that I want. I didn't realize how deeply I craved them until they were dangled in front of my face like a carrot. Now I long to make more memories with this man and our son. I'm holding on tight to what could be, and I don't want to let go.

I don't think I'll ever be able to let go.

Chapter Twenty – The Past That Haunts Me

Reid

I pull into Dani's driveway, the mood in the vehicle solemn and quiet. When it came time to load up the car and bring Dani and Ryan back to her house, everyone's mood turned a little sour. I, for one, am fucking miserable. Like an inmate walking towards the electric chair, my legs are leaden and a weight sits squarely in the middle of my chest, making it damn near impossible to catch a deep breath.

Ryan was uncharacteristically quiet the entire ride. Gone is the rambunctious, talkative little boy from earlier. This boy is forlorn and sad, as if he dreads going back to his day-to-day life.

And that slices me right down the middle of the chest.

"Come on, Ryan," Dani says as she slips out of the passenger seat. Ryan all but drags his chin on the ground as he mopes up the walk and follows behind his mother towards the back door.

"Hey, Ryan," I start. When he turns around, I drop to my knees in front of him, anxious to do everything I can to put a smile back on his face. "I had a great time this weekend. I want to do it again very, very soon."

Ryan's smile is wide as he drops his bag and throws his arms around my neck. "I want to do it again, too, Dad! Can I come over tomorrow?" he asks, his anxious eyes searching my face.

"Not tomorrow, buddy. I have work to do, but I promise to come over when I'm done, okay? I'll come over again every night I

220

can, just like before. And if it works with my schedule and your mom's, you can come spend the night again next weekend," I tell my son.

"I can't wait," he exclaims as Dani lets us in the house.

"Drop your bag in the laundry room, and go get ready for bed," Dani says to Ryan. His mood appears better now that I've reassured him that we'll be spending more time together soon, but Dani's appears just as gloomy as before.

I help Ryan get ready for bed and let him read me a book about Michael Jordan that we found at a local bookstore. Tucking him into bed, I hear those four words that rock me to the core. "I love you, Dad," Ryan says sleepily, his dark hair sweeping down a bit on his forehead.

"I love you, too, Ry." It's automatic. Natural. Heartfelt. And I mean every word. I love him, and it's the first time I've vocalized that emotion since I was a boy myself. As scary as it is to say, I feel no remorse. I don't feel the gut-churning fear that I expected I would with saying those words. In fact, it felt quite the opposite. It felt good. As hard as I've fought it, Ryan and Dani have chiseled away at every carefully constructed wall I've erected around my heart.

I find Dani in the living room, folding a load of towels that must have been in the dryer. "Is he out?" she asks, those crystal blue eyes full of some unspoken sentiment.

"Yeah," I say hoarsely, clearing my throat of the remaining emotion I carry from Ryan's words.

"Good. He's had a long weekend," she says without looking up at me.

"Dani, what's wrong?" I ask, taking a seat next to her on the couch.

Her blue eyes find mine, and the sadness within them leaves me unsettled. I fear that I'm the cause of such sadness, and it instantly pisses me off. "What? Tell me," I demand with a little more authority than I would have liked. I instantly try to calm myself down a bit and remind myself that I'm not in a boardroom, right now.

"I had a great time this weekend, Reid," Dani says as she sets the towels down on the floor. "Ryan had a great time. I'm so thankful that you're willing to spend this kind of time with him, getting to know him, and letting him get to know you. It's important to me that you two have a strong relationship."

"I get that, Dani. You've said that all along. And I'm happy to have this time with him. I'm enjoying the hell out of spending time together," I say.

"Good," she whispers.

"But?" I start, leaving the rest open-ended.

"But, I just wonder how long this is going to last? How long before the newness wears off or you're pulled back into the life you knew before we came along? I know you usually work crazy hours. I know you're devoted to your work and the company, so when does that start to settle back into your routine, and where does that leave Ryan?" Dani's eyes are torturous. She looks torn between saying what she needs to say, and fearing that I'll run the other direction. But it's her next words that strike the deepest. "Where does that leave me?" Her words are almost inaudible.

I move before I even comprehend that I'm moving. I pull her into my lap and wrap my arms around her. "Dani, I can't say where all of this is going to leave us. Yes, I tend to work crazy hours. Yes, I have taken some of that time off to spend with you and Ryan, and I'll have to pick some of those back up at some point. But don't ever doubt that my priorities have changed. Ryan. He's my number one. For the first time in my adult life, I let something–*someone*–besides my work fill that number one spot. It's going to take some getting used to on all of our parts, but I'm not going back to the man I was before. Ryan changed me. *You* changed me."

The words rush from my lips as if I fear I won't be able to get them all out quick enough. Dani stares up at me with those big, blue eyes, and I'll be damned if I don't want to claim every part of her body, mind, and soul. I want more with her. While the thought of loving Ryan seems so natural now, the thought of loving Dani, and having the courage to let her love me back is terrifying. And it's that fear that keeps holding me back.

"I don't know anything about you," she whispers against my chest as I hold her tight.

"You know all the important stuff," I defend, knowing that she's going to want to know things I've never told a soul. Tara and Steven. They're the only ones who know how truly heartless I am, and how willing I am to bleed, how low I am willing to stoop, to get what I want.

"What if it's not enough?" she asks. I'm not surprised by her question. Shit, I've already acknowledged that it was coming. I just wish it didn't.

"What do you want to know?" I ask, afraid and nervous all at the same time.

"I want to know who you are. I want to know who Reid Hunter is, and why he thinks he's a heartless bastard." Dani takes a deep breath but keeps those eyes trained right on me. "Unless this is nothing more than a few rolls in the hay. Then I guess I have no right to ask these things of you."

Gutted. Bleeding all over the fucking floor.

"Dani, first off, as the mother of my son, you can ask any question you want. But as the woman in my life, you've earned the right to ask anything and everything and get the truth in return." The shock on her face is evident.

"That's right, sweetheart. You're the woman in my life. The *only* woman in my life. I've never had that, Dani. I've never really dated; had no desire to. But there has always been something different about you. From the very beginning when I found you crying in the dirt, you grabbed ahold of me and refused to let go."

I take a deep breath. "I'm bad at this shit," I tell her. "I don't talk about my feelings or where I come from." Taking another deep breath, I decide to let Dani in and share my sordid past. The real Reid Hunter.

"I grew up to a privileged family. With the help of his father, my grandfather started a casino when he was in his thirties, and shared it with his daughter, my mother. Even though she came from money, she fell in love with a nobody from the wrong side of the tracks. Now, before you start with the whole fairytale bullshit, there was nothing fairytale about it. My father instantly became obsessed with the business, doing everything he could to ensure he took over The Chameleon. He married my mother and instantly became the next in line to inherit one of the city's most lucrative casinos."

Deep breath. "My father was always a heartless bastard. But it wasn't as bad in the beginning. He ignored my mother, my sisters, and me, sure, but at least he would spend time with us every once in a while. At least he did until I was six."

I'm lost in the memories and pain of my past. My gut tightens almost painfully, like the fist of a boxer gripping and twisting my insides, knowing what I'm about to say. I've only spoken of it out loud once. A time that I chalk up to one of my infamous drunken moments with Steven where the weakness and torment finally grabbed ahold of me.

"My twin sister, Reagan, loved the museum. My mom took Reagan, Tara, and me as much as we wanted. Tara was still pretty little, and I didn't care what we did. I was happy just to be with my

224

mom and sisters. And the museum was Reagan's favorite place in the whole world, so I went readily every time it was her turn to pick.

"On this rare day, my father decided to go with us. I remember him bitching and moaning the entire time about all of the walking and about all of the shit he should have been doing instead of taking his family to the fucking children's museum. Even at six, I was so pissed off at him. He was ruining the trip for all of us. Well, all of us but Reagan. She happily ignored our father, and continued to look over the exact same exhibits she'd already seen a hundred times. Each time, it was with the same excitement and enthusiasm as if it was her first time there. I envied her so much for that. Her ability to forget all the shit and just enjoy the moment of being there.

"We were leaving when my father started in on me. He was upset about something stupid, taking it out on me. My mom was pushing the stroller behind us, and trying her best to intervene as much as she could. No one was paying attention to Reagan. Before we knew what happened, she ran out into the street, chasing a fucking butterfly. I didn't see the car that hit her, but I heard it. I'll never forget that sound. The screeching tires, the scream, the thud. It replays over and over again on some fucked up loop in my head. It has for twenty-four years. I'll never forget that day. The day half of my heart died in the middle of a busy Las Vegas street."

I don't even realize I have a tear on my cheek, not until Dani uses her finger to wipe it away. This is exactly why I never talk about Reagan. Hell, I never think about her. Because when I do, I can't stop the emotions raging inside of me. Anger. Sadness. Despair. And more anger. Usually, a lot of anger.

"I'm so sorry," Dani whispers, her voice and eyes filled with concern and sorrow that mirror my own. I don't see pity, which I'm thankful as hell for. I only see her sadness. Sadness for the little boy who lost his twin sister. Sadness for the man who can't seem to let it go.

"Thank you," I finally whisper and mean it. "I wish that was all," I tell her. The way she wiggles in my arms lets me know that she's not prepared for any more. But that's the thing: I wasn't prepared for anymore shit, and it didn't stop fate from laying it at my feet. So, I go on.

"It was hell at our house. Mom cried all the time and Dad drank when he wasn't at work. Tara was too little to really understand what was going on, so she just stayed back, oblivious to the self-destruction around her." Deep breath.

"I was twelve when I discovered my mom's secret. She had breast cancer, stage four. She hid it well, but I could tell something was wrong. I asked and asked, but always got the same answer. Nothing. Finally, she became so ill that she was bedridden. There was no hiding it then. Mom had to tell us because my father was too busy fucking everyone at the casino. She withered away to nothing right before our eyes, and no one could do a goddamn thing about it. Three months later, she was gone. It was right before my thirteenth birthday."

"Holy shit," Dani whispers, her tears streaming unchecked down her face.

I remember the funeral, the way my father shook hands and cried along with all the elite assholes that didn't really give a shit about my mother. He played the part of grieving husband, and he played it well. No one knew he had a bottle of bourbon and his piece of ass waiting for him in the parking lot. But I knew. And I hated him for it.

"I was born to take over The Chameleon one day. It was bred into me from my earliest memories. When I graduated college, I knew my life was his. If it weren't for my grandfather stepping in and giving me one final summer of freedom, I wouldn't have even have been at that festival that night. That weekend was my last night of independence before I finally sat in the seat next to him. My grandfather was officially retired, but still held the majority shares. He refused to hand them over until I was settled in the company. I hated that fucking place. It wasn't the company my grandfather started and nurtured. It was tainted and spoiled with my father at the helm. I wanted nothing to do with it."

"Then how did you get out of there? You're obviously not still working there," Dani says while rubbing her hand up and down my back in a calming fashion. I love the feel of her hands on me, but this is one of the only times she has touched me and it didn't feel sexual. It feels comforting.

"About two years after I started, I snapped. He wanted me there because it was required of me in the contract from my grandfather. See, my grandfather wanted to make sure I was taken care of and set within the company. Well, my father found a way to keep me involved without actually involving me. He cut me out of everything until one day I flipped. It actually came to blows between us. My father lay on the floor, his lip busted the fuck up, and I told him I was out. I told him all the things I had wanted to tell him my entire life, and before I walked out that door, I vowed to take him down.

"The Chameleon was the first company I purchased and took over. It was the first company I disassembled and destroyed, piece by fucking piece. I watched as he sat there and everything he worshipped, cared about, crumbled around him."

"But, your grandfather -" Dani started, but I cut her off.

"My grandfather gave me his blessing. When I left, he changed all of the contracts and paperwork to ensure my father didn't cut me out of anything from then on. Financially, I was set. Grandfather didn't turn over full reigns of the company because he hadn't truly trusted my father. That's why it was so important for me to have a place within the business. I was his way of keeping things right. But when he realized that wasn't going to happen, he helped me start Hunter Enterprises and take down The Chameleon. He even bought the first round of drinks that night at the bar," I tell her with a small smile, recalling my grandfather's toast to my success.

"My grandfather passed away a few years ago, and Tara is all I have left. My sperm donor is around still, living off of what little money he has left from the purchase of the company. I rarely hear from him, though it does happen on occasion."

"Reid, I don't even know what to say," Dani says, wrapping her arms so tightly around me that it's hard to breathe.

"I don't want you to say anything. You can't change my past any more than I can. You have to understand that I don't visit that part of my life. *Ever.* I get your need to know more about me. I'm not a saint, Dani. I've done lots of things that I am not proud of; things so horrible that you wouldn't even recognize the man before you. But when you're here, all of that seems trivial. It feels like I can put it all in the past where it belongs. For the first time, I feel like my past doesn't have a hold on me."

"It doesn't have a hold on you, Reid. You can let this go and just be you. You can be whomever you want to be."

"I want to believe you. It's going to take time for me to be able to, though," I confess, squeezing her body within my arms. I know this battle may be my biggest struggle of all. Letting go.

Can I let go of my past demons? Can I let go of the hurt and the anger and the rage I've carried around like luggage for the past two decades? Ever since I was a little boy, I've hated my father. Hated The Chameleon. Hated that I couldn't save my sister. Hated that cancer took my mother. Hated my life.

Everything I've ever loved has been taken away from me. That's why I will always keep Tara at arms-length. Maybe if I don't love her as much, I won't taint her beauty with my shit. Sure, I know I'm wrong. I know that's not how love works. I remember how love works, can see it plainly when I think of my mother and Reagan. I know it in my heart, but I can't seem to get my fucking head to agree.

And then there's Ryan and Dani. I love my son more than anything in this world. In a month, I've learned what real love is. I've felt it. And Dani? I feel like part of my soul is missing whenever she's not near. I know I love her too, but I still can't seem to make myself say the words. They're too hard. Even now after confessing my past to her, I still hold back.

I know it.

My entire adult life, I've profited off my rage and anger. I've made a living–a damn good one, at that–off taking down everyone and anything littler than me. I became the bully, only interested in beating down the little guy whose business is weaker than mine. To benefit off their failure. Win.

Now I guess it's time to figure out if I can profit off something else, something other than the ugly. Time to find out if I can make a life with something beautiful.

Something like love.

Chapter Twenty-One – Falling Down

Dani

Listening to Reid share his past with me last night was excruciating. Not only could I see the pain in his eyes, see it written on his face, but I could feel it radiating from his body. He's held onto so much hurt and anger for so long, and it has molded the man he is today. But even though he shared so much with me last night, I still had this nagging feeling that there was more; something else that was left unspoken.

After our talk, he invited me to dinner tonight. He seemed eager to steal a little alone time with me, and I'll admit I am excited for the same. He has a late conference call today so I'm meeting him in his apartment above his office. It's the first time I've ever been there, but he told me that the receptionist downstairs wouldn't give me any trouble.

When I step through the revolving door at the entrance of Hunter Enterprises, I'm suddenly aware of the fact that I'm underdressed. I'm still wearing the tan slacks and light blue silk top that I wore for my day of dealing with third graders. My shoes are more for comfort than anything else. Standing on your feet for seven hours a day makes you carefully weigh all options when it comes to footwear.

Miss Congeniality is sitting at the front desk when I step inside the cool entrance of the building. "Can I help you?" she asks. Either she doesn't recognize me or she's choosing to be difficult. I'm going with the latter.

"Miss Whitley," I hear over my shoulder before I can answer. Turning, I take in Steven's handsome, smiling face, and can't help the smile that spreads over my own.

"Steven," I say as he pulls me into a hug before placing a gentle kiss on my cheek.

"I'm so happy to see you again," he says with a wink. "Reid asked me to make sure you are shown upstairs," he says as he starts to lead me towards the elevator. Again, we slip into the one situated away from the others; the one that takes us straight to Reid's office and private apartment.

"Well, I'm happy to see you again as well. And thank you for seeing me up."

"Reid was just getting into his conference call when I came down. They can last anywhere from thirty to sixty minutes on average," Steven says as the elevator door opens, giving me my first view of Reid's apartment. "Please, make yourself at home."

I take in the lush space before me. Where Reid's house is expansive and somewhat clinical, this space is full of rich colors and lush textures. Even though at first sight it appears void of any real personal touches, you can clearly tell that Reid spends most of his time here.

"The chef already delivered dinner. It's in the warmer. There are a few bottles of wine that Reid requested on the counter. Help yourself to anything you want," Steven says.

"Can I snoop?" I ask playfully. Though the more I think about it, the more I realize I'm fully on board with a little snooping.

"Knock yourself out," he says with a wink before heading over to the elevator.

I turn and head towards the living room, anxious to kick off my ballerina flats. "Dani?" I hear behind me and stop to turn towards Steven. "I just wanted you to know that he's different since you

231

walked back into his life. A good different. A happiness has settled over him, and it's something I've never seen before. Thank you for making him smile," Steven says, keeping those blue eyes trained on me.

I can't seem to speak over the lump of emotion lodged in my throat, so I just give him a quick head nod. "I wish you both nothing but the best," he adds before slipping into the elevator and leaving me in nothing but silence.

After setting down my satchel on the table, I take off to check out Reid's space. The couch is plush, brown leather with a matching chair. The tables are a dark, rich wood, and the television is massive. Yet, if I know Reid at all, I bet it isn't on very often.

The kitchen appliances are bright chrome and look brand new. Obviously Reid isn't much of a cook, if yesterday's breakfast fiasco is any indication, so I'm assuming he doesn't use the kitchen much at all.

Down a hallway, I find three doors. The first one leads to a large room filled with workout equipment. This must be where Reid goes to keep his impressive body in top form. Just the thought of him sweating while running on the treadmill or grunting while lifting weights has heat rushing to the apex of my legs.

The second door I find leads to a bathroom with a massive tile shower stall, and the third door hits jackpot. Reid's bedroom.

The room instantly smells like him as I step over the threshold. The bedding is all black and situated perfectly atop the biggest bed I've ever seen. A single nightstand with a lone alarm clock sits on the left side of the bed; from what I discovered during my weekend visits to Reid's house, that's the side he prefers to sleep on. I can't help myself; I walk over to the nightstand and peek inside. Condoms. Lots and lots of condoms. More condoms than a corner pharmacy, to be exact. Every color and texture you could possibly imagine. The only thing that's the same is the size. Magnum.

My breath catches in my throat. Instantly, I understand what this place is. This is his screw pad. This is the place where he entertains his lady friends. Now I understand why his house feels almost clinical, yet this place feels warm and inviting. Even lacking the personal touch, this place feels like someone lives here. Suddenly, I'm wishing I hadn't snooped at all. Shutting the drawer with a loud bang, I high tail it out of there and make my way to the living room.

Forget snooping and checking out the rest of the place.

Sitting on the sofa, I try to calm my rapidly beating heart. Is that why he brought me here? No, it can't be. I've already been to his house and spent the night with him there. I know Reid has a past. He's admitted to it. He's no saint. But sitting here and imaging all the women who have come and gone from this apartment brings out every insecurity a girl could possibly have. Hell, I'd be a liar if I said even jealousy wasn't rearing its ugly little head right now. It makes me wonder if Reid has a "type" and where I would fall into that category.

The thing that brings me a bit of comfort is remembering that he doesn't do relationships. Reid's confession last night only reiterated the fact that he's just as much in unchartered waters with me as I am with him. I've dated, but that's it. Casual dating. And it appears that Reid has only ever done the same thing. Hell, he really hasn't done much dating. It sounds like he's more of the screw them and get the hell out of dodge kind of man.

I can do this. I can open myself up completely to Reid, and show him that there's a possibility of more between us. He's already shared so much with me, more than he's ever shared with anyone before. I know that Reid holds my heart, even if I haven't told him yet. I need to trust him. There's no room for doubt.

I do trust him, I realize.

I need to tell him.

Three little words.

I just got myself calmed back down, my self-esteem firmly in place, and hope bubbling in my heart like champagne, when I hear the elevator open. Hopping up off the couch, I'm suddenly very anxious to get my arms wrapped around him. At this moment, telling him that I'm falling for him seems like the most urgent thing in the world.

I practically run into the kitchen only to have my steps falter a bit. Reid isn't standing in the kitchen. The woman before me is tall with long legs, perfect brown hair, and hazel eyes. Her makeup is heavily applied to perfection, and she reeks of money, class, and expensive perfume.

"Hi, can I help you?" I ask, unable to keep the timid out of my voice. There's something about this woman that screams viper, and if I don't stay on my toes, she looks like she could eat me for breakfast.

The woman before me lets her eyes run up and down my body, and if the look of disdain she gives is any indication, she definitely finds me lacking in style and appearance. "I'm meeting someone," she huffs before inspecting her manicure.

"Oh, okay. Who are you waiting for?" I ask. As far as I know this was Reid's apartment, but maybe someone else, like Jon, uses it from time to time?

"I'm waiting for my fiancé," she claims without looking at me.

I'm not sure who she's waiting for, but it is obviously not Reid. I exhale the breath that I didn't realize I was holding and give her a smile. "Well, I'm the only one here right now. I'm sure your fiancé will be along shortly," I say stepping into the kitchen to grab a bottle of water.

"I'm sure he'll be here any moment. We're having dinner this evening," she says before setting the world's smallest purse down on the table. I catch her looking at my satchel bag and rolling her eyes in annoyance.

"You're having dinner here?" I ask, not quite following. Did Reid not realize that his apartment was being used this evening? Is there some sort of sex schedule to book this place?

"Yes," she says, exasperatingly. "Would you get me a glass of wine?" she asks while digging in her mini-purse. Okay. I make my way over to where two bottles of red wine are waiting on the counter. Grabbing one of the two glasses, I pour her a bit of wine.

"Thank you. What is for dinner this evening?" she asks, making herself comfortable at the table.

"Excuse me?" How in the hell am I supposed to know what's for dinner tonight?

"Dinner. Tonight. What did you make for dinner?" she asks, her annoyance with me and my seemingly irritating answer to her questions with another question evident.

"I…I didn't make dinner," I stumble. What the hell is going on here?

"Are you or are you not the maid?" she asks, again, not bothering to look up at me.

"I'm not the maid. I'm meeting someone here," I tell her defiantly.

"Well, you're going to have to meet your little friend somewhere else. My fiancé is finishing up a conference call and then he'll be up. We want a nice, quiet night in this evening," she says.

My brain is trying to process what she's saying, but it's stuck on one part of the statement. Conference call. "Who is your fiancé?" I whisper, suddenly unable to speak normally.

"Reid Hunter."

Her words crash into me like a tsunami. My gut tightens and I fight the nausea setting in. "Reid is your fiancé?" I ask, again my voice barely above a whisper.

"Yes. We're to be married by the end of year," she says, looking up at me with a perfect little smile. Yet her smile is filled with malice and rudeness. Almost evil.

"Reid Hunter?" I ask, my mind trying to process what she's just told me.

"Who else lives in this apartment? Reid and I have dinner often here. He's been working so much lately that I couldn't pass up his invitation to join him this evening. My man works so hard," she bites out through lipstick stained lips.

My mouth opens and closes like a fish out of water. Reid is engaged? I want to dismiss her claims, but something doesn't feel right. Just when I'm about to ask her further questions, I hear the ding signaling the arrival of the elevator. The door opens with a quiet swoosh, and Reid steps through the door looking frazzled.

"Reid, darling," the woman says before flitting towards him, her heels echoing in the quiet room.

Reid appears shocked as he looks from me to the woman who now has her arms wrapped around his waist. My jaw is practically hanging on the ground as she extends herself upward and places a kiss on his silent lips.

"Cynthia, what are you doing here?" he asks, never taking his steel eyes off of me.

"I missed you, baby. I thought I'd surprise you with dinner tonight," she coos as she runs her hands up Reid's chest. My stomach clenches with the desire to retch.

The movement jolts him a bit causing him to jump back. He disentangles himself the rest of the way from her claws before turning back to me.

"How did you get in here, Cynthia?" he asks, turning and looking at the tall woman who stands between us like an anvil.

"That nice woman downstairs let me up. When I explained who I was, she showed me to the elevator," Cynthia says. "I'm sorry, I've been rude. My name is Cyn," she adds while walking over to me, hand out. Sure, she drips with politeness now that Reid is here.

"You did not have permission to come up here, Cynthia. I'll deal with Erica," Reid fumes angrily.

"Oh, don't be a bear, darling. She knew who I was." Turning back to Reid, she says, "I was just telling the help here about how hard my fiancé is working." She waves another dismissive hand in my direction, but it isn't her reference to me that causes my blood to run cold through my veins. Reid doesn't dispute her when she refers to him as her fiancé.

My stomach starts to drop to my knees as realization starts to set in. I struggle to find enough air in the room to fill my lungs, and I quickly turn away. Blinking back the tears that are threatening to fall, I keep my gaze locked on the wall of windows. The sun is setting and the lights of Vegas are bright with life.

Yet, I feel like I'm dying inside.

"Dani," Reid starts, but I cut him off.

Turning back around I say, "Fiancé?" My words are clipped as I focus my fiery gaze on him.

"Of course I'm his fiancée. We're to be married by the end of the year. We've been waiting so long for this moment, right, dear?" Cynthia asks as she walks back up to Reid.

"Cynthia. I need you to leave."

"But, Reid, I thought we could enjoy an evening in tonight. We have so much catching up to do and so much planning to do for the wedding," she says, her voice dripping with sugar.

"I said go," he seethes. His hands are firmly positioned on his hips, and his steel gray eyes are focused solely on me.

"I don't understand why *I* have to leave, darling," she says while planting her feet firmly in place. She mimics Reid's stance, tapping her designer heels on the polished hardwood floor.

"She's right. I should leave," I say as I turn to grab my satchel bag off the table.

"No." Reid's voice is firm. Final. "Cynthia, you are to leave immediately. If you want to see me again, please make an appointment with Carly." His tone holds so much authority to it that no one dare argue. The way Cynthia opens her mouth I can tell she's considering it. But then Reid trains those intense eyes on her, and she must think better of it.

Cynthia walks over and retrieves her purse before turning back to Reid. "I don't know why you are pushing me away. We will be married within the next six months, so you better get *this* out of your system before then," she says before turning and walking away. When she said "this," she looked at me as if I was just a minor inconvenience she would get past.

Reid continues to stare at me until her heels retreat to the elevator and the door closes behind her. When the quiet around us threatens to swallow me whole, Reid turns and walks over to the wine. He pours a little in the second glass and retrieves a clean one from the cabinet. When he has two glasses filled, he approaches me and offers a glass. "Drink?" he asks.

What?!

"Excuse me?" I ask, not understanding how he can be standing before me, offering me wine, while sending his fiancée away temporarily. *Who the hell is this man?*

"Wine. You look like you need a drink," he says. Still holding one glass out for me, he takes a heady drink from the other glass while keeping his eyes focused on me.

"No, I don't want a drink, Reid. I want to know what the hell that was. Who was that woman? Is she really your fiancée?" I ask, happy that I actually got all of that out before crumbing. The way my vision blurs from oxygen loss, I wasn't sure if I'd be able to speak at all, let alone ask the questions burning in the forefront of my mind.

Reid exhales loudly and closes his eyes. Turning around, he sets both glasses down on the counter. "Let's go sit in the living room so we can talk," he says. Dread bubbles to the surface. Why do I suddenly feel like I'm not going to like the outcome of this conversation?

Without saying a word, I follow Reid into his living room. "Do you need anything?" Reid asks, stalling no doubt.

"No, I don't need anything. What I need are fucking answers, Reid."

Another loud exhale. "Fine. Almost a year ago, I was presented with insider information that Bravado Resorts was considering a change in leadership. It's a massive company with a beautiful portfolio, and from the first moment I saw it, I wanted it. Jon set up the initial meeting, and I instantly knew that Bravado would be mine.

"We worked tirelessly for months, hell the better part of a year, to secure this deal. Every time we came close, Cruz would throw up another red flag and we'd find ourselves renegotiating."

I'm doing everything I can to follow. This is about a business deal?

"Cruz presented me with an offer too good to pass up. It was exactly what we had been hoping for and more. The only catch -" he says, but stops. He seems to be struggling to say the words he's trying to say.

"The only catch was what?" I ask, knowing that I'm not going to like this part. Not one bit. I can feel the way the air is sucked out of the room like some big vacuum.

"The only catch was that the company must always remain in his family. He had no sons, no nephews, no brothers. The only way to get it was through his daughter," he says, not able to look at me suddenly. As I absorb his words, it's probably a good thing that he isn't looking at me. I'd hate for him to see how crushed I am from those few little words. How bad they hurt.

"So you are marrying his daughter," I state. It's not a question, really. I already know the answer.

Reid looks at me and I can see the angst in his eyes. I can see the battle raging, the heartache, and the sadness. Sure, I can see how difficult this is for him, but I can also recognize defeat when I see it.

"And this deal is already done?" I ask, looking for the confirming words. He wouldn't be looking like death, and Cynthia wouldn't have been in this apartment calling him her fiancé, if it wasn't already done.

"I signed the papers the day you walked into my office. That's why I was such a prick to you. I had just signed my life away and promised myself to another woman. For a company. For money."

I'm not going to lie. His words slay. They hurt so bad, I'm afraid the sun might never shine again. "And there's no way out of this contract?" I whisper, hating myself for sounding so small in this moment.

"No. It's final."

"And you've kept this from me the entire time?" I whisper, unable to mask the pain in my voice. His silence is the only answer I need.

Then that's it. I need to get out of this room. I need to get out of this apartment and out of this building. I need to be as far away from Reid Hunter as humanly possible, because when I breakdown–and lord knows the breakdown is coming–I don't want him to see it. I don't want him to know how bad this is going to affect me. I don't want him to see the devastation and destruction, the ruins left behind.

"I need to go," I tell him, getting up and looking for the bag I dropped somewhere along the way.

"Don't go," he says, panic laced in his voice.

"Why? I can't stay. You're engaged, Reid. How could you have forgotten that one little detail? A month we've spent together getting to know each other. You've spent a month getting to know your son," I tell him, suddenly sick with consideration on how this will affect Ryan.

"This affects nothing," he says.

"How can you say that? This affects *everything*, Reid. But it won't affect your relationship with Ryan. Don't worry, I won't keep him from you. You can see him as often as you'd like, I'll make sure of it. I know he'll love to stay with you on weekends still, when your schedule will allow. I won't stand between you and your son," I tell him, holding myself together the best I can. The only problem is the glue is starting to slip.

"I don't want Ryan without you," he says, the words both so sweet and excruciatingly bitter at the same time.

"You can't have us both anymore. Ryan is all you have left."

He looks defeated. His eyes look haunted suddenly as the realization sets in that our time together has come to an end. I can't stay. I won't be the other woman while he's married to someone else. The only thing I can do is walk away with as much dignity as I can gather.

Grabbing my bag off the floor, I head towards the door. I have no idea how I actually manage to walk because my legs are numb and lifeless. Before I can call the elevator, I feel his presence behind me. His arms wrap around me one last time, and I'll admit that I revel in the feel of his strong arms and the way his body molds to mine. One last time.

"I don't want you to leave," he whispers, his arms still firmly around me.

"I can't stay," I tell him. Taking a deep breath, I gather all of the courage I can muster, and turn in his arms. "I need you to do one last thing for me, Reid."

"Anything," he says, his eyes pleading with me to stay.

"I need you to walk away. I need you to let me go and never look back. I need you to forget everything. Every moment, every second we've shared, I need you to forget them. Because I'm not strong enough to walk away. So I need you to do it for me, for the both of us. I need this one last thing from you, please. Walk away."

The tears are falling in earnest now, and I don't do anything to stop them. Reid's face is full of his own hurt. "I don't want to," he says; unshed tears gathering in his eyes.

"You have to. There's no other way," I whisper.

We stare at each other for what feels like a lifetime, but in reality, it's probably only a few seconds. When Reid leans forward, rests his forehead against mine, and closes his eyes, I know this is it.
Goodbye.

"It was always you, Dani. Always. I love you."

Closing my eyes, I feel the daggers of his words pierce my mangled heart with so much force that I know it'll never be whole again. His lips press firmly against mine, but there's no heat, no passion. It's full of sadness. It's a kiss of goodbye. It's absolute.

I can't even respond. His words weigh so heavily on me that I feel like I'm drowning in the darkness suddenly surrounding me. And as much as I want to hang on and pray he won't let me go, Reid does what I asked him to do. He gives me this one final thing. The one thing I knew I wouldn't be able to do myself.

He walks over to the elevator, gets on, and walks away.
Forever.

Chapter Twenty-Two – Hell On Earth

Reid

I have no idea how I actually make it outside. I don't remember anything about the elevator ride down, nothing about walking through the lobby. As I stand outside, in front of the building I worked my entire life to achieve, all I can think about is the despair and angst in Dani's eyes. A look that will haunt me for the rest of my life.

A look that I put there.

Suddenly, that big glass and steel building feels emptier than before I moved in.

"Reid?" Steven asks, walking up next to me on the sidewalk. I hold up my finger while digging my cell phone out of my suit jacket. Without saying a word, I dial Jon's number.

"Hello?"

"Fire the receptionist in the lobby. I don't want her to ever set foot in my building again," I say to my right hand man.

"Done. Are you gonna tell me why?" he asks.

"She allowed Cynthia Cruz upstairs and into my apartment without notifying Carly."

"Ahhh."

"Take care of Human Resources for me," I add.

"Consider it done," Jon says moments before I hang up.

I start to walk down the sidewalk. Fuck, I have no clue where I'm going but I do know that I can't be here when Dani comes downstairs. Everything good inside of me is telling me to turn around and go back to her. To take her in my arms and promise her it will be okay. But then reality sets in and I know that it won't be. Nothing will ever be okay again.

"Reid," Steven says behind me again. I stop, but don't turn around. "Where are you going?" he asks, his voice filled with concern.

"I don't know," I whisper.

"Come on," he says as he leads me towards the Town Car.

When I made plans to spend time with Dani in the apartment tonight, I gave Steven the night off. What he's still doing here now is a mystery, but I'm thankful as fuck to have him here.

"You should be home," I tell him as I slip down into the backseat.

After securing the door, Steven walks around and gets into the driver's seat. "I was just heading there when I saw you getting off the elevator," he says as he signals and pulls into traffic. "Where to?"

His question sits like a ton of bricks on my chest. Where to? That's the question of the century, isn't it? Like so many of the other questions heaved at me tonight, this one is one I can't answer.

"I don't know. Not home. Somewhere with alcohol," I tell him, not even noticing the buildings we pass along the way.

Twenty minutes later, we pull up to a modest white home that I don't recognize. Steven gets out of the vehicle and walks towards the front door. I'm left sitting there in the back seat of the car wondering where the hell we are, and why the hell he just left me here. When he uses a key from his pocket to unlock the front door, I finally have my answer. Slipping out of the back seat, I head towards the doorway that Steven just disappeared through.

Inside, the house is warm and inviting. There are pictures on the walls, knick-knacks on most flat surfaces, and well-worn, comfortable looking furniture. It smells clean with hints of fresh bread and apples. Seeing light filter through a doorway at the end of the hall, I head that way in search of Steven.

"Pick your poison," Steven says, motioning towards a decent display of alcohol in a cabinet behind a wooden desk. I point to a familiar bottle and watch as he pours several fingers into two glasses.

Taking the seat across from his desk, Steven surprises me when he comes around and takes the seat beside me. "Spill," he directs as he hands me a glass.

After a sip of strong bourbon, I look over at my driver, seeing him–really seeing him–for the first time. Gone is the professionally dressed man who caters to my every need and chauffeurs me around town. In his place is a man with his leg casually slung over the other leg, and sparkling eyes. He looks as comfortable as the old furniture in the living room. The wrinkles around his eyes hold worry, but he appears calm and happy. I can see how easily he slips into a cozy form of tranquility when he's home. He's at peace.

"What happened after I took Dani upstairs?" he asks, breaking the spell I slipped into.

I breathe another deep sigh and a large gulp of bourbon before I begin. "When I finished the conference call, Shannon, the temp who's filling in for Carly while she's on her honeymoon, was already gone. I knew Dani was going to be there, so I turned off all the lights and headed upstairs. When the elevator opened, Cynthia was there. She was telling Dani all about the contract. Fuck, she thought she was the hired help," I mutter, still unable to fully process what went down tonight.

"I take it you hadn't told Dani about the deal with Cruz?" Steven asks with no accusation in his tone.

"No. Honestly, I never really thought about it too much. When I was with her, everything just sort of faded away. The bad day, the business deals, the hours of monotonous phone calls, it all just disappeared. The only time I ever really thought of the Bravado deal was when someone brought it up, and Dani wasn't anywhere near."

"So what happened when you told her?"

"You mean how did she take the news that I'm contractually obligated to wed another woman? About as well as you can imagine," I mumble before taking another drink.

"What next?"

"Nothing. Nothing happens. The deal goes on as planned, and I'll be a married man by the end of the year. If I'm lucky, I'll still get to spend time with my son when I can. She promised she wouldn't keep him from me," I respond and even to my own ears, my voice sounds monotone.

When the quiet seconds turn into uncomfortable minutes, I turn to face one of my only real friends in this world. "Really? That's it?" he asks, the question evident in his eyes. They're not accusing or angry, just concerned. It's as if he can't understand what I'm saying.

"That's it. I signed the deal. I've wanted Bravado from the minute I laid eyes on that company. I've waited my entire adult life for a deal like this to come along, and I'm not about to let it slip through my fingers now. I've worked too hard to lose this deal now," I defend.

"The deal. That's all that matters?" he asks, perplexed.

"What else is there?" Clearly my friend isn't listening to me.

"Your life!" Steven's outburst startles me, and I damn near drop my glass. After taking a few deep breaths himself, Steven faces me squarely. "Let me ask you this, Reid. Do you love Cynthia?"

I don't even have to answer that question. The look I give him is glacial.

"Exactly. Now, do you love Dani?"

I don't have to answer him on this one either. I know the answer, and so does he.

"Deals are broken all the time, Reid. Contracts are renegotiated, penalties are paid. There's always a way out. The question for you now is this: Do you want to find a way out? Is your business still the most important thing to you? Profiting and getting ahead? Is that what you want for the rest of your life?"

I watch as Steven drains the rest of his glass and sets it on the corner of his desk, not even bothering to wait for my answer to his question. "The door across the hall is the guest bedroom. Help yourself to anything you want, and let me know if there's anything you need. We'll head into the office around seven," he says before turning and heading towards the door.

When he reaches it, he stops, but doesn't turn around. "This is your chance to have everything you want, Reid. You just have to decide what it is you *really* want."

And with that, Steven walks out of his study, leaving me alone with my thoughts.

And my thoughts right now are jacked the fuck up.

How in the hell do I walk away from everything I've ever wanted? Hunter Enterprises was built from my own blood, sweat, and tears. I've given my soul to the very company in which I created from nothing. This deal–this merger–will catapult Hunter Enterprises into untouchable territory. Bravado will be mine. The sky will be the limit. The bottom line, nothing but black zeroes.

A loveless marriage to a woman I can barely stand. Endless nights wrapped around the wrong woman. A son who will spend every other weekend at my house. A life that's empty on the inside, despite what my bank balance says.

Fuck! There's no clear winner here, no cut and dried, black or white answer. Whichever decision I make will be the wrong one. Someone will be hurt. Something will crumble.

My company.

Or Dani.

As I slip into the guest room at Steven's, I'm no closer to resolving the issue as I was when Steven left me alone. The only difference is now I'm slightly drunk. As hard as I tried, the bourbon just didn't seem to take away the pain in my chest. It didn't mask the excruciating emptiness I've felt since I left Dani alone in my apartment.

Walking away from her tonight was the hardest thing I've ever done. I'll never forget the look, the hurt, in her eyes before I left her standing in my apartment. The kiss I took before leaving was purely selfish. I needed that one final taste of her sweetness, that one final touch of her perfection.

I don't even strip off my clothes before I fall onto the top of the bed in the guest room. As hard as I try, I can't shut off the replay of tonight in my mind. I knew I was going to have to let her go. From the very beginning, I knew that I wouldn't be able to keep her.

But, damn does it fucking hurt now that she's gone.

Right there in the center of my chest, where my heart beats wildly, it breaks into a billion pieces. As hard as I've tried to keep everyone at arm's length, push everyone away so that I wasn't able to hurt them, I failed. One woman. One beautiful, energetic, perfect woman wormed her way into the hollowness of my chest and proved to me that I do, in fact, have a heart. With her laughter and light, she showed me that there was more to life than money and profits. Together, with our son, she showed me that there's more to me than just a coldhearted asshole who only cares about where his next business transaction is coming from. And now I've lost that heart.

Dani was my heart.
Dani was my soul.
And now she's gone forever.

Chapter Twenty-Three – School's Out

For Summer

Dani

The last week of school passed by in a blur. I wish I shared the same energy as the kids when it came to the final days of school, but knowing that I'd be trapped at home with my thoughts wasn't as appealing as it usually is.

Reid has called every night to talk to Ryan. When I see his name appear on the caller ID, I don't answer. I can't. I'm not sure how I would react to hearing his voice. Just seeing his name displayed on the phone is enough to send me into another crying fit.

At some point in the conversation, Reid always asks Ryan how I'm doing. I know this because Ryan tells me. I can't figure out if the pain in my chest has to do with that little tinge of excitement I get when he asks, or the pain that takes over once I remember that they aren't anything more than simple gestures of politeness.

I do all of my crying at night when the house is silent and the moon taunts me through my window. Trysta, being the stellar sister that she is, curses his name, vowing to decapitate his man-parts every chance she gets. I always make sure to smile and pretend to agree with her, even though cursing his name and threatening to de-man him doesn't seem to help any.

What's worse is that tomorrow is Ryan's eighth birthday. The party has been in the works for a couple of weeks now, and everyone is invited. Carly and Blake, along with their daughter

Natalia, will be here. Reid's sister, Tara. My dad and sister. A handful of Ryan's school friends. And of course, Reid. Just the thought of him being here makes my stomach turn. Especially when I start to wonder if he's going to bring his new fiancée with him.

The school bell ringing pulls me out of the abyss in my head. As I scan the room, the kids gather up their books for the last time. This moment starts their summer vacation, and technically, I guess it starts my own. Vacation. Woohoo.

"Mom, are you ready to go get the stuff for the party?" Ryan asks, bouncing into my classroom like he just downed a dozen pixie sticks.

"Almost ready, Ry," I say as I shut off everything in my classroom. I'll be back early next week to make sure everything is cleaned up and ready to sit for the summer.

"I can't wait til Dad sees my Batman cake," Ryan says as I lock up my door.

"He's going to love it," I tell him absently.

When we climb into my hot car, Ryan turns to me and asks, "Why hasn't Dad been by to see me?"

"He's been busy with work, Ryan. He calls you every night, though." My heart breaks for my little boy. I can't even imagine what he feels like right now. He just found out about his father, who was suddenly active in his life, and now he's absent again. Oh, sure, he calls every night, but that's not the same. Not for an almost eight-year-old little boy who just wants to spend time with his dad.

"I know. He tells me that all the time. Last night he said I might be able to spend the night this weekend. Maybe after my party I can go home with him? And you can come too like last time," Ryan suggests as I pull out of the parking lot and head towards the bakery that I ordered the cake from.

"Oh, I'm not sure if I'll be able to come this time, buddy. But if your dad says it's okay that you go home with him after the party, I don't see why not," I answer. Great. A night where no one will be around to hear my agony and witness my breakdown. Splendid.

"What do you think Dad got me for my birthday?" Ryan asks. "Maybe he'll take me to the Lego museum. Chad says they have a superhero display and I'm sure they have Batman. You can't have superheroes without Batman," he adds. I tune out the rest of his ramblings because I can't seem to get past the fact that in less than twenty-four hours, Reid is going to be in my house. In my backyard. Swimming.

God is cruel sometimes.

* * *

"Where is he?" Trysta mumbles next to my ear as I help my dad pull the hotdogs off the grill. I scan all of the faces in the backyard one more time, making sure his face hasn't magically appeared in the few seconds since I last looked for him, before turning towards her.

"I don't know," I whisper.

"Surely he wouldn't stand up his own son on his birthday, would he?" she asks as I set the platter of dogs down in the middle of the table. I have buns, fruit salad, pasta salad, and even potato salad all ready to go. I tried to slow down the cooking to give Reid a little more time to get here, but how slow can you cook hotdogs?

"I wouldn't have thought he would do that up until a week ago. Now, I don't know what he's capable of doing," I quietly reply to my sister. Never in a million years would I picture Reid as the type of man to miss his son's birthday party, but as we hit the two-hour no-show mark, I'm starting to think I was way off base with this guy.

Disappointment sets in like a knife to the lungs, making it almost impossible to breathe. Disappointment for me, sure, but so much disappointment for Ryan. He's trying to put on a brave face, but I can tell the absence of his father is hurting him. He hasn't smiled in the last hour; even when all of his friends played Marco Polo in the pool with him.

"Time to eat," I holler over the cheers and screams coming from the pool. I hired Trysta's friend to lifeguard the pool so that it was one less thing I had to worry about. Heaven knows my mind isn't capable of keeping up with a bunch of kids in a swimming pool.

After making Ryan a plate and helping half a dozen other boys get food, I turn when Carly and Blake walk up behind me. "Great party," she says with a sheepish smile. I give her a friendly smile, but focus my attention on their daughter in Blake's arms. I was so happy they were able to make it to Ryan's party. They're all going to be a part of his life, so the more time he gets to spend with them, the better.

"Thank you so much for coming. Are you enjoying the pool?" I ask the dark haired, green-eyed beauty wrapped in her father's arms.

"She's having a great time," Blake answers for his daughter.

"It appears someone is missing," Carly says as she casually looks around the yard.

"Yeah, it appears that way," I reply, going for casual. Unfortunately, I think casual stepped out the door and was replaced by fury about thirty minutes ago.

Neither one of us have time to say anything else before Tara walks up, her shoulders tight with tension. "Where the hell is my brother?" she barks to no one in particular.

"We were just wondering that," Carly says.

"I tried his cell phone again and it just goes to voice mail. I can't believe he would miss this," Tara says, her voice a combination of anger and worry. "Do you think something has happened?"

"No, I'm sure he's fine. You know Steven or Jon would have called you as soon as possible if something happened. I'm sure he just got…sidetracked," Carly says, but I can't tell if she's trying to convince Tara or herself.

"I tried to call Steven and Jon but their phones went to voice mail, too. I'm so pissed off at him right now, I could wring his neck," Tara says before stomping off and fixing a plate.

"I'm sure he's fine," Carly says, trying to reassure me. "He gets so focused on work sometimes, that I'm sure he just lost track of time."

"I'm sure you're right. Thank you both, again, for coming. Excuse me," I say with a forced smile that I hope appeared friendly before slipping into the house to collect my thoughts.

Inside, I work on opening packages of small plates for the Batman cake. At this point, I have to keep my hands busy, in addition to my mind. If I focus on the mundane task of organizing plates and napkins for dessert, then maybe I'll stop fretting over the fact that Reid no-showed at his son's birthday party. Maybe if I stay inside long enough, I'll be able to avoid the looks of pity from his friends and family, and the look of devastation from his son. Oh, he's doing everything he can to cover up his desolation, but there's no hiding the damage done in his fragile little eyes.

When the back door opens, I blink repetitively, trying to will away the tears threatening to spill. I told myself I wouldn't cry. Not today. Not on the day that is supposed to be a celebration of my son's birthday.

"He seems to be having a great day," my dad says behind me.

Turning slightly and giving him a small smile, I say, "Yep, it's a great day."

"I can't help but notice Reid's missing," my dad says. Leave it to Dad to not beat around the bush and call a spade a spade.

"You're not the only one who has noticed his absence," I tell my dad, finally turning around and facing him.

"And?"

"And what? I've called. He didn't answer. His sister has called and nothing. He knew what today was. I overheard Ryan telling him last night all about his cake and all about the games we were having. Reid knew, and he knew what it meant to that little boy." I can't help the bitterness in my voice. I'm blanketed in it.

I've been angry with Reid all week for what he did to me. His lies and his deceit. How can a person completely omit the fact that they had entered into a business deal to marry another woman? How can you overlook that while you're bedding one and planning to marry another?

The worst part is that for every ounce of anger I possess for Reid, I love him that much more. And *that* I hate. I don't want to love him. I don't want to miss him. I don't want to wish he were here, not only for our son's sake, but for my own as well. Because at the end of the day, no matter how many times I ignored or denied it, I miss him and wish he had picked me.

"Maybe something came up? Why else would he choose to not be here for his son's birthday?" My dad, always the peacemaker.

"Yeah, maybe. It still doesn't change the fact that tonight, I'll be left repairing the damage and wiping the tears for my heartbroken little boy."

Dad is silent for several minutes. If it weren't for the fact I could hear him breathing, I would think he already slipped back outside. "You're a great mom, Danielle. I know things were difficult for you growing up without a mom around, but you persevered. I never had to worry about you like I did Trysta. I didn't have to worry then, and I don't have to worry now. Not about Ryan. Because at the end of the day, I know he's going to be okay. He's going to be okay because he has you."

I don't stop the tear that slides down my cheek. Instead, I walk over to my dad and wrap my arms around his chest. Breathing in his familiar scent, I say, "I turned out to be the woman I am today because of you. Because *you* were my dad. As long as I had you, I had everything. Still do," I mumble against his shoulder.

"I don't know about that, but we did alright, didn't we?"

"Yeah, we did."

"And you and Ryan are going to be alright, too."

"Yeah, we are."

The door opens behind my dad, and I quickly bat away the tears on my cheek. "Hey, Dani, sorry to interrupt. Ryan and his friends are ready to get back in the pool if that's okay with you," Tara says from the doorway. The look she gives me is full of sadness and nervousness. I have no idea if she knows what happened between Reid and me, but neither her nor Carly have said anything. Yet there's melancholy in their eyes when they look at me that lets me know they're aware.

"Sure, that's fine. I'll be back out in just a minute," I say, giving Reid's sister a friendly smile.

"Get outside with your son. He needs to see your face right now," my dad says with a knowing smile. Following another hug from my dad, I head back out to the patio with a fake smile on my face and a pain deep in my heart.

An hour later, I sing with all of those near and dear to us on the back deck.

"...Happy birthday to Ryan...Happy birthday to you!"

Ryan's Batman cake is ablaze with eight black, flickering candles. After several long seconds, I look down and notice him staring at the fire dancing across the top of his cake.

"Ryan, blow them out," I prod with an encouraging smile.

"Where's my dad?" he whispers, but loud enough for everyone to hear. Audible gasps echo around me, but I keep my eyes trained solely on my son. The sadness in his eyes guts me, the pain like a dull knife to the chest.

"Your dad got called to work. He wanted to be here more than anything in the world, Ry, but sometimes he's just pulled away and can't get out of it," I reply. I'm not sure why I felt the need to defend Reid in Ryan's eyes, but it felt like the right thing to do. Even after everything that happened between Reid and I, I made a promise to myself that I would never stoop so low as to badmouth and belittle his father the way so many angry, bitter women do. Hell, and it's not just the women. I vowed that Ryan deserved better than that, and that he would form his own opinions of Reid based off his experiences; not based off what he hears me say about him.

"Okay," Ryan whispers. I watch helplessly as the black wax continues to pool around the base of the eight candles.

Walking up to where he's sitting, I bend down next to him. "Make a wish, sweetheart." His gray eyes shine with so much hope and pain, that it steals the very breath I take. I watch with all of the other guests as Ryan looks around at the family and friends gathered around the picnic table, closes his eyes, and after a few moments, blows out his candles.

The crowd cheers, but my heart does anything but.

When the cake is nothing more than crumbs on a piece of cardboard, I start to clean up the icing smeared on the tabletop and the scraps of wrapping paper littering the deck. One lone piece of cake sits on a plate next to all of the opened gifts. Reid's piece of cake. Ryan insisted.

"Mom," Ryan exclaims as he runs up to me, soaking wet from another dip in the pool. The party is winding down and the guests are gathering up their belongings to head home. I made Ryan get out of the pool to say goodbye to his guests and thank them for coming to his party, which he has graciously done.

"What's up, Ry?" I ask moments before his wet body is wrapped around me.

"Nothing. I just wanted to give you a hug and tell you thank you for the party," he says. I wrap my arms around his wet body and squeeze until I'm sure he's running out of air.

"Mom!" he laughs.

"I love you most in this world, Ryan," I whisper before bending down a little and kissing the top of his wet head.

"I know that, Mom," he says with that smile I know and love.

Squatting in front of my son, I say, "You are my entire world, and there is nothing I won't do for you."

"I love you, Mom."

"I love you, Ryan," I say before pulling him into another hug. I hold on with everything I have, knowing that someday, there's going to come a time where he isn't going to welcome my hugs as easily. Someday, I'll have to fight with him just to steal a little bit of his time. Someday is going to be here before I know it, and I'm not about to let these little moments slip by.

"Mom?" Ryan whispers, his voice full of humor and wonder. "Batman is here."

His statement catches me off guard. At first, I think he's referring to his decorations or the new toys he received. But when he taps me on the shoulder and points in the direction of the gate, I do a double take.

Batman is here.

Chapter Twenty-Four – Rubber Pants

Are Itchy

Reid

Have you ever worn a black rubber suit, head to toe, in the month of June in the desert? Here's a piece of free advice: Don't do it. The material doesn't breathe; therefore your body basically sweats profusely until you find yourself drowning in your own perspiration. In a fucking rubber suit. That's what they'll focus on in my obituary, too. *This dumbass drowned in his own sweat while wearing a superhero costume.* Fucking great.

But the moment I rounded that corner and saw Ryan's face? Nothing. Else. Mattered. His smile was so bright it could power a casino for days. That smile makes all of the discomfort and teasing I received from Jon, Scott, and Steven all worth it.

"Batman!" Ryan exclaims as he peels himself out of his mom's arms and runs towards me. I gingerly squat down and brace myself for impact. And the moment Ryan's little body slams into mine, everything else melts away all over again.

"I heard someone was having a birthday today," I say in my regular voice because there's no way I can mask it over the lump lodged in my throat. And even if I wanted to, I have no clue what Batman sounds like.

"It's *my* birthday today," Ryan screeches while all of his friends start to gather around.

261

"It *is* your birthday today," I reply and look him square in the eye. "I knew it was your birthday because you are the most important person in the world to me. Every superhero needs a sidekick, so I thought I'd see if you wanted to be mine?"

"Really? I can be your sidekick? But what about Robin?"

"Well, Robin is getting older and is ready to take a break. He thinks it's time that maybe he should settle down and have some kids." Okay, so not my most creative explanation, but I'm winging it here, alright?

"So I can be your sidekick now? Cause I'm your biggest fan. Even bigger than Robin," Ryan says with that big toothy grin. God, I've missed that smile this past week. Hearing his voice on the phone was nothing compared to seeing his face light up as we talk face to face.

"And I'm your biggest fan," I tell him honestly. "I'm sorry I missed your party."

Ryan looks at me with confusion for only about two seconds before recognition sets in. "Dad?" he whispers.

"Yeah, buddy, it's me."

Ryan starts jumping up and down and laughing. "I knew it! I knew you were Batman! Mom, Dad is Batman! Dad is really Batman! *THE* Batman!"

I look over Ryan's shoulder and see the love of my life standing there with tears in her eyes. At least this time, they seem to be happy tears. That makes the ache in my chest only slightly better at the sight of her crying.

"My dad is Batman," Ryan exclaims as he turns to his friends who all have starry-eyed goofy smiles on their faces.

I actually spend the next ten minutes having my picture taken with Ryan and his friends. As parents arrive to pick up their kids, I see them off alongside Dani. She has yet to speak to me, but I have yet to speak to her either. I have so much to say, so much to tell her, but I don't want to do it while we have an audience.

"Batman, big brother?" I hear the chuckle behind me and can't fight my own smile as I turn around. Tara is grinning ear to ear as she snaps a picture on her cell phone. "That's going out to everyone in my contact list," she smarts off.

"Come here," I say as I pull her into a hug. Tara is stiff at first, but it doesn't take her but a few seconds to loosen up. "I'm sorry I've been so cold and distant. For so long, I've been a shitty brother to you."

"You were fine. I know you went through a rough time with Reagan and then Mom. I don't blame you for closing the rest of us off," she says.

"Yeah, but it's no excuse. I promise to do better." I give my sister one more hug and add, "I'm probably going to mess up a few times. This whole being a better person thing is harder than I thought."

Tara's laughter erupts from her belly. "Apology accepted."

As I pull away, I can't help but ask, "Scott Dixon, huh?" Tara instantly blushes a deep red and looks away.

On our way here, Scott and Jon rode along, declaring their intent to not miss the opportunity to see me grovel...and wear a black rubber suit. Steven drove while Jon and Scott helped me get zipped up in this monstrosity. As soon as we stepped into the backyard, Scott's eyes zeroed in on Tara, and I watched with new eyes as hers did the same. They've been standing off in the corner talking ever since.

"It's okay. Scott's a great guy. You may not have noticed, but I've seen the way he's always watching you. He can't take his eyes off you."

"Yeah, well, it's too bad your friendship comes before anything else. He won't make a move because he's afraid of pissing you off," she says with a sad smile.

"You let me worry about that," I tell her, vowing that my next conversation will be with my buddy, Scott. Well, after I talk to Dani.

"Aunt Tara, did you know my dad was Batman?" Ryan asks, coming up behind us.

"I didn't know that. He hid his secret very well."

"I knew he had to have a super cool job. When I was little, my mom always told me that my dad had to be gone a lot for work but that he loved me and was always watching out for me. I knew it was something totally awesome like a superhero."

"Your mom is a very wise woman," I say, looking over his shoulder at the woman standing on the deck cleaning up the remnants of the party.

"I'm going to head home. I'll see you both soon," Tara says.

"I'll walk you out," Scott says, walking up to us, wearing a shy grin.

After watching my sister and one of my good friends walk away, I turn towards the backyard and start moving chairs and taking down tables. Steven, Jon, Scott, and Dani's dad, Robert, join me in the yard and before I know it, we have the backyard back in pre-party order. Every once in a while, I catch a glimpse of Dani in the kitchen cleaning up the dishes and whatnot with her sister. It kills me not to go in there now and demand to explain myself. If she only knew the real reason I was late to the party...

"I'm going to run Jon and Scott back to the office to get their cars. Do you want me to come back for you?" Steven asks.

"No, go ahead. If I need a ride, I'll call. Or better yet, I'll take a taxi."

"Well, son, let's hope you don't need a ride," Steven says with a smile.

"Yeah, well," I start and look up at the kitchen window once again. Dani is laughing at something with her sister. I've never seen a more beautiful woman than when Dani is laughing. "Let's pray she doesn't kick me out and lets me explain."

"She will," he says with a hard slap on the back. "She will because she loves you too." I give my friend a half-smile, then turn to watch them leave.

A few minutes later, Robert comes out and takes a seat next to me on the deck. "Ryan's in the shower," he says casually.

"Good. I bet he'll sleep good tonight," I say in way of small talk.

"Oh, I'm sure. The Batman costume was a nice touch," he says with a smile.

"It's hotter than hell," I tell him, resulting in a hearty laugh.

"You could probably change now."

"Yeah, about that. I thought about it, but I just realized my clothes are in the back of my car that left about ten minutes ago." That makes Robert laugh even harder.

"Laugh it up now," I reply, unable to fight the smile.

"Well, this could get interesting then. I'm almost sad I have to leave."

We both sit in comfortable silence as we watch Trysta and Dani scurry around the kitchen. "You know, when Danielle was little, she had the biggest heart. She'd bat those baby blues at me, and I was a goner. She has always worn her heart on her sleeve, and would give the very shirt off her own back for someone who needed it.

"The day she told me she was pregnant, I smiled. Not because she was making me a grandfather and not because she was crying happy tears of joy, but because she was destined to be a mother. I knew that she would be the best mother possible for her son or daughter. She's caring and sensitive and loves with her entire heart. When she's mad, you'll know it, but if she loves you, it won't take much to gain her forgiveness." Robert pauses and gives me time to soak up his words. "Do you love my daughter?"

It's a simple question and requires the utmost truth. "With my entire being."

"Then get your ass inside and make this right." I watch as Robert gets up and walks inside. He throws his arms around Trysta first, then Dani second. Though I can't hear the words he's saying, I can see the reaction to them on her face. She nods her head up and down a few times before he slips back outside.

"Ryan is already in bed, and Trysta is going to watch a movie upstairs. I think that leaves you and my daughter with some time to talk," Robert says. I jump out of the chair, the rubber suit squeaking a bit against the plastic seat, but before I can go inside, Robert sticks out his hand. "Good luck to you, Reid. I hope I see you again soon."

And with that he slips out the gate and heads to his car.

I give myself a few minutes to get my thoughts in order before I go inside. Like the bullet points I review before a meeting, I need to have them organized and ready to fire at the drop of a hat in case Dani isn't hearing me.

When the kitchen light goes out, I tuck my tail between my legs, grab ahold of my Batman cape, and open the back door.

Ready to duke it out with Dani.

Ready to fight for my family.

Chapter Twenty-Five – Not All Superheroes Wear Capes

Dani

I flip off the light a few moments before I hear the backdoor open. Knowing that my dad walked out just a few minutes ago, I turn around fully expecting to see him coming back inside. What I wasn't expecting was to see Reid.

"I thought you left," I mumble the first words to Reid since his arrival at Ryan's party earlier this evening. The truth was I had hoped that Reid would have talked to me before he left. When I didn't see him around the backyard and thought he had cut out, the sadness that had evaporated when he arrived had started to return. And that's just silly talk because Reid is here for his son. Period.

"I told Ryan I'd give him a hug good night," he says casually, those eyes focusing all of their energy on me. They're like little laser beams burning into my bruised and battered soul.

"He's in bed. Go on back," I tell him as I step aside to allow him to pass.

"I'll be right back," he says as he slips around the corner and heads down the hallway. I realize instantly that Reid is still wearing the superhero costume from earlier. He took the mask off when they were cleaning up chairs and tables, but he has yet to remove the rest of the suit.

Grabbing a bottle of water for my parched throat, I head into the living room and tuck my legs underneath me on the couch. The deeper into the evening we went, the more exhausted my body became, so sitting down right now is almost orgasmic. My muscles are all sighing in sweet relief. It was a hot day and I still feel grimy and sweaty in my jean shorts and tank top. A shower is definitely in my very near future.

Ten minutes later, Reid comes into the living room. He seems hesitant to cross the threshold of the room. I can only assume he has other plans for his Saturday night. Maybe plans with Cythina. Planning their pending nuptials.

And suddenly I'm nauseous.

"Dani, do you think I can speak with you for a minute?" he asks, taking a tentative step into the living room.

"Sure," I reply, forcing my voice to sound chipper. I'm sure he wants to talk about Ryan, maybe work out his weekend schedule from this point forward. "Have a seat." I expected him to take the rocker recliner, but he doesn't. Reid walks over and slides down onto the couch next to me. Even through the squeaky plastic of his suit, his unique scent permeates my senses. I have to close my eyes briefly as the memories of our past flood my mind. It's the worst kind of torture.

Grabbing my foot, Reid absently starts to knead at the soles of my foot. "Dani, I have so many things to say to you," he starts with his head and eyes cast downward as if watching his hands work my sore muscles. "First off, I never meant to hurt you. You have to know that." Reid's eyes focus back on mine. They appear to be carrying the weight of a whole mixture of emotions, and the intensity causes me to swallow hard over the lump in my throat.

"It's okay, Reid. You don't have to explain anymore. You explained it all Monday night. We really don't need to go through it again," I tell him, not sure my heart could take a repeat performance of Monday night. His hands are still on my foot, and it takes everything I have not to moan from the pleasure of skin on skin contact.

"Dani, Monday night was a hundred ways of fucked up."

"Reid, it's okay, really. We share a son, and you're welcome to stop by whenever you want to see him. We'll work out a schedule that's convenient for both of us. I just can't do this tonight. I don't want to rehash any of this right now. I'm exhausted and gross from the party. I just want to go take a shower and go to bed. Besides, I'm sure Cynthia is waiting for you," I say, her name biting my tongue, as I pull my foot back. With that, I stand up and wait for Reid to follow suit.

"You're beautiful," he whispers, almost audibly.

"What?" I'm sure I misheard him.

Reid gets up and stands directly in front of me. "You heard me. You're beautiful. You said you were gross, but all I see is the most beautiful woman in the entire world, with her long, gorgeous blond hair and mesmerizing blue eyes. Long tan legs and a stunning smile. And this birthmark. Right here," he says as he touches the side of my hip. Even through my shorts, I can feel the heat of his touch.

"You can't say that to me anymore," I whisper. God, it hurts too much to hear him say this, yet my heart is screaming "more, more."

"Yes I can. Do you know why?" I can't answer with real words, so I just shake my head. "I can say that to you because it's the truth. And do you know what else is the truth? That I'm in love with you. One hundred percent, crazy in love…with you."

Holy shit. Kill me now.

"Reid," I start, his name choking me along with the air I try to breathe. "Please don't do this. Please don't say that. It hurts too much."

"I don't want to hurt you, Dani. That's the last thing I want to do, sweetheart." And because I'm weak, I let Reid pull me into his arms when he steps forward. I don't want to. I know I should disentangle myself from him as soon as possible. It's the only way to walk away with any of my heart, even if it's only a sliver.

"Then why are you here?" I look up into his eyes, trying to gauge where he's going with this entire conversation. Of course, the fact that I haven't moved out of his embrace hasn't gone unnoticed. By either of us.

"I'm here for you and our son."

"But you can't have us both. You will always have your son. I am your past; a distant memory that should be kept there from now on."

"See, that's where you're wrong, Dani. You are my future. Do you want me to prove it?" I can't answer him. Part of me is screaming at the top of my lungs to have him prove it, while the other part doesn't want to hear what he has to say for fear that, at the end of the day, he'll still walk away.

"Today, I missed one of the most important days in our son's life. Do you realize how much it pained me to do that? I would rather go ten rounds with Mike Tyson than ever experience the pain I felt today when I was stuck in the office instead of helping you celebrate our son's birthday. And knowing that it caused Ryan an ounce of hurt? Excruciating. Do you know what I was doing today?" Again, I can't answer, so I just wait. "I was meeting with Cruz. I've spend the past two days, eighteen hours a day, with my legal team figuring out how to get out of the contract that I already signed."

Okay. Now he has my full attention.

"That's right, sweetheart. I wanted out. I wanted out so damn bad that I was willing to risk everything, lose everything, to be with you. I was ready to go into this meeting and renege on that very contract I signed. The one that I wanted more than anything in my world because all I saw was what I was gaining. The one I was willing to sell my soul to the devil himself for. Profit. That's what I was after. Well, I'm tired of living my life like that. I'm tired of letting business and returns and my overwhelming need to win rule my life, because the way I see it, if I let you go, I'm not winning; not in the least bit. I'm the biggest fucking loser of all." Reid continues to gaze down at me, his eyes bright as I shake with nerves. I wish I knew where this was going.

"When you walked into my office, I knew in that moment that I had made the third biggest mistake of my life. I signed the contract mere hours before you showed up, and I knew I was wrong."

"The third mistake?" I whisper through my desert-dry throat.

"Yeah, the third. The first mistake was the night I let you slip out of my tent without finding out your name or how to get a hold of you. That mistake is quickly followed by walking out of my apartment Monday night without fighting to the death for you. All mistakes that I plan to rectify right now.

"Today, my team and I met with Cruz who owns Bravado Resorts. We found the loophole that I've needed. We were able to get out of the contract without being dragged into court for a yearlong litigation and breach of contract lawsuit. Oh, this whole mess won't go away without some sort of financial loss on my part, but no amount of money is enough if it gets me out of that damn contract."

"I don't know what that means," I state, trying to keep the hope from bubbling to the surface.

"It means the contract doesn't exist anymore. Hunter Enterprises is not acquiring Bravado. There is no merger planned. But more importantly, I'm not engaged to that woman."

I can't fight the tears that leak from my eyes by this point. They fall in earnest, unchecked, as Reid swipes them gently from my cheeks.

"I'm not marrying her because there's only one woman I want to spend the rest of my life with, and it sure as fuck isn't her. I want to marry *you*, Dani. I want to wake up next to you, fall sleep with my arms wrapped around you, spend every waking moment with our son, and maybe even give him a few brothers and sisters. I want a life, and I want it with you."

"You're not marrying her?" I whisper, afraid that the words he's saying will somehow disappear or I'll suddenly wake up from whatever dream I'm having.

"No, Dani. I'm not marrying her."

Sobs erupt from deep in my throat as my vision blurs from the tears yet to escape. Reid reaches up again and strokes my cheek, wiping away the seeping tears. "I don't know the exact moment my life changed, but I know it was for the better. I was nothing but an asshole, money hungry and desperate to dominate everything and anyone I could. I don't want to be that man anymore, Dani. I want to be the man you need and one you can be proud to call your own. I want to be everything you need because you are everything I need. You and Ryan are everything to me. I don't deserve you, but I'll be damn sure I prove myself worthy every day that you give me."

I stare up at him for several tense moments, while my heart tries to explode from my chest. I'm sure he's waiting on me to say something, but for some strange reason, I can't form a single sentence. I want to say so much, but have no clue how to begin.

"Please say something, sweetheart." His words give me just the jolt I need.

"I love you, too," I whisper. It seems like the only thing to say in this moment as I stand before the man I'm crazy in love with as he professes his love to me, saying everything he can to prove it. And finding out he found a way to break that contract sure is the best way to prove it.

A small smile spreads across his devastatingly handsome face. "Say it again," he orders.

"I love you, too," I say a little louder this time.

"I will never get tired of hearing you say that," he mumbles moments before claiming my lips with his own. It's the sort of kiss that curls your toes and soaks your panties. It professes love and commitment, and even dirty things to come.

"I can't promise I won't mess up a time or two, but I promise that I will always do everything in my power to make it right and to be the man you deserve." Reid claims my lips once more in another searing kiss.

"You did an amazing thing for Ryan today," I tell him, pulling back from the kiss.

"I'm sorry I missed most of the party. I'm even more sorry that I had a reason to miss it."

"It's okay, Reid. I understand why you did what you did–all of it. I may not agree with it, but I get it."

"I'm a different man, babe."

"No, you're not. You're the same man I met in the desert almost nine years ago. You just kept him buried deep down and refused to let him out."

"But I couldn't hide him from you."

"I knew there was more to you than the facet you showed the world." Reid gives me another of those panty-melting kisses that steals my breath and makes me forget my own name. He's so damn good at that.

"Babe?" he asks, pulling back ever so slightly without breaking much contact.

"Yeah?"

"This suit was built for a smaller man," he says with a smile against my lips.

"Smaller man?" I'm sure my face shows my confusion.

"Down below," he adds with a laugh.

Dropping my eyes down, I take in the very tight plastic suit stretched tautly over Reid's impressive bulge. The sight makes me laugh. It looks like his dick is being strangled by a big, black condom. "I'm pretty sure *that* wasn't included in the original Batman costume. Why are you still wearing that thing?" I ask through my laughter.

"Uh, because my clothes are still in the back of the Town Car that left about thirty minutes ago."

"So you need to borrow clothes?" I ask, unable to control my laughter.

"If you thought an adult men's black vinyl Batman suit was hot, you should see me in a pair of woman's yoga pants," he says with a wiggle of his eyebrows.

"Or we could just forget the clothes altogether," I suggest, running my hands down the chest of his suit.

Instantly Reid's eyes heat up. "Even better. Let's go with your idea," he says with a wicked grin.

And before I realize what's happening, Reid picks me up and hoists me over his shoulder like I weigh nothing. "Reid! What are you doing?" I exclaim.

"Taking Batgirl to the Batcave so Batman can ravish her body from head to toe," Reid says moments before he slaps my ass hard enough to sting. And because I'm staring at his delectable ass as well, I give him a playful swat on his rear in return. "I have big plans for us tonight," he adds as he walks straight into my bedroom.

Big plans that involve a lot less vinyl.

Profited

Chapter Twenty-Six – Reclaiming

What's Mine

Reid

Waking up next to Dani is heaven. Her soft skin caresses me from my shoulder all the way to her blue polished toes. Fucking heaven on earth. I can feel the heat from her core against my leg, and it makes me harder than granite. Best way to wake up. Period.

Waking up with a pair of gray eyes that belong to your kid staring at you…not so much.

"Hey, buddy! What are you doing up so early?" I ask casually, trying not to rouse Dani from sleep. Besides the fact that I kept her up pretty late with our mattress aerobics so she could use a little extra sleep, but I'm also afraid that she'll jostle the sheet and expose her mouthwatering tits to our son. They're barely covered up by the sheet as it is.

"I'm hungry," Ryan says with a sleepy smile.

"Okay. How about you and I make breakfast for your mom."

"Remember what happened last time?" Ryan asks with a huge smile.

"True. How about we start the coffee and run down the street and get bagels?"

"Probably a better idea," he says with one of those smiles that you can't help but reciprocate.

"Go get dressed and brush your teeth, and I'll meet you in the kitchen in a few minutes," I instruct.

"Okay!" he yells while running out the door without shutting it.

"It's only six," Dani mumbles next to me.

"I know, and apparently, Ryan is hungry. We're going to go grab breakfast and be back. Get a little more sleep," I say before placing a kiss on her forehead.

"What exactly are you going to wear? Your Batman costume?"

"No, Steven dropped off a car last night and included a change of clothes for me. He put a bag by the back door."

"Do you want me to go get them?" she asks without opening her eyes.

"No, I'll slip on a towel and get them."

"You're going to make my eighty-year-old neighbor very happy if she sees a hot young man streaking by her kitchen window."

"Then I better keep the towel on, huh," I say just before giving her another kiss, this time on her lips.

"Don't forget the blueberry cream cheese," she mumbles as I slip out the bedroom door, my laughter the only response I give.

"Ready, Dad?" Ryan asks after I retrieve my bag, throw on a fresh set of clothes, and brush my teeth and hair.

"Yep. Let's go, buddy."

Ryan talks the entire ride to the small corner deli and bakery four blocks away. We've discussed everything about his birthday yesterday, from the cookout to the swimming, and especially the presents. And when I say we discussed it, I mean I listened intently as Ryan filled me in on everything starting the moment he woke up that morning.

On our ride home with a bag of fresh, delicious smelling bagels with a variety of cream cheese, I steer the conversation back towards the birthday that I missed. "Hey, buddy, you know I didn't want to miss your party, right? Sometimes adults have things that come up and they can't get out of them. I wanted to be there in person so that I could give you my present," I say.

"You got me a present? What is it?" he asks. Of course he would focus on the gift aspect of the conversation.

"You'll have to wait until later today to get it, okay? I thought maybe you, your mom, and I could go for a ride later. That okay?"

"Yep!"

I have one more thing I want to discuss with him, but this one is proving to be a little more difficult subject to broach. I'm running out of time, though, since we're almost back to Dani's house. "Hey, Ryan. Can I ask you something?"

"Sure."

"This morning, when you woke up, I was in your mom's bed," I start, not really knowing how to start this.

"I know," he says casually with a shrug of his shoulders.

"Are you okay with that?" I know he isn't going to get the full meaning of the statement, and I sure as hell am not going to tell him, but it seems important to make sure he's okay with finding me in his mom's bed. I'm sure if Dani was fully awake, she would have been just as concerned as I am.

"Yeah. I mean, you're my dad and she's my mom. Aren't you supposed to sleep in the same bed? All of my friends' moms and dads sleep in the same bed. Brenden told me that one time his mom was sitting on top of his dad in bed and -"

"Okay, I'm glad you're alright with our sleeping arrangement," I interrupt. I'm pretty sure I know exactly where that story was headed, and it's not something I want to hear my kid share. I also make a mental note to ensure the door is thoroughly locked every time I consider getting naked with Dani. In fact, I think I need to install a second lock.

"So, when are we going to get my present?" Ryan asks as I pull into the driveway, breaking my train of thought away from the idea of our son busting us getting busy in the bedroom.

"Soon, buddy. Soon."

* * *

"Do I want to know what you got him? I mean is there a reason we had to come to your place and then trek to the back of your property?" Dani asks as we walk past my in-ground pool, past the pool house, and towards the acres of flat, manicured grassy area that surrounds my pond.

"There is a reason, yes." As we reach the pond, a dog barks, drawing Ryan's attention.

Steven is standing by the pond, holding the leash of a rescued Labrador that I purchased from a shelter Carly helped me find online. "Dad! There's a dog back here," Ryan exclaims moments before taking off and running towards the animal.

"You didn't," Dani whispers, shock and maybe a little anger evident in her voice.

"Uh, I might have," I reply with a sheepish grin.

"A dog? You got him a dog? After I told you no?"

"In my defense, you told me no before we really discussed it."

"We *didn't* discuss it, Reid," she says.

"True, but in my experience, it is easier to ask for forgiveness than to ask for permission. So, this is me asking for forgiveness in purchasing a gift for our son that he really, really wanted. I've discovered in the past few weeks that I'm unable to tell him no."

"Oh, he's well aware of that fact and is using it to his advantage."

"If it helps, Sam is housebroken and has been through all of his obedience training. His previous owner kept him up on shots and whatnot, and he's fixed. There will be no baby Sam puppies popping up in the neighborhood following his wild nights of humping."

"How old is he?" she asks, the anger completely void from her voice.

"He's almost a year old. The owners had to move to a heavily populated part of town and he wasn't able to get the exercise he needed. When I stopped by the shelter–just to look–he had only been there about two hours. I knew as soon as I saw him that I wanted him. For Ryan."

"Where are you putting this dog?" she says as we start to walk over towards where Steven and Ryan are playing with Sam.

"Here at my house," I tell her. "And I'm hoping that Ryan will come over all the time and help take care of him. A dog is a great way to teach responsibility, Dani. It's a valuable lesson that he can't learn just anywhere," I add. I'm pulling out all the stops right now, including throwing in one of those charming smiles that melts her annoyance away and helps drop those panties.

"Okay," she says defeated.

"But that's just temporary," I say, crouching down and grabbing the ball that Ryan just tossed for Sam.

"What's temporary?" she asks.

"Ryan visiting to take care of his dog. That's the temporary arrangement until you're ready to make this his permanent residence," I add confidently. I'd call a moving company and move them in today if I thought she would go for it.

"Permanent?" she asks, her voice just barely over a whisper.

"Yeah. When the time is right for you and Ryan, I want you both to move in here. With me."

I can practically see the wheels turning inside that beautiful head of hers. She's considering what I said and dissecting it from every angle imaginable. It's one of the many things I love about her.

She doesn't just jump in with both feet like so many. She looks at every aspect of whatever it is she's considering.

"You want us to move in with you?"

"When you're ready, Dani. I won't pressure you, but I want you here. Both of you. I want forever, and I want it with you." I reach for her, and pull her perfection into my arms. She links her slender arms behind my back and rests her cheek against my chest. I can't help it, and I take a whiff of her hair. Yep, I turned into that fucking doe-eyed, sappy guy, and I don't care.

"I kinda want that, too," she says against my chest. Her words vibrate through my entire being. I feel peaceful.

"Good, because I'm not letting you slip through my fingers again," I say honestly before claiming her lips with a kiss.

"Dad! Steven says the dog's name is Sam. Can he sleep in my room?" Ryan asks as he tosses a stick towards where Steven is standing.

"He sure can, Ry. Every day you're here, you'll have to feed him and provide him with fresh water, take him for walks and play with him, and even help brush him. And if he wants to, he can sleep on the floor by your bed," I tell Ryan.

"Yay! Sam, you want to sleep in my room, buddy?" he asks as Sam jumps on him and knocks him down. Dani and I both laugh as the playful pup starts to lick his face relentlessly.

"I think you did good," she says as she wraps her arms around my midsection.

"As long as I have you two with me, I can't go wrong," I say before twisting in her arms.

Sliding my hands across her cheeks, I bend down and graze my lips across hers once more. I could kiss this woman every day, and if I have anything to say about it, I will make sure that I do.

Love isn't just a feeling, but an action. It's in the way I touch and hold her in my arms, and talk to her with words that reflect my affection. I've never wanted love; I ran from it my entire life. But with Dani, I didn't have a choice. Love is inevitable; like the sun rising in the East every morning. It's in my heart and burrowed into my soul. It's forever.

Life without love isn't a life at all.

It's a prison sentence. Slow and painful.

In this moment, with my arms wrapped around the woman I love more than my own life, while we watch our son play with his new dog, I know that my life has only just begun. My love for her is infinite, and the love she gives back so effortless and abundant. Her love is pure, and it's all mine.

That's my greatest profit.

Epilogue – My Fairytale Ending

Dani

2 months later

The Vegas sun is definitely brutal. The entire month of July was hot enough to fry an egg on any outdoor flat surface, and it's proving to be just as scorching as we roll into August. Since school released, we've spent a bit of time in the pool. Okay, so we've basically camped out in the pool for the past thirty days. And not in my own pool either. No, Ryan and I have spent as much time as possible with Reid at his house.

Today, we are heading over to Carly and Blake's house to celebrate Natalia's second birthday. I've gotten to know Carly quite a bit over the past couple of months, and she has quickly become a close friend. She's well organized and as much of a detail-oriented person as Reid is, and she definitely keeps him structured and orderly. Plus, she loves to tease him about the whole Batman costume, so she wins mega points for that alone.

Ryan is already out of the car and heading around to the backyard before Reid gets his car in park. Ryan has proven himself a father hen where Nat is concerned. Every time he takes her by her little hand and leads her towards the swing set to play, my heart melts a little bit more. He's going to make a great big brother.

And that thought brings me right back to my surprise for Reid later tonight. He has been talking a lot in the last few weeks about adding to our family. Since Ryan is already eight, we're both eager to give him a little brother or sister. I've been putting him off, not really commenting when he brings it up. It's not because I'm not ready or not excited to grow our little family, but because I'm anxious to do it right this time around. And my decision to have more kids with Reid falls into my planned surprise for later.

"I see he didn't even wait for us," Reid says, pulling my attention from my thoughts.

"He usually doesn't. And did you notice that he grabbed her present? He wants to be the one carrying it up so she knows who brought the gift."

"Smart man. Already workin' to impress the ladies," Reid says with a laugh as we get out of the car.

"Yeah, just like his father. Always thinking of a way to sway the female population." The smile on my face is contagious. I've had it plastered there since the night Reid told me about getting out of the contract to acquire Bravado Resorts, and subsequently the woman he was contracted to marry. That's also the night he told me he loved me. He's held up his promise and told me every chance he's gotten since that night as well. There's nothing better than hearing the one you love profess their love to you.

"There's only one female I want to sway. And I plan to do a little swaying later tonight after our son goes to bed," he says, his voice laced with enough heat to melt the panties off a nun.

"You have a date," I say just before his lips descend upon my ear. When his tongue snakes out and swipes the shell of my ear, I can't help the involuntary shudder that rakes through my body. It's the same bodily response. Every time.

"We could probably drop him and run. No one will notice we're missing. That's the good thing about having a few friends and my sister here. Built in babysitters," Reid says as serious as ever.

Just when I get ready to burst his sexually filled bubble, Blake walks around the house. "How did I know I'd find you two making out in my front yard. This is a family neighborhood, man," he says sarcastically.

"Yeah, yeah. I was just convincing Dani to slip back into the car and head somewhere else for a bit. I'm sure you'd be fine with watching Ry," Reid says while fighting a smile.

"Yeah, I don't think so. Get your ass back there before Carly has to come up here to get you." Blake shakes his head while smiling as he turns and heads back the way he came.

"Let's go. It's clear that I'm not about to get any front yard action right now," Reid says, feigning disappointment. At least I hope he's feigning.

The party is lively with adults, and only a few kids in attendance. Blake's brother, Luke, is here, along with his parents whom I've not met until today. His dad appears like a decent guy, but his mom looks to be a touch on the overbearing side. And not as much to Blake as she is to Luke. I'm surprised to see that she didn't go up and make his plate or cut his meat for him when we ate dinner.

"Did you tell him?" Carly says to Blake as she slips down into the lounge chair with him.

"Not yet," he mumbles. Blake wiggles a bit in the chair as if he's uncomfortable with the attention Carly brought to him and Reid.

"Tell me what?" Reid asks, looking between Carly and Blake.

"I quit the Bureau last week," Blake says confidently.

"Seriously?" Reid asks. Clearly he's as surprised as I am by this news. Carly hasn't said anything about Blake being unhappy with his job within the Las Vegas division of the Federal Bureau of Investigations.

"Yeah. It was time. Right before we were married, they wanted me to go to Tucson to consult with another team on a big case. I was actually considering it until they told me it was for three to four months. I couldn't be gone that long from Carly and Nat, and definitely not right before the wedding.

"Then, they offered me another assignment undercover a few weeks ago. I just couldn't do it. I want to be home with my wife and daughter every night, not halfway around the country doing God knows what to bring down a criminal. I've already missed too much of Natalia's first half of her life. I'm not missing anymore." He says it so confidently and with so much love.

"So what are you going to do?" Reid asks.

"Actually, I thought of starting my own security business. I've spent the last week talking with some contacts in the industry, and I think there's a growing need in Vegas."

"And I want in," Luke says next to me. I didn't even hear him walk up. Carly says that Luke hasn't been the same since Blake was shot last year when she and Natalia were kidnapped following an undercover assignment that went wrong. Even though Blake wasn't hurt severely, Luke hasn't gotten over seeing his brother shot.

"What kind of security are you thinking?" Reid asks, clearly very interested in the direction of this conversation.

"Corporate security mainly, but I won't rule out personal security as we start to grow and if the need is there." Blake has that authoritative, take-no-shit appearance. He's clearly good at his job if the FBI hired him at such a young age. I can definitely see him being successful in whatever direction he decides to take this venture.

"Corporate security, huh? What if I told you that I might know of a company looking to hire a firm to coordinate security between headquarters and a few smaller satellite offices and businesses? Would you be interested?"

"Hell yeah, I'd be interested." Blake's face lights up like a Christmas tree.

"Why don't you meet me in my office Monday morning. Set up a time with your wife," Reid says as he takes a drink of his Corona.

"Do you mean -" Carly starts before Reid cuts her off.

"No. I don't want any favors, Reid. I don't want you to think you have to give me a job just because we're friends and my wife works for you." Blake seems adamant about forging his own way in the industry.

"Lucky for you I met with my security team this past week and discussed outsourcing the job to a company specializing in security. Right now, we have our own guys hired in-house who take care of everything. They're good—damn good—but it would be nice to not have to worry about that aspect of the company. In fact, if you're interested, I might have a few names I'd be happy to pass along for when you're ready to hire more employees."

"No shit?" Blake asks as he stares wide eyed at Reid.

"Looks like the perfect opportunity has presented itself on both accounts, Blake. You need clients and I need security. Meet me in my office Monday morning," Reid says with a smile.

"Deal." Blake stands up and shakes Reid's hand firmly. I can tell their working relationship is going to be mutually beneficial for both of them.

* * *

"Big man in bed?" Reid asks as I join him in his bedroom after making sure Ryan is asleep. He's reviewing a stack of work papers in bed. His chest is bare, and even with the sheet pulled up to his waist, I can tell he's wearing a pair of shorts. Ever since a naked

Reid woke up to find Ryan in the bedroom with us, he's been paranoid about making sure he keeps his junk covered, as he puts it.

"Yes. Sam is passed out on the floor next to him. I love how that dog snores when he's exhausted."

Reid laughs as he sets the papers down on the nightstand next to his side of the bed. "You coming to bed?"

"Yes, just give me a minute to freshen up," I say as I slip into the adjoining bathroom suite. I make quick work in the shower to make sure all of my bits and parts are smooth and clean. Then, I slip into the black negligee that I found online from a New York based lingerie shop.

When I slowly open the door, I see Reid has all of the lights out except the small lamp on his nightstand. He's lying back on the sheets with his hands casually resting underneath his head. The muscles of his arms and chest are pulled deliciously taut, and suddenly the brand new g-string I'm wearing is soaked.

"Dammit, you are fucking hot," he says as his eyes greedily watch me walk towards the bed.

"You're not so bad yourself," I say as I reach the end of the bed.

I give the negligee a little tug so that the material is gathered around my upper thigh, and I slowly kneel onto the foot of the bed. Releasing the material, I crawl my way up Reid's body. His impressive bulge is strained against the material of his shorts and my mouth waters to explore his body with my tongue.

"This is new," Reid says huskily as I slide my hands up his thighs.

"It is."

"I like it."

"I can tell," I reply, nodding towards his hard-on.

288

"That happens every time you walk into the room. It doesn't matter what you're wearing."

"I had something I wanted to discuss with you tonight," I say. I'm using my best Sex Kitten voice, and I'm just praying it doesn't make me sound too nasal.

"You want to discuss something now?" he asks. Even though his eyebrows are both skyward in question, both of his eyes are locked firmly on my girls. Like missiles zeroed in on their targets.

"Do you remember when you said you wanted Ryan and me to move in with you?" I ask, holding my breath as I wait for his response.

Reid's eyes shoot up to my face. "Yeah," he chokes out. His voice sounds gravelly and deep.

"We're here so much anyway, so maybe it's time that Ryan and I make this place our permanent residence," I say. My heart feels like it's about to beat out of my chest. "I mean, if the offer still stands," I add.

"Are you kidding me? Of course the offer still stands. You really want to move in?" he asks, his face full of surprise and hope.

"Yeah. I talked with Trysta last night about renting the house from me. She has a friend at the casino who is looking for a place, so she'd like to bring in a friend and both of them rent it."

"You've made me the happiest man on Earth right now, Dani," Reid says as he pulls my face down and plants a firm kiss on my lips.

"That's not all," I say bravely.

"There's more? Don't keep me waiting. If it's anything like your first surprise, I'm ready for whatever you have to say." His gray eyes are bright and his smile wide.

"You've mentioned a lot lately about giving Ryan a brother or sister," I whisper. This one is more emotional for me so saying these words is a little bit harder than telling him I'll move in with him. Reid is apparently unable to speak words as well, and answers my statement with just the nod of his head.

"Well, I was thinking that maybe we could do that."

"You want to have another baby?" he asks, his eyes, once again, wide with shock. Now it's my turn to nod my head up and down.

"Nothing would make me happier than to have you move in here, and to give you another child."

"What if we were to get married first?" I ask, fearing that he'll say no.

God, what if he says no?

Maybe he doesn't want to get married? We've talked about forever, but never marriage. What if Reid is one of those guys who is content with living together and shooting out offspring without the commitment of a formal marriage?

"Did you just propose to me?" he asks, incredulously.

"Maybe?"

"You did not just propose to me," he mumbles, closing his eyes. The look on his face is sad with a hint of something I don't want to dissect. Oh my God, he's going to turn me down and call off everything else.

Suddenly, Reid whips us around so that I'm beneath him. He plants a firm kiss on my lips before he gets up out of bed. This is it: the moment he walks away. My heart slams into my chest with so much force, I'm afraid I might have cracked a rib.

I keep my eyes closed, but I hear Reid open up a drawer. He must be dressing, and I don't want to witness it. A moment later, I feel the bed dip as Reid kneels next to my unmoved body. "Get up," he says.

Opening my eyes, I see Reid isn't dressed. He hasn't added any more clothes to the shorts he was wearing moments ago. His chest is still gloriously on display as he takes my hand and helps me stand.

"I can't even believe you just proposed to me," he says with a smile.

"It just came to me, I didn't mean to upset you. I mean, if you don't want to get married, that's okay. I don't want to force you or for you to think that I have to have a marriage to make this work," I say, swallowing over the emotion lodged in my throat.

"I can't believe you proposed to me before I could propose to you," he says as he brings his forehead down to mine.

Wait. What?

"I love you so much, Dani. You and Ryan. When you agreed tonight to move in with me, I didn't think I could get any happier. Then you told me that you wanted another baby, and I thought my happiness was going to literally burst through my damn chest. But now? You've gone and done the one thing that I was planning to do soon. The one thing that would make my life complete. I could survive without more kids. I could survive with just you and Ryan forever. But what I couldn't survive without, is you. I couldn't survive without making you mine forever."

That's when Reid drops down to one knee. He pulls a little black velvet bag from behind his back, unties the strings, and drops a diamond ring into his hand. The stone sparkles brightly even in the darkness of the room.

"Danielle Whitley, you have shown me what love is. You give it freely and take it fearlessly. You are my heart and my love. You are my forever. Will you marry me? Spend the rest of your life with me?"

I have no idea when the tears started, but they did. They fall in earnest down my face landing where our hands are joined. Reid holds an immaculately sparkling diamond at the tip of my ring finger, patiently waiting for the sign to slip it on my finger. There's only one answer to his question. "Yes."

Suddenly, the rock is on my finger and Reid's arms are wrapped around me. He's kissing me passionately as his hands slowly wipe away the remaining tears. This moment is better than anything I could have possibly imagined.

And the proposal was so much better than the one I did moments before.

"Now I'm the happiest son of a bitch in the world," he whispers against my lips. "Do you know what would make this night ever more spectacular?"

"No," I whisper as I slide my tongue along the crease of his lips.

"Taking my fiancée, my future wife, to bed so that I can give her the baby we both want."

The next thing I know, I'm being hoisted up into his arms and carried to our bed.

Our bed.

In our house.

Reid slides his hands up my thighs, pushing the material up as he goes. "I love you, future Mrs. Hunter."

"I love you, Mr. Hunter," I reply.

Reid's eyes fire to life with my words. His lips are urgent as he pushes the rest of my negligee up and helps pull it over my head. He removes his shorts in one swift motion and throws them somewhere into the darkness.

"Please forgive me for being rushed and skipping the foreplay, but I just need to be inside of you, Dani." Reid rips the thin material of my g-string panties and pulls them quickly from my body.

Seconds later, he's positioned at my entrance and sliding inside. For every moment of hurried passion, he's now slow and steady. He slides all the way in, my body stretching to accommodate him. When he's seated all the way, we both exhale deeply.

"I'm going to love giving you a baby," he says as he slowly pulls back until he's almost all the way out.

"And I'm going to love being pregnant with your baby again," I tell him as he pushes back in.

The slowness of his motions starts to turn hurried as we make love for the first time as an engaged couple. With each pump of his hips, he pushes me closer and closer to the edge of the cliff until I'm barely hanging on by my fingertips.

"I love you so much," he whispers and slides all the way in with the right amount of force. With a firm rotation of his hips, he hits that delicious place inside me, and I'm sent soaring above the clouds, blinded by the bright lights of my orgasm.

"I love you, too," I yell as he joins me in release.

We lie in bed, wrapped in each other's arms, and my heart feels content and full. Reid doesn't get up to clean up, but instead continues to lie with me, his body still linked with my own.

"Do you think it worked?" he finally asks when his breathing is under control.

"Did we make a baby, you mean?"

"Yeah."

"I don't know. We'll find out in a few weeks."

"I'm pretty good at this, you know. It only took once the last time. I'm pretty sure you're already knocked up." I can hear the smile in his voice.

"You're awfully cocky, Hunter. And how do you know it was done on our first time out in the desert? It could have been the second or third time that sealed the deal," I say with my own smile.

"Oh, I'm sure. I have super Bat-sperm." My laughter fills the room, bouncing off the walls in our bedroom.

Reid's arms pull me in close and his lips trail tender kisses over my chin, cheeks, and lips. I've never been so content in my life. I have the man I love next to me, a wonderful son that we created together, and a whole life to look forward to.

What more could I ask for?

"We better do it again. You know…just to make sure," Reid says as he pulls me back underneath him once more.

Okay, so maybe a little more of this.

~ The End ~

Stay tuned for the third book in the Bound Together series, Entwined, coming late 2016 and featuring Blake's brother, Luke Thomas.

Acknowledgements

As always, this entire process wouldn't be possible without with the love and support of so many!

Thank you…All of the bloggers who share reveals, release information, and take the time to read and review; Nazarea and the entire InkSlinger PR team; Sara Eirew for another amazing cover; Mat Wolf for gracing this cover; Brenda Wright, the formatting queen; Kara Hildebrand, for your editing expertise; Sandra Shipman, for your valuable input while this story was developing and for beta reading; Amanda and Jo (Sugar T*ts x 2); Taryn Clatterbuck, for beta reading; Holly Ward-Collins, for your love and support and for being the bestest friend a girl could ask for; My family and friends; Tiffany Marie (AKA my #1 Stalker), for planting the seed of a concert one night stand in my head; Leah Joslin for the many laughs in Louisville; Danielle Palumbo, for your amazing graphics; Lacey's Ladies, for EVERYTHING you do; My husband, Jason, and our two beautiful kids, thank you doesn't seem like enough. I love you.

And to all of the readers, THANK YOU for reading!

About the Author

Lacey Black is a Midwestern girl with a passion for reading, writing, and shopping. She carries her e-reader with her everywhere she goes so she never misses an opportunity to read a few pages. Always looking for a happily ever after, Lacey is passionate about contemporary romance novels and enjoys it further when you mix in a little suspense. She resides in a small town in Illinois with her husband, two children, and a chocolate lab. Lacey loves watching NASCAR races, shooting guns, and should only consume one mixed drink because she's a lightweight.

Email: laceyblackwrites@gmail.com
Facebook: https://www.facebook.com/authorlaceyblack
Twitter: https://twitter.com/AuthLaceyBlack
Blog: https://laceyblack.wordpress.com

Made in the USA
Middletown, DE
23 April 2017